March 2004,

Dear Ann,

I thought you would like

In Praise of What Persists

to have a copy of your friend Joyce's book. I went to a reading at the Writers Center in Bethesda last week, at a celebration of its publication, and Joyce's daughters Robin and Susie were there. They remembered you with great fondness and wanted me to send you their regards. Robin asked me to send you her address, which I've included at the back of the book. Hope this finds you well.

Cecilia

ALSO BY JOYCE RENWICK

John Gardner: An Interview (with Howard Smith)

In Praise of
What Persists

BY

Joyce Renwick

RENWICK, JOYCE (1942-1995)

For Joyce's daughters, Susie and Robin,
who showered this book with blessings.
They are the keepers of the flame. Mucho thanks
for allowing me to compile this collection from your
mother's surviving stories and manuscripts.

First Edition
ISBN: 0-9-31181-12-7

Richard Peabody thanks all of the following people for their help in making
this project come to light: Julia Alvarez, Rafael Alvarez, Richard Bausch,
Molly Bennett, Kate Blackwell, Holly Carver, Michael Collier, George Core,
Cortney Davis, Lucinda Ebersole, Anne Edelstein, Barbara Esstman, Paul
Grant, Patricia Browning Griffith, Margaret Grosh, Laurie Klemme, Karen
McCaney, Kevin McCaney, Tania Pryputniewicz, Bob Shacochis, Barbara
Shaw, Gail Shields, and Virgil Suarez.

Sunflower photo © 2004 by Molly Bennett
Check out her work at www.mollybennett.com

Paycock Press
3819 North 13th Street • Arlington, VA 22201

ACKNOWLEDGEMENTS

"Crispy Critters" was published in *Damascus Works*.

"The Goat" appeared in *The Louisville Review* and in *Mahogany and Molasses*.

"The Beast" was published in *Phoebe* as "Ronguers."

"Cuatro Casas" appeared in *Gargoyle* and was nominated for a Pushcart Prize.

"Sportin' Life" appeared in *The Green Mountains Review*, *The Pearl*, and on *Story Time* radio, WCVT 89.7 FM.

"In Praise of What Persists" was published in the *Sewanee Review* as "At Sea."

"Cane" was published in *Dead White Mountain*.

"The Man Who Loved Chekhov" was published in *The Antietam Review*.

"Where Are You Now, Ella Wade?" was published in *Michigan Quarterly Review* and in *Between the Heartbeats: Poetry & Prose by Nurses* (University of Iowa Press, 1995).

"Animal Mischief," a winner of a Cecil Hackney Literary Prize and runner up in the *Stand Magazine* (U.K.) International Fiction Competition, was published in *The Southern Review*, and anthologized in *Finding Courage: Writings By Women* (Crossing Press, 1989).

∽

In "The Goat," the epigraph is from "Oda a Salvador Dali" by Frederico Garcia Lorca, translated by Paul Blackburn. Excerpts are from "Madrigal: 1919" and "Anda Jaelo" by Frederico Garcia Lorca, translated by Paul Blackburn.

In "Cuatro Casas," a few lines are quoted from *Gilgamesh: Translated from the Sin-Legi-Unninni Version* by John Gardner and John Maier.

The journal excerpts in the story "In Praise of What Persists" are from the Merchant Marine travel diary of Eugene Wilberforce Titus, Jr., Joyce Renwick's father.

CONTENTS

REMEMBERING JOYCE

When she was young, and I was young, we were at George Mason University together, studying English and wanting to write. We spent time in the newspaper office, and the office of the literary magazine, *Phoebe*, named—we had been told—for George Mason's mistress. I remember that she often came to school from her work, wearing the nurse's uniform, and that she seemed to me then to be too nice ever to write anything good. That was me, then. Callow to the point of an absurd cool—I was the sort of young writer who wouldn't be caught dead at the scene of an emotion, and whose pretensions to seriousness included a delectation of despair, a kind of glib enjoyment of the terrible facts of existence. Joyce would look at me with her softly crinkled, smiling eyes. She had to look up, since I was at least a foot taller than she was, and the tilt of her head made her seem faintly puzzled, or bemused. She spoke so softly, and was so kindly, that I remember being surprised at the tough intelligence that was in her words.

Along with my romantic enjoyment of existential gloom, I was a fairly adept hypochondriac, and I'd conceived the notion that I was fatally ill. This was my last semester at Mason, and I was a new father, unready for the responsibility, scared deep down, and losing weight. I had a bad cold that became a flu, and then I couldn't digest anything properly. I missed classes, and there was a frantic feeling to the days. And I began, for the first time, to fear for my sanity. Joyce was a nurse; she had medical training. She spoke to me in her direct way, in that quiet voice, about what one's nerves can do to one's digestion, about how the flu makes people lose weight, about her own battle with the frights that come. I felt surprised to learn that anything at all upset her or worried her, and of course this was a function of my stupid self-absorption, my inability to see the kindly, and richly insightful person herself—the one who shows forth so powerfully in these pages.

Well. She was already an artist, then, and I was a fool, incipient at best. And she, who was already saying her vision in her own voice, without pretension and with utter honesty, accepted me even so, and was kind. How I wish she was still with us; how I wish she had been given these years to do more of what she loved so passionately, and could do so well.

Here is that kindly person herself, in all we have of her now—what she did do in the short time she had: the beautiful work.

—Richard Bausch

Crispy Critters

The paramedic raised his booming voice. "Picture this. Spanky and I are barreling down the Interstate doing eighty and on the radio, old Tennessee Ernie Ford's singing 'Nearer my God to Thee—'"

"Who? Come on Bill." Amy squinted up at the red-faced man in the blue uniform as he held forth under the influence of three cups of middle-of-the-night coffee. "Don't ambulances have to obey the speed laws too?"

"Nah." Bill took another swallow from his Styrofoam cup. He glanced over at Officer Bancroft who was sitting in the corner by the coffeepot.

The Emergency Room's examination bays were empty. The spillover from Evenings had accounted for the usual off-and-running first few hours of the shift, but by three a.m. the scrapes brought in after the bars closed had had their stitches and gone home, and the intern had shuffled back to his quarters to sleep.

"Yeah," Bill picked up his story, "me and Spanky were going hunting in West Virginia."

Spanky and Bill, two of the paramedic ambulance drivers whose area included the hospital, and Officer Bancroft, a local patrolman, had stopped into the Emergency Room to join Amy and Carolyn as they waited out the middle of the night.

"Sure, Bill," Amy said. She went to the coffeepot and came back with a steaming cup of black coffee. Each night they sat together like three-year-olds in a sandbox, she thought, in staring parallel play.

Each night caught together in the waking dreamtime their bodies couldn't let go.

"Hunting in the ambulance?" Carolyn asked. The young blond nurse was in her usual chair, turned into the corner to avoid the glaring overhead lights.

Bill grinned at her. "Why sure," he said. He stood in front of her, both hulking and boy-like, while his partner Spanky—short and square with wire-rimmed glasses on a freckled face—sat on the plastic couch wearing an old man's intensity like a badge.

"Bill just wanted to tramp around in the woods," Spanky said. "Don't let him fool you, Aim."

"Oh, I'm not easily fooled."

Amy, now brown-haired and pale at twenty-eight, knew she was rarely fooled, and never noticed. In fact, no one had noticed her on the street, or anywhere else in the last couple of years. After the baby, her hair had darkened and so had everything else in her life. She worked nights because eleven to seven paid better than the other shifts and her husband Ronnie's work as a carpenter was seasonal, sporadic. She never got enough sleep during the day, and she often worried that her three-year-old son might be home alone at night while Ronnie stepped out for a beer.

"Hunting." She raised an eyebrow to Bill, then eased down onto the green Naugahyde beside Spanky, careful not to spill her coffee.

She stared down at her scuffed white shoes. Even though Carolyn, an ex-Navy nurse, sometimes changed her uniform twice a shift to withhold a pristine standard, Amy's shoes were her small rebellion. Polishing her shoes, she thought, would be denying the reality of her job, the time on her feet, the effluvia she walked through. She would keep them scuffed.

She took a sip of the bitter coffee. "Come on Bill," she said quietly, "carnage every night and you still go hunting?"

"Has nothing to do with it." Bill rode his chair like a horse. He peered down at his large hands spread open in front of him. "It's fate, Aim." He laughed. "Look, I was born in those hills. A gun in hand is just natural."

"Sure." The walkie-talkie on Officer Bancroft's belt rattled and died. The tiny patrolman was sitting on a molded plastic chair. At five foot five he had just made the town police department's height requirement. "Firearms aren't a problem when you know what you're doing." He winked at Bill and patted his service revolver.

"I've seen too much of it," Amy snapped. "Take that gunshot wound last week."

The patrolman checked his watch. "Old guy caught him breaking and entering?"

Amy nodded. "And carrying away his TV."

"Yeah," Bill said, "we remember it, don't we, Spanky? Brought him in babbling. Silent as stone once he got here."

Amy stared down into her coffee. "Is a TV worth that? Guns, Bill. And we get the leftovers."

"Amy, honey, you've got the wrong perspective."

"What perspective should I have?"

Bill lifted his hand, finger extended, and fired a shot into the light fixture overhead.

"Oh, drink your coffee and get out of here," Amy said. "You're not making the connections. Why do I have to put up with you every night?"

Carolyn, who had been staring at the wall, turned in her swivel chair and smiled. "Amy, you're just burned."

"Sure I'm burnt, and what about you?"

Carolyn shrugged, her large face flat with a studied calm.

Yes, she was getting burnt out already, Amy thought. She had seen it in the older nurses, their coldness. No, not coldness exactly. They're numb. Yes, that's it. Numb. As if they've felt too much, done too much that mattered, and they can't acknowledge them anymore, those feelings worn thin from overuse.

Amy glanced around the room. A smiling Santa Claus beamed at them from the red and green crepe paper twists that draped the receptionist's desk. Somebody had sprayed the lounge with pine scent.

"Just another crispy critter," said Spanky.

"Yeah, that reminds me." Bill cleared his throat. "There was this fire last week up on 28th Street. Remember Spanky?"

Spanky nodded. "Oh yeah."

"We got called up there to accompany the trucks, Aim. Got into this burnt-out house and saw this woman sitting there big as life at the kitchen table. She was black, her eyes big white marbles."

Amy yawned, quickly covering her mouth.

"Now I thought," Bill said, "this sure is strange, 'cause I knew it was an entirely white neighborhood. I just wasn't thinking." He shook his head. "'Cause when I got close, I saw she was burned to a crisp. She was just sitting there—all stacked up, I guess—because when I reached out to her, she fell into ashes at my feet."

"They really look like that?" Amy asked.

"Sure," said Spanky.

"You all are ruining my concentration!" Carolyn wailed. She swiveled around in her chair. "TM—I'm taking a class."

"Geez," Amy said. She stood and walked to the nurses' station, tossing her empty cup into a trash can on the way. Static crackled on the rescue monitor, then the phone rang out.

Amy picked up the receiver. "Here we go again." She listened a moment. "Okay, we'll be ready for you." She hung up. "Bleeder coming in," she called over to Carolyn who jumped up and headed across the hall.

"We'll need the larger room." Carolyn propped open the door to the minor surgery room and pulled back the curtains.

"Rescue Ten is bringing him in." Amy turned to Bill and Spanky. "Want to stick or split?"

"We'll hang around," Bill said, "maybe you'll need some muscle."

"Okay—just no more stories, right?"

"Swear to God," Spanky answered.

"See you folks," Officer Bancroft said. He pulled on his hat and was gone out the side door, the walkie-talkie on his belt screeching in the static-laden voice of the dispatcher.

The old fear she always felt when a case was coming in pawed at Amy's throat. It didn't matter that she'd worked in the Emergency Room for two years, or in nursing over eight. Each time the same metallic taste came to her tongue; the same stage fright pounced on her and made her breathless. She stomped the familiar back. Don't think. She hurried to the ambulance entrance and latched open the double doors. A December chill filled the hallway.

Carolyn had already set up the IV fluids, monitors, and suction and alerted the night supervisor, saying they might need her. She rejoined Amy in the cold hall. A light dusting of snow was falling outside.

"Have you called the doc?" Carolyn asked, glancing out the doors. She handed Amy two pairs of gloves.

"I'll wait a little," Amy said as she pulled on the vinyl gloves. "You know how pissed Joseph gets if we wake him too soon."

"Once the case is here, he's okay. We'll get this guy in the room first." Carolyn snapped on her gloves.

"You got it."

Rescue Ten backed into the entrance ramp, beeping and flashing. The paramedics rolled the stretcher out of the ambulance, up the ramp and through the doors into the tiled hallway where Amy and Carolyn were waiting. One of the paramedics pulled a bright blue blanket off the patient as they came in and threw it into a wheelchair sitting in the hall. On the stretcher a grey mound of a man—a worn forty-five or fifty—lay motionless, his grimy T-shirt rising and falling almost imperceptibly, above a mother-of-pearl belt buckle.

In the doorway to the minor surgery room, Carolyn gestured to the younger paramedic at the back of the stretcher.

"Was he conscious when you found him?"

"Nope," the small man said, flicking a shock of blond hair out of his eyes, "smells like he's been celebrating."

"Third bleeder this week," Amy said, coming in behind them. "Merry Christmas. How's his blood pressure?" She rolled an IV up to the table.

"Barely there. Sixty over zip."

"Okay, get him on the table fast."

Amy ran to the wall phone, took a deep breath, and dialed the intern's quarters.

As she grabbed the end of the stretcher, Carolyn shouted over into the lounge, "Hey, Bill, two hundred fifty pounds of dead weight here."

Carolyn turned back to the men from Unit Ten. Both were splattered with the coffee-ground-like separated fiber and liquid of old blood.

"Have a hard time getting him out?" Carolyn asked. She rewrapped the blood pressure cuff around the patient's arm as the paramedics pulled the stretcher beside the table.

"You don't know the half of it," the older, dark-haired paramedic said. "Walk-up. Room full of crap. Got the picture?"

Bill and Spanky hustled into the room, nodded to the men from Unit Ten, and helped them heave the unconscious man onto small operating table that stood in the center of the room.

"Heavy bastard," Bill said. "Good luck, guys. We just got called. Fire on 35th." He motioned to Spanky.

"Any family coming in?" Carolyn asked the blond paramedic who was stripping the soiled sheets off the stretcher.

"Don't think so." The paramedic threw the sheets in one of the hampers along the wall. "Guy lives alone. The Resident Manager heard him fall and called us. Manager's been through this with him before, and doesn't want to have anything to do with the guy. "

"Pulse is thready," Carolyn said, her fingers on the unconscious man's wrist. "Where's the doc?"

Carolyn pulled out her bandage scissors and split the man's T-shirt and trousers. She grimaced as she peeled away the clothing. The grey trousers were fouled, the man's legs plastered with dry blood.

"Aim," Carolyn called over to Amy at the phone. "This one needs blood right away—lots of it. Look at this." Carolyn held up the soiled clothing. "Check out his nail beds."

"Already called the lab." Amy picked a packet off the equipment cart and tore it open.

Amy glanced at the man's bluish fingernails as she stuck adhesive disks to his hairy white-skinned chest and attached the wire leads to the heart monitor. His chest rose and fell in shallow breaths above his bloated abdomen. She noted his closed eyes and ashen face.

Here we go again, Amy told herself, don't think. She had turned some kind of corner in her life she knew; her nerve had fallen away from her like some flimsy plastic film. Acting out of habit, she ran her hands over the man's taunt abdomen.

"Belly's like a drum," she said to Carolyn. "There's still a lot in there." She picked up a clipboard. "Got a name for the chart?"

"Wallet's there," Carolyn said, cocking her head toward the stool. She pumped up the blood pressure cuff.

Dr. Joseph strolled in wearing a rumpled green scrubsuit. The intern pulled the curtain across the doorway.

"What do we have here?" he asked. He glanced at the unconscious man. "Looks like a John Doe to me." He wrinkled his nose. "Smells like an alky bleeder."

"Name's Timothy Whalen," Amy said, the patient's black leather wallet open in her hand. A plasticised card fell to the floor. She dropped the wallet and a bunch of keys into a yellow plastic bag and shoved the bag toward the paramedic who was at the closet getting replacements for the supplies they had used.

"See if the supervisor's out there," Amy said to him, "and give her the wallet so she can call the family."

The young paramedic nodded. "Just for you, sweetheart." He took the bag.

Amy shot him a frown. "Cut it out," she said.

"Got a chart going?" Dr. Joseph asked.

Amy gave him the clipboard. He glanced at the chart and handed it back to her.

"Start another IV on him," the doctor said as he leaned over the man, a stethoscope dangling from his neck, "and get the lab in here, stat."

The lab technician came in as he was speaking. Dr. Joseph glanced at Amy. "You're anticipating again."

"Sure," Amy said, "I've done this before. Want me to start the bloodline?"

"Do it," the intern said. "And put that rate at 120 drops per minute." He gestured toward the IV Carolyn had started.

Dr. Joseph glanced again at the chart Amy had propped on the cart in front of her. "Any history?"

"He's been out, but I can guess," Amy said. "Lonely alcoholic, holiday season. One binge, one office party too many. Why doesn't anybody ever tell drunks about bleedouts?"

"Any vomiting?"

"Not here, but the paramedics found him in a room-size mess."

"Diarrhea?"

"Yeah," Carolyn said, pointing to the clothing on the floor at her feet. "Black. Old blood mixed in. Lots of it."

The huge man stirred on the table. He groaned as the doctor slid the stethoscope over his chest and abdomen. "Mr. Whalen," the doctor said, "do you hear me?"

The man mumbled and began to choke. He raised his head and shoulders, vomited, then fell back onto the table with a thud. The dark brown coffee-ground-like material spread from his chin and neck onto the sheet behind his head, wetting his hair. An acrid smell of sour whiskey and old blood filled the room.

"Let's get him on his side," Dr. Joseph said, "pronto."

Amy and Carolyn rolled the heavy man onto his left side. As Carolyn steadied him, Amy pushed a kidney basin against his cheek. She quickly ran water onto some gauze squares at the small sink and wiped off his face.

"There you go, Tiny Tim," she said.

"You'll need this." Carolyn threw her a towel.

"Well," Dr. Joseph said as he stood back and watched nurses clean up the man. "We can be pretty sure those fragile vessels in the esophagus have been leaking for some time. Stomach bleeding too, by the looks of him. Abraded bowel. Booze just eats those tissues up."

Feeling something on her leg, Amy glanced down and noticed dark liquid was dripping off the table onto her shoe. The man vomited again. She jumped back too late. Her face and uniform were splattered, her eyes suddenly wet.

Amy remembered her arrival at the Intensive Care Unit after a rough flight to the Coast. Her husband Ronnie had decided not to accompany her. It had been after midnight when she arrived, and her brother was already unconscious on a ventilator.

"Hello, Paul," she had whispered, leaning over him. "Hello friend. It's Amy. Do you hear me?"

She glanced down at Timothy Whalen. He looked terrible. She turned to wipe off her face, hit the propped clipboard, and the chart clattered to the floor.

"Have the lab type and cross match three units of whole blood," Dr. Joseph said to Carolyn. Amy stooped to pick up the clipboard.

"Yes, sir," Carolyn said, shooting Amy a puzzled look. "Anything else?"

"Three more units of blood, standby."

Carolyn picked up the wall phone and dialed the lab.

Dr. Joseph avoided Amy, the scattered papers, the dark puddles on the floor, and walked over to study the cardiac monitor mounted on the wall.

"What's his pressure?" he asked.

There had been no response in her brother's face, Amy remembered. No movement of his body except for the steady rise and fall of his chest in response to the ventilator.

"70/45," Carolyn answered, her fingers palpating the artery inside Timothy Whalen's elbow.

The man coughed, followed by an explosive flow of projectile vomiting which shot across the room, splattered the x-ray light boxes, and the green tiled wall.

A diminutive Asian lab technician entered the room, glanced at the wall, then at the choking man lying on his side. She skirted around the table, and as soon as he quieted, from behind him drew a vial of blood from his right arm, which rested on the ridge of his hip.

"Those blood vessels holding up?" Dr. Joseph asked her.

"Yes, sir," the lab tech said in a small voice. "Okay for now." She left quickly, watching where she walked.

Amy put a clean towel and a suction tube at the patient's head and wiped off the man's pale lips. There was an explosive sound and a fetid smell rose in the air of the small room as a mahogany ooze appeared below the patient's hips.

"Oh!" Carolyn said, pulling a stack of incontinence pads out of the metal closet behind her, "here it comes." She yanked a pair of gloves from the box beside her and tossed them to Amy.

"Mr. Whalen." Carolyn shoved a few plastic pads and several towels under the patient's buttocks. "You're not going to do this to us, are you?"

The man moaned in reply.

Her brother had looked young to her, Amy thought, incredibly youthful, even handsome. His face was clear, unwrinkled, relaxed on the life support, as he no longer fought for breath. His wavy hair had been brushed back from his high forehead uncharacteristically. In contrast to the calm of his face, there was more grey in his brown hair than she remembered when she had last seen him only a few months before.

"He looks so good," she had said aloud to the quiet nurse who stood behind her.

"Looks like internal bleeding for some time," Dr. Joseph said. "Some of this is black. Really old stuff, not bright red new blood."

Dr. Joseph glanced up at the wall clock. "Why me, Lord?" he asked the ceiling. "I've been on for forty-eight and this is my second bleeder." He turned to Carolyn. "Any frank bleeding? New stuff?"

"No," Amy said answering for Carolyn. "Christmas week, every year. I've been here long enough to see the patterns. Bleeders—holidays and springtime."

"Yeah," the intern said. "Scientific study." He percussed the man's hard abdomen. "Liver's like a rock," he said. "Those small belly vessels that take over get overtaxed and *carumba!*"

"*Carumba!*" said Carolyn. "Teddie, is that your considered medical opinion?"

"Dr. Joseph to you," he said.

A deep rumble came from the patient.

"Get that blood going," Dr. Joseph said. "Where is that nursing supervisor?"

She had sat at her brother's bedside, Amy remembered, and tried to orchestrate his care. She watched the dosages change on his IV medications, followed the monitors, asked numerous questions, made a pest of herself—

A square, wire-haired woman in a white lab coat rushed into the room carrying a rectangular plastic bag of packed blood cells.

"Here we go," the supervisor said. "Who will check the numbers with me?"

Amy ran over and read off the blood label. "HL 102450—0 Positive," she called out. "Okay?"

"Sign here," the supervisor said, "and I'll go get the next unit. Should be ready by the time I get back to the lab." She rushed out.

If someone ever asked her to describe the smell of a bleedout, Amy thought, what would she say? Imagine an outhouse, and a slaughterhouse. On a hot day. Stop, she told herself.

"Line's ready," Carolyn said. She ran a saline flush through the tubing and hooked up the blood.

"Open it up," Dr. Joseph said, "he's lost a lot."

Bill popped his head around the curtain. "A shitload."

"Bill, you still here?" Amy said. "Get to the lab, find the supe, and be sure the guy's family has been called."

"Aye, aye, sir."

Amy glanced at the patient. A rapidly enlarging halo of bright red blood pooled at Timothy Whalen's head.

"New bleeding," Carolyn shouted.

"Blood pumps," Dr. Joseph barked to the nursing supervisor who burst into the room carrying another unit of blood.

The woman stood for a moment and stared down at her highly polished sticky-bottomed shoes before she turned to go.

"Frank bleeding," Dr. Joseph said, "and still oozing. Start another bloodline. We'll try a Blakemore to stop the throat hemorrhage."

"Okay, doctor," the supervisor said. She left running. Amy heard Bill's booming voice follow her down the hall.

Her brother had aged before her eyes, Amy thought. He never regained consciousness. Finally, the hard decisions were her's to make, and she made them.

"What's his blood pressure?" Amy asked.

Carolyn took the stethoscope out of her ears. "Fifty-four over zip."

"Not good," Dr. Joseph said. "Get that Blakemore tube going. Where's that other blood? We'll do a lavage—rinse him out with ice water. Increase the IV—150 drops."

"Okay," Carolyn said, a thermometer in her hand, "but his temp's up now, and he's chilling."

"Scrap that blood and put up another. Bad blood, or he's allergic."

When he died, Amy thought, Paul looked seventy. In three weeks she had seen the future become the present in her brother's face. Ronnie had not understood this when she told him. The last time she stood at her brother's bedside and touched his cooled skin, he had looked like their grandfather. Enough, she told herself, stop.

Amy moved in to take Timothy Whalen's blood pressure. "58/30," she called out. She went to the equipment cart and set up the Blakemore tube.

"Hell," Dr. Joseph said, "let me start that new line."

"Gladly." Carolyn handed him an IV start pack. "His veins are collapsing."

"Damn, I was afraid of that."

Dr. Joseph turned the patient onto his back to palpate the veins in the crook of his left arm. As he leaned over the man there was a new rumble, and Dr. Joseph jumped away as projectile vomiting hit the tiled ceiling and the light fixture overhead. The vomiting came in paroxysms, as the black ooze continued from between Timothy Whalen's legs.

Bill poked his head in the door. "Need a cork? Doc, there's some guy out here with a cold demanding to be seen. Says it's the middle of the night and from the look of the waiting room we obviously ain't busy."

"Look," Dr. Joseph yelled, "we've got a trainwreck in here. Tell him to go to an all night drugstore or wait." He paused. "Sure it's a cold?"

"Yeah."

"Get out of here, Bill!" Amy shouted. "Get us towels. And a mop."

The supervisor came in with two blood pumps and another unit of whole blood. She handed Carolyn the pumps and checked the numbers on the blood with her.

"You okay?" the supervisor asked, coming up to Amy after Carolyn took the blood. She put a hand on her arm.

Amy nodded. "I'm fine."

"I know your brother just . . . I'll get the ice for the lavage," the supervisor said, turning to the doctor. "Want the next unit of blood?"

"Yes," Dr. Joseph bellowed. "Ice. And four more units."

"Don't think they have that much on hand."

"Then get on the horn to Red Cross, damn it."

Carolyn attached the pumps onto the units of blood going into the left and right arm sites while Amy helped Dr. Joseph put the Blakemore tube down the patient's nose to the junction of the esophagus and stomach where the blood vessels were the most likely to have ruptured.

Once assured of the tube's correct position, they injected the liquid mercury into the Blakemore tube's blind outer tube, so the heavy fluid would press against the bleeding varices in Timothy Whalen's throat. While they were doing this, Carolyn pumped in the blood.

Bill came in with two more units of packed cells that Carolyn hung as soon the first units were empty.

"Super says Red Cross will have more blood here by special messenger in ten minutes," Bill told them.

"Good," Dr. Joseph said, "we'll need it. Pressure?"

"Forty-five over zero," Amy's voice was almost inaudible.

"What did you say?" Dr. Joseph shouted. "Got a hemoglobin?"

"Four," the supervisor said, coming in.

Timothy Whalen vomited, wrenched by a projectile stream, which hit the overhead light above him. His splattered face was grey.

They rolled him onto his side so he wouldn't choke as the red blood and coffee ground material dripped down on them from the light fixture. A thick cloud of odor—of vomited whiskey, old blood and black waste—hung in the room.

"The tube still in place?" Dr. Joseph asked.

Amy adjusted the Blakemore tube. "It's okay now." She touched her hair and then glanced down at her stained uniform and shoes. She grabbed more towels from the metal closet and threw them on the floor. "How about more IV lines?" she asked.

"You've read my mind," the intern said. He pulled a clean patient gown out of the closet and threw it over his splattered scrubs. "Take one foot and I'll take the other. If you can't find a vein, try the ankle. You," he said pointing to Carolyn, "set up more tubing."

Carolyn rolled over two IV poles on which saline and blood tubing were already hanging. "What do you think I've been doing over here?" she asked.

"Okay, okay. The stink's got to me."

"You!" Carolyn glanced down at her stained uniform. She ripped off her gloves and put on new, double gloving. She pulled the towels away from under the patient's hips and stuffed them into a plastic trash bag, which she tossed into a corner. The black ooze continued as she pushed clean pads under the man's buttocks.

"It's a blessing this guy's not awake," she said. "Aim, did you get the last pressure?"

"Yes." Amy leaned over the patient's yellow feet. "The chart's up to date."

Amy ripped off her gloves so she could feel the cool surface of Timothy Whalen's skin, searching by touch for a vein that had not collapsed. She stuck the large number eighteen needle into a vein at the top of his left foot. "Best I can do," she said as she attached the blood tubing. She grabbed a sterile towel and pressed it against her face.

After a few tries, Dr. Joseph got a bloodline going into the inside of the man's right ankle.

"We need blood pumps on all four lines," Dr. Joseph said.

The supervisor came in with a basin of ice and more blood pumps. "Found the pumps," she caught her breath, "on Ward B. Knew you'd need them."

"Good. Get two more units of blood, pronto," Dr. Joseph said. "Stat."

"Okay," the supervisor said, "I know what pronto means. Red Cross should be in by now. Is this going to work? Want some Vitamin K? I can get it."

"Why not? And some cimethedine. And get the lab tech here for another hematocrit."

"The fool has blown every blood vessel in his entire gut," Carolyn moaned, looking down at Timothy Whalen, "he's losing it."

The lab tech came in with two units of blood. As she took another blood sample, Carolyn hung the units on the new lines going into Timothy Whalen's feet.

Amy looked at the ashen man on the table. Four units of blood were hanging like red clouds above him, spilling bloody rain into his veins as quickly as they were able to pump it in. No matter how hard they tried, they weren't replacing his blood loss fast enough.

Carolyn put on fresh gloves and injected ice water into the inner chamber of the Blakemore tube that projected like a rubber snake from Timothy Whalen's nose.

A burned out nurse isn't callous, Amy thought. She glanced over at Carolyn who still seemed to believe she could stop the tide. A burnt out nurse knows too much and too little at once. She isn't unfeeling. Amy thought of the hardened nurses of old movies. Damn, she thought, the opposite is true. As time goes by she doesn't feel less, she feels more. Each case is a new assault on her emotions, more painful to bear. Each time more courage is needed to stand fast. Each patient is again, her brother.

"Timothy Whalen never planned on this," Amy said to the air. "How long do you think he's been bleeding?"

"A week, ten days maybe," Dr. Joseph said. "Denying he had a problem the whole time, I'd guess. Give the K and the cimethedine as soon as it arrives."

Carolyn stopped running the ice water through the nasal tube briefly to pump up the blood pressure cuff. "Oh no," she said.

Dr. Joseph glanced quickly at the cardiac monitor.

"Forty," Carolyn called out, "and I'm just palpating."

"Let me see." Dr. Joseph moved in front of Carolyn, pumped up the BP cuff and listened. "Get the dopler," he said.

The supervisor came in with the medications. "Ready for the next units?" she asked.

"Lab girl brought them in," Dr. Joseph said. "Get the dopler. We'll amplify the sound of his pressure."

"Anything else?"

"What's it now?" He looked over at Carolyn. "Let me do that lavage."

"Look," Carolyn said, "five pints of blood in so far and there's no sign of this bleeding stopping." She pulled down an empty unit of blood and hung another. "The human body only carries what? Ten to twelve pints?"

"We'll give twenty if we have to," Dr. Joseph said. "Thirty. What's his heart rate?"

Amy looked at the monitor. "Fifty-two," she called out. "PVC's, lots of irregularities."

"Good thing we don't have other patients down here," the supervisor said, pulling back the curtain. "That's it. That's all the blood there is. We called all over. Red Cross. Other hospitals. Nothing more available in less than an hour." She looked over at the man on the table. His lips were white, colorless. "I'll try again," she said.

Amy glanced at the splattered green walls, the stained ceiling. The floor of the minor surgery room was three layers of sticky towels.

Well, she thought, Christmas week riddle: What's a little eggnog among friends? Answer: soiled death. Sick, she told herself. Stop.

The supervisor turned at the door. "Want me to get the Intensive Care bed ready?" She looked at the patient, then at Dr. Joseph. "He's not going to make it, is he?"

"Found any family? They coming in?" Dr. Joseph asked.

"I called every number I could get from his wallet."

"No one?"

The supervisor shook her head.

Amy looked up at the mahogany-colored stain on the overhead light.

"Why do we do this?" she hissed to Carolyn who stood by her, changing gloves. "Why aren't we all dressed up and selling cosmetics at Saks? Or home with our families? My son would love to see me home one Christmas of his life. Why, Carolyn?"

Looking at the ashen man, Carolyn rewrapped the blood pressure cuff around his arm. "He's like one of the hairs on my own head," she said quietly.

～

The man on the table stopped breathing as the thirteenth unit of blood was being pumped into the one remaining open vein on the top of his bruised right ankle. In the air of the fetid room hung a familiar silence.

"I gave him all the coagulants known to man, Blakemore, ice

lavage, thirteen pints of blood, for Christssake, then a code." Dr. Joseph sat down in the nurses' station. "Let me do the papers."

Amy and Carolyn nodded. They went back to minor surgery and first restocked the CPR cart. Another one could come in any moment, unannounced.

They removed the Blakemore tube from Timothy Whalen's nose, the IV and the bloodlines from his extremities, pulled the dirty sheets out from under him, washed him, and diapered him with five layers of pads. They covered him to the chin with a clean sheet, laying him out just in case someone decided to come in.

Carolyn knelt to pick up a plasticised card from the floor. "From his wallet, I guess," she said to Amy. She held up the card. "'God grant me the serenity—'" Carolyn read. She studied the card a minute. "At least he was trying." She tossed the card into the wastebasket.

After an hour, Amy and Carolyn wrapped Timothy Whalen and moved him down to the morgue. They came back to mop the minor surgery room. Amy glanced at the stains on the ceiling and the upper tiled walls. She tried to ignore the fetid smell. During the day the housekeepers would have to reach the stains. She and Carolyn had cleaned up the worst, but Amy knew the housekeepers would still complain, not knowing what the worst was. Nobody knew about the black shit and old blood of a bleedout. Nobody wanted to know. Amy didn't blame them. She bombed the room with disinfectant spray and closed the door.

≈

About six a.m. Amy and Carolyn moved into the nurse's lounge with their Styrofoam cups of coffee. Bill and Spanky sat in the lounge grinning, their bulky blue jackets across their knees.

"Morning time!" Bill said as Amy and Carolyn eased themselves onto the Naugahyde couch. "We just got back. That guy make it?"

"Nope," Amy answered.

"Didn't think he had a chance," said Spanky. "You know the odds."

They heard the door close as Officer Bancroft came in with a draft of cold air. There was snow on his shoulders and cap. He went directly to the coffeepot, filled a cup and started out the door again with a wave.

"Have a busy night?" Bill called after him.

"Nothing much. A robbery and an assault. Some guy with a tire iron." The patrolman raised his coffee cup and headed out the door. "Got to go. A load of paperwork to do."

"Got a story for you!" Bill said turning to Amy.

"No, I don't want to hear one of your stories," Amy said shaking her head.

"Oh, you'll like this one," Bill said, "it's about a little dog."

"No," Amy said. She took a sip of coffee and glanced at Carolyn who was smiling. "Well, all right," she said, "but be quick about it. Day shift will be in soon."

"Well," Bill said. He paused a moment and glanced at Spanky, who got up to get a cup of coffee. "There's this seafood restaurant down by the docks, and this couple—friends of mine—went down there for dinner. And they saw this little friendly white dog without a collar in the parking lot outside the restaurant. They said to themselves, 'If this little dog is still here after we eat, we'll take him home.'"

"And darned if he wasn't there," Spanky said, coming back to sit down.

"Yeah," said Bill, "so they took him home. My friends already had a cat, but that wouldn't be a problem with such a little dog. So they went to bed thinking they'd take the little fellow to the Vet the next day for his shots and all. In the middle of the night they heard some noise, but they thought that the little dog was strange and he'd be okay once he got used to them."

"Okay, Bill," Amy said, "will you speed this up?"

"Well," Bill said.

"Come on," said Carolyn, grinning. She lit a cigarette.

"Well, in the morning the couple found the little dog frisky as ever. They couldn't find their cat, but they thought he'd just gotten lost out of jealousy. Then they saw there was a great mess of things under the dining room table—small bones and fur—and they got concerned."

"Yeah," said Spanky, "animals get jealous."

"They took the little dog to the Vet and the Vet asked them, 'Where did you get him?' They told the Vet about the seafood restaurant and all. Then they told him about the bones. The Vet looked at them funny. 'This isn't a little dog,' the Vet said, looking at the little white long-haired fellow, 'it's a long-haired Siberian rat.'"

"Must have been a pet of the sailors," Spanky said.

"Get out of here, Bill!" Amy shouted. She leaped to her feet. "Get out of here! Take you, and your stories, and get out of here." She pointed to the door.

"Okay, Aim. See you tonight." Bill laughed as he grabbed his coat. "Come on, Spanky, sun's up."

The Goat

Pero también la rosa del jardín done vives.
¡Siempre la rosa, siempre, norte y sur de nosotros!
Tranquila y concentrada come una estatua ciega,
ignorante de esfuerzos soterrados que causa.

—Lorca

Yes, I'd often hear him singing, although John Nokes usually reserved the singing for the times he was out in the pasture rounding up that black and white renegade goat, Pie Face, or sitting under a tree by the dry creekbed, summers. But it was nearing winter. "Ain't no excuse for this cold in October, Eugene," he'd say almost every day and I'd say, "No, sir," and leave it at that, even though it was just like any October in Virginia and didn't feel especially cold to me.

John Nokes was my grandfather, but I called him "Pa" or "John Nokes," the whole name in one breath connected as a statement: "Johnnokes. Johnnokes." The farmhouse was unpainted, Dwight Eisenhower was President, and we had a garden, some hives, and a few sheep and goats. For most of my life we'd had each other and our share of stewed tomatoes over slabs of Nellie Ross' white bread, and a lot of pea soup that was nothing more than green garden peas swimming in goat's milk with a yellow starburst of butter floating on top.

I think even Pie Face missed not seeing John Nokes outside much that fall, because I kept finding the goat wandering in the dining room, or standing on the front room fireplace mantel just like she was

30

wild on some mountainside—her udder bulging out from the wall—
and only John Nokes could get her down. He'd coax her with a tea
biscuit in his hand, "Good Pie Face, sweet Pie Face, that's a girl," he'd
say, "come on down here." And she'd jump down off that mantel grinning her goat grin, her tail waving at him like a flag. He'd milk her
right there in the house, or sometimes he'd call me to do it.

Pie Face was not one of those mysterious-looking Nubian goats
with hooded eyes and a turndown Roman nose. She was just an ordinary American mongrel milk goat, mostly black with white wedges
under her eyes that gave her the name, and turned back, twisted horns
that are not unusual for a female goat. She weighed about a hundred
pounds and would chew or lick anything in sight that might contain
minerals. She bit me every time I milked her so I'd gotten to expect
it, and I knew John Nokes would always ask for "a tad of that pre-
scription milk" when I was through. He'd say, "Now shoo out this
house," and the goat would mind him every time, just like I did.

John Nokes was getting so quiet I began to worry about him at
night as I watched the moon out my window inch by behind the trees.
I tried to get him roused by imitating his singing in a disrespectful
way—"Old Johnnokes got splinters in his elbows leaning on the fence
post so long. . . ." Songs like that. Then I'd watch him close and listen. But most of the time I didn't see anything but that deep line I
hadn't noticed before between the bushy grey wings of his eyebrows.

Once after I had been imitating his singing, sitting at the kitchen
table with John Nokes staring off into the distance in front of me—
really pushing at his patience with a song I called "The Cow Died and
I'm so Sad"—he turned as if he could feel my eyes on him. After a
minute he said, "Eugene, you ever see a stereopticon?"

"What's that?" I asked, wondering how my song would make him
think of something like that.

"Let me show you, boy." He limped away and came back from the
attic with it—a magic lantern he said his father gave him. He put it on
the table next to the empty plates and showed me how to direct the
light sources in the tin cylinder. He said if I studied it long enough I
would learn something.

～

One Monday morning when the sun was barely up there was a knock at the back door and our neighbor Nellie Ross was there to tell me she'd come to pick up the honey. I told her that John Nokes wasn't himself, and rubbing the back of her hand across her mouth she said she'd noticed. She was a short wide woman with wiry grey hair who ran her farm by herself. She had so much energy she made you tired.

"I have news for you, Eugene," Nellie said peering at me through the screen door we hadn't gotten to changing yet. "Is John Nokes around?" Her thick fingers tapped on the doorframe.

"No ma'am, he's gone down to the creek. I think."

"Well, all right then. You don't have that goat in the house again, do you?"

"No, ma'am."

"Just not proper." She gave the door a single tap.

"No, ma'am."

"Well, came to tell you there's a new doctor over in Upperville. Got himself a clinic there. Heard he treats folks in exchange for things like barrels of mangoes, carts of rhubarb, or stumbly horses."

"What kind of doctor is that?"

"Well, he's a foreign man, here from somewhere in South America cause it's the best place to be." She gazed across the field toward the green and yellow trees that hid the creek from view. An early morning haze rose from behind them. "If that doc had been around maybe your Gran would have done better."

"Yes, ma'am."

Nellie squinted at me through the screen door into the dark house. "Do I hear something in there?"

"Don't think so."

"He speaks proper English too, this doctor."

"Nellie," I looked down at my hands, "do you think he'd see John-nokes? We don't have money."

"Nobody does, Eugene," she said. "He knows that. Accepts payment in kind. A cart of hay, a fence repair will do. Somebody did give him a stumbly horse, though Lord knows who that was."

∽

Huge white clouds were moving in fast to crowd the sky that chilly October afternoon a couple days later when I got John Nokes into the cab of the old green pickup we called Jezebel. He was cold and he thanked me when I covered him with a scratchy Army blanket. I was sorry I didn't have something else to wrap him in. Across our driveway I could see the goatsuckers flying wide-mouthed and low in the pasture, scooping the air for insects around the half dozen black-faced sheep that were grazing there. The last thing I did before we left was round up Pie Face and tie her in the rear of the pickup, as far back from the cab as I could. She protested some, bit me on the finger as I knotted the rope into the rib of the flatbed and then, satisfied, grinned her wicked grin at me and quieted down.

"I don't want that goat to kick the cab and jostle you," I said to John Nokes as I got into the truck on the driver's side and slammed the door.

John Nokes pulled the blanket around his broad shoulders and glanced at the goat through the truck's rear window. "Oh, I don't mind kicking," he said, and he turned to me with a little smile, "but Pie Face must have gotten into something a trifle old this morning."

I didn't say anything at first but the dank odor that lingered around us reminded me of the abandoned slaughterhouse near the reservoir. "Never mind," I said finally. I leaned under the dash and touched two wires together to get the engine started.

"You're getting pretty good at that, Eugene. Someday the state is going to let you drive."

"I'll be tired of it by then."

He smiled and looked out the window. As we drove out to the road a clump of black-faced sheep in the pasture broke into a run, and filed one after another along the fence beside us. We passed the stand of yellow-brown cottonwoods and the weathered shed at the edge of the property. The clouds were stacked high above them, their edges gold-rimmed with the afternoon sun.

John Nokes hummed to himself for a while and then got quiet, and as I drove I thought about him always saying that there were extra clouds in his pocket for our part of the valley. In the evening the old man liked to stand alone and watch the sky, and sometimes he told me he'd have visions of folks singing up there—singing the fine old songs he'd learned walking beside his father when he was a boy. The songs were his only inheritance, he said. As we drove along, I heard the jarring cries of the goatsuckers coming out of the woods on either side of the road, as they anticipated the dusk, bristly bird mouths open, and I imagined them swooping under Pie Face at the back of the truck to suckle her blue-white milk away.

I never did understand why John Nokes liked that goat so much. He told me that when she was only a few days old Pie Face had boldly come up to him out of the flock one evening when he was standing at the fence. She started nibbling at his sleeve and then nuzzled at the crook of his elbow, as lusty and persistent as if she was nursing there. She could run and kick four hours after she was born just like the rest of them, he said, but she didn't have any fear of him in her, unlike the other newborn kids, no fear right from the beginning. And John Nokes did admire fearlessness. Later he said to me that watching Pie Face always reminded him that God didn't need to drink the blood of goats—or eat the flesh of bulls either. I didn't know what he meant by this, and when I asked him he just leaned back and looked up at the sky and said, "Now, Eugene, you'll just have to look for it." So I suspected it was in the *Bible* somewhere.

When we lurched into a pothole I couldn't avoid, John Nokes woke with a start. He sat stiffly next to me in the cab staring straight ahead and then turned toward the window.

"Look at those clouds, Eugene," he said. He pointed through the mud-splattered glass at clouds roaming like white buffalo on the horizon. "You ever see them pile higher?" He rolled down the window so I could see them better.

"No sir," I answered. I looked through his window and then ducked down so I could see under the visor. "Higher than most days."

"Eugene, you may think this silly," he said, "but I saw a lot of people in those clouds last night after supper." He scratched one bristly cheek with an index finger. "I see too well; that doctor's going to wave me goodbye."

"No, Johnnokes." My scalp felt like a prickly pear. "You're fine."

I glanced in the rearview mirror. Pie Face was shaking her head and grinning. A goat doesn't know anything.

In the bouncing pickup the old man dozed after I called back once or twice through the opened window for Pie Face to quit chewing whatever it was she was chewing.

"It's just her cud," John Nokes said quietly before he fell asleep.

After ten or twelve miles winding by woods, pastures and an occasional farmhouse, we reached the doctor's one-story cinderblock clinic on the outskirts of Upperville. There was a small hand-painted sign at the edge of the gravel parking lot, which said, "José Alegría, Physician." The late afternoon air was brisk and the sun was hiding behind the clouds, throwing the whitewashed building in shadow.

"We're here, Johnnokes," I said pulling Jezebel off the road. As the engine sputtered out I pulled the hand brake tight.

"So soon?" he said. "Somehow I thought it would take more time."

"Well, snoring helps make the time pass," I said.

John Nokes chuckled at that. We sat in the truck for a while just looking out the windshield studying the hood ornament and the few dusty cars parked in front of the clinic.

"Remind me, Eugene," he said, "I have something to tell you." He took the green blanket off his shoulders, slowly folded it and placed it between us on the seat.

"What is it, Pa?" I was looking off down the road.

"Can't tell you now."

I turned back to him. He studied me for a bit and then smiled. "I'll tell you later." He turned around painfully to look at Pie Face through the back window of the cab. "That's some goat," he said.

I glanced down at my bloody thumb. I quickly hid it at my side.

"It sure is," I said without enthusiasm.

I jumped down from the truck and went around to the passenger side. For once when I took his arm John Nokes didn't remark that he always got his feet tangled up when people walked so close. As we were going across the parking lot in the chill air I noticed an empty pasture to the left of the cinderblock building and a white wall to the right with a black wrought iron gate. I guided John Nokes into the clinic. He stumbled on the narrow step going in and I caught his elbow, then held the door open on its strong spring and eased him toward one of the empty seats. The small dark reception room smelled like a barn after three days of rain. John Nokes was in a cold sweat by then and he wilted into the chair.

"Leave me alone here, Eugene."

I gazed around at the tan cinderblock walls, the magazines thrown open on the laps of the silent slack-shouldered people who sat there waiting. A skinny, hollow-eyed fellow with a rag around his hand looked away when we came in, and a redheaded child about three years old watched me with wide yellow-green eyes. After a few moments she put her forehead on her mother's arm.

"Shoo out of here, Eugene."

"But—"

"Do as I say, boy."

~

I shut the clinic door behind me and took a deep breath of the cool, musky air. The trees across the road were brilliant in a swath of after-noon light, scarlet against green. After a few minutes I took the path along the clinic until I got to the gate I had seen earlier. I peered through the dry vines that wound around the wrought iron and found myself looking into a garden courtyard.

There was a patio with a ceramic birdbath in the middle and two cement benches on either side, in front of a low slung white house set back in the trees. Several large magnolias with giant buds like uplift-ed fists flanked the patio, their glossy dark green leaves thick amidst the twisted short evergreens which pushed their way between them. Half hidden among the trees were small statues on pedestals, their blind eyes turned onto the patio. I noticed some of the statues were of delicate-featured women, others of naked creatures playing reed pipes, their hoofed feet dancing in the air. In the sunny corner to my right was an overgrown vegetable garden. Pole beans hung dry their stick tripods, and the gold backs of pumpkins curved out of leafy vines. Here and there overloaded white rose bushes seemed to jump from the ground to compete with stunted dogwood and mountain laurel—the natural growth, so familiar to me—which was creeping back into the courtyard through the gate and under the crumbling walls. Above, on the walls, hung a jumble of dry vines and climbing red roses still in bloom.

The wind threw brittle leaves at my feet as I turned from the gate. Wishing I had thought to bring a jacket, I went to the truck to check on Pie Face.

The goat was mincing around at the back of the pickup, chewing on the rope I had used to halter her. I pulled myself up onto the flatbed and went over to pat her side, taking care to keep my fingers away from her mouth and her twisted horns. I cooed as convincingly as I was able, "Good Pie Face, sweet Pie Face," but she kept her head turned away. I gingerly pulled the rope out of her mouth by its frayed tail. She peered over her shoulder at me with her head tilted skyward, her black eyes wild.

As soon as I re-entered the dark waiting room, a thin swarthy man came up to me and put his hand on my arm. In the dim light I saw he had sleepy, close-set eyes. Thin lines crossed his hollow cheeks. He was quite tall, and was wearing a white coat over a dark blue suit. When he extended a long hand I noticed his slender fingers and clean nails.

"Eugene?" he said. He stood overly close to me and his voice was low.

I nodded and backed up a bit.

"I'm Dr. Alegría." He nodded his head slightly to me. "Your grandfather is in the room for examination. Please sit down."

"But—I just brought him in."

"Yes, I know. Please sit down."

I searched the faces of the people in the waiting room but as I did their expressions changed, and they became like pictures turned to the wall.

Dr. Alegría did not look at me directly as I sat down, but at some point next my ear. "I have something to tell you," he said. He put his hands deep into his white coat and eased himself empty chair next to me.

"Johnnokes is seeing things, sir," I said quickly, "I know about that."

The doctor's dark brown eyes held me steady. "I took your grandfather in to be examined right away." Dr. Alegría's voice was soft and I leaned forward to hear him. "For a long time he has been passing blood, did you know that?"

"I suspected it, sir," I whispered. The redheaded little girl began to cry.

"A bleeding ulcer, perhaps," the doctor said. "He'll have to go to the hospital and he has already agreed."

"But I'm just—" I looked up at the ceiling. "Johnnokes never did believe in insurance."

"There is nothing else I can do," the doctor said.

"I'll take him in Jezebel—I mean in the truck."

"It's a long ride, he'll be more comfortable in the ambulance."

"But—"

"This is the truth, Eugene," the doctor said quietly. "Everywhere 'clocks keep the same cadence and nights have the same stars.'"

"What?" I asked.

"A poem. Everywhere it is the same," he said. He rubbed his hands over the shiny knees of his dark trousers. His voice was barely audible. "It follows us everywhere."

"I'm sorry sir, I didn't—"

"He has lived well," the doctor said brusquely. He rose to his feet.

I jumped up to catch his look before it disappeared, but his face was like a flat grey stone. The others in the waiting room seemed to be twittering to each other in a language I didn't understand and the woman with the redheaded child in her arms stood when the doctor motioned to her to follow him.

I felt like a sparrow sent out to fight hawks. I followed the woman into the back of the clinic and peered into the small rooms on either side of the hall until I discovered John Nokes in one of them lying on an examining table. In the cramped space he looked so unfamiliar I didn't recognize him until he raised himself I went in and sat down on a chair by the door.

"Hello, son." He smiled. "You found me." He eased himself down. His hair stood out in grey wisps on the white pillowcase.

"Yes, Pa." In the small stuffy room I smelled the sharp odor of rubbing alcohol.

"Eugene," he smiled at the ceiling. "Did I tell you where I found Pie Face yesterday?"

"No." I glanced around me. "Where was she?"

"Up on the hood of the pickup." He waited a minute then chuckled. "Butt to the windshield. Licking the hood ornament. He paused. "Can you imagine that?"

"No," I said, "imagine that."

"Wanted to lick the silver paint off, I guess."

"I guess."

I moved to the straight chair next to John Nokes and ran my eyes over every inch of the examining room—the brown and yellow patterned drapes on the high windows, the speckled brown floor tile, the blue plastic covered chairs and table, the small metal desk. I inspected the dry blood on my thumb.

"I don't like that doctor," I said at last.

John Nokes was lying with his eyes closed, hands resting on his belly. "That doctor's just weary," he said without opening his eyes.

"Worse than that."

"Sometimes if you listen close singing, Eugene, you can hear the trumpet."

I picked my finger until it bled.

"You know I don't carry a tune anywhere, Pa."

He started humming to himself so low I couldn't tell which song it was. After a while I heard loud talking in the hall and two men in bright yellow uniform jackets came in rolling a narrow stretcher. I noticed the emblem on their jacket sleeves, a sword with some snakes wound around it, and the words "Middleburg Rescue." They continued to talk as they maneuvered the stretcher.

"We went by too fast I told you," the large blond man said.

"Don't know what it was." The freckled-faced man pushed his glasses back against his nose. "Just something in the woods by the road."

I felt my face go red and hoped John Nokes hadn't heard. I

imagined Pie Face in the woods along the road, her hooves braced against a tree trunk, nibbling leaves.

The freckled-faced attendant silently indicated John Nokes with his head.

"Geez," the other man said, "how ya doin'?" When John Nokes didn't answer, the blond man turned to me. "What's the matter with him?"

"Just quiet."

~

The people in the waiting room looked up from their magazines as we came through. They didn't seem to notice me, but they watched the ambulance attendants. I thought any moment they would break out into a run and file one after another right out of the room. John Nokes remained silent until we were outside. He opened his eyes and inspected the afternoon sky. The wind brought a pungent whiff of pasture.

"Listen to me, Eugene," he said, "I know what you are feeling, son, and don't you come with me." He shut his eyes to let me know the matter was settled. "Go home," he said.

I hurried beside the stretcher. I couldn't say a word. An old 1947 blue and white Chrysler ambulance with rusted wheel wells was parked at an angle in front of the clinic building, its noisy, powerful-sounding motor idling fast.

"Don't forget about the goat," John Nokes said to me as the men lifted him into the ambulance. He began to sing to himself as the freckled-faced attendant got in the back with him. When the man leaned forward to pull the double doors closed, his highly-polished glasses caught the late sun.

"Yes, sir," I mumbled to the air as the ambulance made a U-turn over the gravel, its red lights flashing. As soon as it pulled onto the road the siren began to wail. I thought about Gram Nokes never coming back once we let her go. As I stood there in the parking lot near the pasture fence where I had moved out of the way, I watched the red Virginia earth rise from behind the ambulance wheels.

Dr. Alegría came out the clinic door, crossed the gravel lot and stood beside me. I ran my hand over the pasture rail. It was grey and splintered.

"He will be all right," the doctor said.

"You hardly looked at him," I said. I turned and saw the cloud of red dust still hung over the road. My voice was as thick as if I had been running in that dust behind the ambulance. I turned to the doctor, a rasp in my throat. "Why didn't you do anything?"

"It doesn't take long to see what is true," the doctor said quietly. He started to go back into the clinic.

I lunged at him, turning him around, and grabbed the front of his white coat, his dark tie with it. "Johnnokes will die," I said.

"No, I don't think he will," the doctor said, "at least not soon."

"Tell me now." I released his coat.

"Your grandfather needs blood, Eugene, that is all." I grabbed his coat again—half threatening him, half hanging on.

Dr. Alegría stood there for a moment looking down and swinging his foot through the leaves at our feet. He seemed to be pretending my fist wasn't knotted under his chin. When I let go of him he looked up into the sparse branches of the black oak that was growing just inside the pasture fence. He turned to go.

"Wait," I said. "Please. John Nokes told me to pay you."

"It is not necessary," the doctor said. I followed his gaze into the pasture. A sway-backed white horse with a yellow mane was grazing there in a shaft of afternoon sunlight, its big pike hanging down. As I watched, the old horse lifted its head. One eye was milky, the other glassy black and shining. I knew it did not see me.

"Wait," I said. I caught up to Dr. Alegría as he resumed his walk to the clinic. "I have a goat for you." I looked over at the horse, which had its mouth to the grass again. In my mind I kept hearing John Nokes.

"She's a very good animal, for a goat," I said. "She's been sung to a lot. And singing is good for the soul of everything, or at least that's what John Nokes says. He says that goats can stand heat, but you have to protect them from wind and drafts, cold rain—"

"That would be fine," the doctor said. His eyes were so dark I couldn't see his thoughts behind them. He put out his hand. Before I decided to shake it he said that he had patients waiting and turned back toward the clinic door.

The wind scattered reddish-brown leaves at my feet as I went to the pickup. When I looked up to check the time, the sun was straddling the courtyard wall. There was a chill dampness in the air. I wanted to ask where to put the goat, but Dr. Alegría had disappeared. I decided to turn the goat loose in the pasture, but when I got to the truck the only thing on the flatbed was a swirling eddy of leaves that had been raked into the corner by the wind. The rope halter was chewed through and Pie Face was gone.

I heard shrieks coming from the courtyard. I cut across the gravel lot and peered through the gate. Pie Face was standing on top of the birdbath, and on either side of her were two dark little girls. The smaller one in yellow was pretty, despite her spindly arms and legs and soiled dress. The other sister was sad-eyed and older, her shoulders softly stooped in her pink dress, her nose and mouth turned down.

"I claim the goat!" the smaller girl in yellow shouted. She had dark braids pinned to the top of her head and a way of holding her chin that told me even Pie Face would have trouble with her. The girl was standing on her toes alongside the birdbath throwing a coil of rope at the goat's head. "I need an animal for practice," she shouted. She hurled the loop into the air and it caught in the branch of a dark magnolia above her. The red roses on the courtyard wall watched her with yellow eyes.

"The goat is mine, Alma," The sister in pink yanked the rope down from the tree. "Use the horse!"

"No!" Alma glared at her sister. "The horse is too old. It runs into things." She pulled the rope from her sister's hands. "And besides," she said over her shoulder, "you're wrong, Corazón, the goat is perfectly able to take care of herself."

"Oh yes? Can she milk herself? Can't you see she needs to be milked?" Corazón, hands on hips, glared at her.

The goat's udder hung low and full as she swayed in the birdbath, making small throaty noises. In my concern for John Nokes that afternoon I had forgotten to milk her.

Alma put her arms down for a moment, the rope slack in front of her, and gazed up at the goat on the birdbath. "Look how well she stands up there!" she said. She swung the rope over her head in a circle. "If this goat were yours, Corazón, it would be prissy and white like a little angel, just like you." She stuck out her tongue. "But this goat is really black."

Alma hurled the lasso. It hung in the air for a moment and then collapsed to the ground, tangling itself around the base of the birdbath. Pie Face looked down at the rope with curiosity.

At the gate, I moved closer against the wall so I couldn't be seen from the house. I was glad for the late afternoon light that hovered over the garden like a brilliant afterthought.

There was a shrill yelp from the courtyard. The goat had her head turned up to the sky and was making yodeling noises deep in her throat. The girls didn't seem to be paying any attention but the delicate statues surrounding the patio followed her movements with blind eyes.

"Alma," Corazón screeched, "the goat is mine, I'm the oldest."

Alma was kneeling at the back of the birdbath untangling the rope. Pie Face leaned down over the side of the bowl and nibbled at the dark braids on the top of her head. Alma swatted at the goat with one hand. She stood, adjusted the loop, then threw the rope into the air. Pie Face snapped her head forward and caught it in her teeth. Alma tugged on the rope, nearly bending over backward as she pulled, but I knew the goat had teeth as tough as the enamel in footed bathtubs. I watched Pie Face shake her head furiously and give one of her sly goat grins. The goat was holding the rope end in her mouth like a cigar, her ears standing out horizontally from her head. The wind fingered its way through the rose bushes, and lifted the leaves of the trees.

"Corazón!" Alma was panting from her tug of war with the goat. "Why don't you help me?"

"Let's be reasonable," Corazón said pulling her dress down at the waist. "I'll have the goat a year, then it's your turn."

"Horsefeathers," Alma said. "Just try it."

Pie Face was holding her hooves together and rocking back and forth in the birdbath as if she were dancing on a single stone in the middle of the creekbed. Her eyes were half closed and the rope still hung from her teeth. Corazón was standing very close to the swaying goat.

"Be quiet, Alma," Corazón said as she stroked the goat's black and white flank. Pie Face dropped the rope and nuzzled Corazón's shoulder. "See," said Corazón, "she likes me. I take better care of everything. Look at your dress."

Alma looked down at her soiled dress. She whirled around and slapped Corazón. The blow glanced Corazón's cheek. After a moment Corazón crossed her eyes. Alma growled, dropped the rope, and gave her another loud slap. Corazón steadied herself on the birdbath.

The goat's eyes suddenly rolled wild on either side of her head. She leaned over and took a bite from Corazón's frilly shoulder. Corazón shrieked and jumped back in alarm. As Pie Face chewed, a pink shred of cloth dangled from her mouth.

My heart jumped in my chest like a winged bird. I moved further back into the dry vines that hung from the gate. At first I thought I caught a whiff of a sweet odor, but no yellow-white flowers remained on the spindly vines, and all I heard was a dry crackle as I flattened myself against the wall wondering what John Nokes would think of this. I looked at the tangle of vines and I thought of him telling me about riding home in the pickup on lush early summer evenings. He'd roll over the hills as the sun went down, the honeysuckle so thick on either side of the road, he said it seemed to be creeping out to meet him—the vines climbing tree trunks and curling around the split rail fences—choking them with a smell so sweet, he said, it entered his head to flood his heart.

"This diablo bites!" Alma shouted to Corazón.

"I know *that*," said Corazón.

I pulled on the gate but it resisted, and looking inside I discovered it was latched from within. Pie Face must have squeezed through the gate, or scaled the wall, or maybe climbed to the roof of the clinic building and jumped down into the lush tangled courtyard. Maybe she had been climbing on the roof above us while we sent off John Nokes. I began thinking of him again in that ambulance, wondering if you think of people suddenly when they have need of you, and thinking he might be at the hospital in Middleburg by now, waiting in some cold hallway, maybe humming "In the Garden" or "Amazing Grace" to himself and keeping his own counsel. I wished I could put all of his misery on the head of this goat, and send her off in a cart into the wilderness, or maybe let her escape into the woods to nibble trees.

It had been John Nokes' idea to use the goat as the doctor's payment, but if I'd had to make a choice between the two of them Pie Face, of course, would be the first to go. I put my hand through the gate, pulled the latch aside, and slipped into the courtyard.

The goat was rocking the birdbath and singing at the top of her goat voice. Her ears perked up as if she had heard me and she began swaying even more lustily, with a gleam in her small black eyes that I recognized. The girls jumped in surprise when I walked up. Alma had untangled her rope, and looking at me intently, she began swinging it in the air.

"Who are you?" Corazón demanded, her hands on her hips.

At that moment the birdbath tipped over and shattered on the patio cement. Pie Face jumped off the debris and ran, complaining at the top of her rusty voice. She crashed through the trees, knocking a statue off its pedestal and then circled wildly through the courtyard, going up and down the maze of tree branches, butting tree trunks when they got in her way, veering around the rose bushes, trampling the mountain laurel. She ran through the vegetable garden, ripping up the pumpkin vines and crushing the ripening globes beneath her hooves. The sisters and I ran after her in crazy pursuit dodging around the silent statues and the whispering trees. Pie Face was grinning and nay-saying at the top of her voice as she circled the courtyard with all three of us stumbling behind her.

Alma stopped, picked up a handful of dirt and pelted the goat, and then me. "Hey! Stop that," I shouted as Corazón joined in.

Stones and snatches of pumpkin flew through the air. In terror at the sudden barrage, the goat let out a raspy cry, shaking her head and braying in protest. Pie Face cut across the patio head down. She plowed through a white rose bush and halfway through the thorny limbs she got caught by her horns. Whole blooms fell apart, their white pedals littering the ground.

The noise in the courtyard suddenly changed. The goat's complaints from the bush continued, but the girls had gone silent. I moved back into the trees. Someone had come out of the house at the back of the courtyard. Good Lord, I thought, another one. I stepped further back into the leafy shadows. In front of the house was a larger girl in a frilly dress. I decided she must be the oldest and maybe the favorite, because her dress was white, and she was very beautiful.

"You are all wrong," she shouted, "the goat is mine."

Alma stomped off toward the house without looking back. Her rope hung around Pie Face's lowered neck as the animal strained against the bush. Corazón ran across the courtyard.

"But Momma," Corazón said.

"There is nothing you can say, Corazón, that would make a difference—*nada, nada, nada.*"

The woman pulled a hairbrush from her waist and began striking it across her palm. I could hear the repeated sharp slap of wood against flesh.

"The goat is mine," said the woman. "You can stop fighting." She dropped the hairbrush into her dress pocket then held the door open. "Come in. It's cold." The woman lifted her chin. "*Un beso,*" she said, lightly tapping her cheek. First Corazón and then Alma kissed her quickly before going in the door. As the woman turned to go back into the house I saw her glossy black hair was pulled back tight. A silver comb above her dark bun flashed like a star of hammered light.

I waited until the door closed and then I went to the bush and untangled the goat. She pulled away from me as soon as she was free, ran across the courtyard and leaped back onto the pile of rubble that had been the birdbath.

I heard a step in the gravel behind me. Dr. Alegría was there, dark and silent. I don't know how long he had been standing behind me, but his manner was stiff and formal. He had taken off his white coat and was wearing a dark suit.

"I don't think you should be in my courtyard," he said.

I nodded.

He cleared his throat.

"Yes, sir," I said. I felt the sparrow flap its wings again in my chest. I looked over at the goat rocking on her perch. "I can replace the birdbath," I said. "But your daughter's dress is torn."

"Dresses, birdbaths—*no es necesario*," he said. "Replacement is not necessary."

"But the courtyard—"

"Dresses can be mended. It is certain the birds can find water."

"But the birdbath—"

"My wife— There are many little rivers, Eugene, aren't there?"

"Yes," I said, "there are creeks. Smaller than rivers."

The doctor surveyed the ruined courtyard, the shattered statues and birdbath, the trampled garden. "Ah," he sighed. "I remember fishing *los rios pequeños* when I was a boy." He looked out the gate. "Then in my country, all life was time."

I ran my hand over my head trying to comb the dirt out of it with my fingers.

Dr. Alegría looked at me closely for a moment. "What is that? Your finger."

"Nothing."

"Let me look at it," he said quietly.

"It's nothing."

"All right, Eugene." He folded his long arms across his chest. "Let me ask you something, *niño*. Are those grand fish out there? What do you call them? Muskellunge?"

"Yes, sir."

"And those little ones. Blue gills. I have heard stories. Someday I will fish for them." He stretched out his arms. "I will say, 'I am sorry, the clinic is not open today.' I will rest for just a little while."

"But what if there was a bad emergency that day?"

He moved back into the honeysuckle vines that wound around the gate behind him. "How old, *niño*?"

"Johnnokes?"

"No. *Usted*." He regarded me seriously. A thought worried his face like wings against the sky. "'*Para mí será el dolor*,'" he said, "'*para mí será el quebranto*.'" Quietly he said, almost to himself, "The loss would be mine as well."

I glanced at him in surprise. "Fourteen—" I slapped the red dust off my clothes. "I'll round up the goat if you don't mind."

"I thought you were older," Dr. Alegria said. "John Nokes has taught you well. "

"Yes, sir." I looked at the doctor's scrubbed hands. "He told me to give you the goat. She was in the truck and got away and then got caught in your rose bush and—"

"*'La rosa, siempre la rosa,'*" he whispered.

I looked at him and then the ruined courtyard, the closed door of the low slung white house, and thought for a moment. "Pie Face is trouble you don't need," I said. "I'll pay you mangoes. I think I know what they are."

The doctor looked at me with a half smile on his face. "John Nokes knows how to live, Eugene. Don't be afraid."

"Or bread," I said. "Bread would be better. Nellie Ross bakes every week. I give her the honey from my hives. I'll get bread for you. Honey too, if you like."

Dr. Alegría unlatched the gate. "An excellent idea," he said. "John Nokes might need the goat's milk for his digestion." He bent toward me for a moment, and then went through the gate toward the clinic.

Now no one had ever bowed to me before, not with a serious face like that, but I guess we understood each other. And as I drove the pickup those miles back to the farm—Pie Face safely tied in the back—from both sides of the road the goatsuckers met us hungrily. In the rearview mirror I saw them swooping at the goat's full udder with open mouths. Quickly, I turned to watch the road in front of me. I started humming to myself, and after several miles I understood— how a joyful song could rise from a sad one.

When I passed our shed the sun had just gone down, and I tried to uncover John Nokes' visions up there in those dark clouds, at least hear folks singing as he told me I would. But all I could hear was the sound of the whippoorwills, as they called from their nesting places in the weeds along our pasture fence.

The Beast

Miss Finney could not stand it another minute. After all, even the Hoot Owl Diner has to have an hour or two in the wee of the morning to shovel out and prepare for the next day. And a hospital is no different. She went striding down the dimly-lit hall. After ten years on the night shift she could see quite well without a flashlight. She had something that had to be done and the silly family vigil at Dude Shank's bedside was getting in the way. She shooed the Shanks out like a bulldozer with a smile painted on its grill. Enough is enough. One of them came back for her coat—the young one—and Miss Finney found a cross-eyed fat woman hiding behind the door in the patient bathroom, but after twenty minutes thin, firm Miss Finney had them all out.

~

Mr. Serle woke when the lights went on. The skinny man looked up from his bed uneasily, his eyes bulging white mounds below his thinning hair. He never knew what the nurses would do when they began to exercise their territoriality. He was relieved when Miss Finney passed his bed and stopped at Dude Shank's bed by the window.

"Good morning, Miss Finkley," Dude said cheerily. It was one a.m.

Miss Finney grunted. Dude Shank still had a distinctive lizard green look to his skin. And he'd mispronounced her name again. She ripped back the covers from the bottom of the hospital bed and exposed Dude's feet. "Unbelievable," she said as she turned and stormed from the room.

"Can I help you?" Dude turned on his side and yawned through his last word. "Honey—ummm."

∽

Miss Finney swung into the nurses' station. "Ronguers," she said under her breath.

"What?" The young nurse's aide quickly looked up from her chair with a wide-eyed, vague expression.

"Ronguers, get the ronguers!" There was a shrill edge to Miss Finney's voice. She pulled a metal chart out of the rack.

"Sure." Cindy, the nurse's aide stood up. "Where?"

"E.R." Miss Finney flipped to the back of the chart.

"Where?" The nurse's aide stretched. Her rumpled uniform rose above her knees.

"Emergency room. Emergency room! How long have you worked here?" Miss Finney slammed the chart back into the rack.

"Can't you use bandage scissors?" The aide knew what Miss Finney had in mind. For once, she had listened to the report at the change of shifts. A call bell buzzed like an impatient bee.

"They tried scissors this morning." Miss Finney tapped the countertop once with her fingernail. "Pulled them apart at the hinges. They tried clippers. Did nothing. I want ronguers. Creative nursing!" Miss Finney banged her fist on the desk. "Ronguers! Bonecutters!"

"All right, all right." Cindy looked at her watch. "So that's—bonecutters. E.R. Be right back." Cindy glanced at the buzzing call panel and gimped out of the nurses' station as if one of her legs was asleep.

Miss Finney answered the call bell and then paced the dimly lit hallway opposite the nurses' station. So far it had been a quiet night. She'd have nothing to show for it. In the morning the other nurses would ask among themselves, "What did Finney *do* all night?" She went down the hall to Mr. Shank's room, the soft soles of her shoes slapping against the waxed floor tiles.

The overhead lights were still blaring into all the corners of the room when she entered, but both Serle and Shank were asleep. Shank was snoring. Miss Finney tiptoed over to Shank's bed, lifted the bedcovers, and looked at his feet again.

She'd heard his toenails hadn't been cut for five years. He just sat in a bar and drank for five years and never cut his toenails. Looked more like ten years to her. The feet were black with encrusted dirt and the toenails were layered, three-fourths of an inch thick and solid as rock. The nails grew down over the ends of his toes and curved under like the claws of a tortoise or some prehistoric beast. Straightened out from the quick to tip they would be five to six inches long. How could he walk? She'd heard he came into the hospital three days ago, barefoot and singing risqué sailors' chanties. Then he'd passed out into an hepatic coma, only to surprise everyone after twenty-six hours by awakening with a beatific smile on his face.

When he roused and it became evident he wasn't going to die, they began soaking him in the bathtub for an hour or two each day—usually when the hovering family members left for meals. Miss Finney had looked the family over suspiciously, but none of them seemed aware of the horror that lie beneath the bedcovers. She looked down at the toenails on the bloated sleeping man. A beast, she thought, a god-damned beast.

The nurse's aide came in the room with the bonecutters wrapped in a green sterile towel.

"Cindy, will you. . ." The gimpy nurses' aide was gone.

She can move fast enough when she wants to, thought Miss Finney, the ronguers heavy in her hand. She looked at the sleeping man. A sudden snore broke the air like the cheek flapping snort of a horse. Mr. Serle turned restlessly in his bed. Oh well, another stroke for human decency, she thought as she unwrapped the ronguers on the overbed table.

She woke Dude by shaking the foot of the bed. With great effort she swung him to the edge of the mattress and then transferred him into the large bedside chair. He was heavy and half-asleep, his big bottom peeking out from the open back of his white and blue print patient gown, but she preferred this to remaking the bed, with both him and all the dirty toenail flakes in it.

"What's this, honey?" Dude said as she pulled him up to a sitting position in the chair. "Ooh hoo, your hands are cold."

Miss Finney lifted one of Dude's heavy yellow-black feet up on top of a wastepaper basket. "Just going to cut your toenails, Mr. Shank." She had a way of not opening her thin lips when she talked.

"At one a.m.?"

"Yep. One a.m." She sat down on a stool she had pulled in front of the wastepaper basket and straightened her white uniform over her knees.

"Why, my feet are just fine, honey, no need."

"Well, I want to do it, Mr. Shank. You'll find it a lot easier to walk."

"Hell, I don't need to walk, honey. Lot nicer to just lay in bed and let all you pretty nurses wait on me."

She grunted and adjusted herself on the stool above his toes. She grabbed the bonecutters from the overbed table. The ronguers looked like a combination hedge shear and rose clipper. Too much of this "waiting on" Miss Finney thought. She positioned the bonecutters one way in the air and then another.

"Hummm. New philosophy," she said looking at the instrument she was holding suspended in the air above his feet. "Help the patient do for himself." She pierced Dude with a quick glance into his rheumy eyes.

"Uggggghh." He grimaced at her. "God damn! I used to fly and now I can't even get out of the bed."

"Oh, Mr. Shank," she looked at last, interested. "Were you a pilot?" The bonecutters were poised over his toes.

"Of course. Flew for the 235th Airborne. 635th Sky Devils. 123 Bi-Plane Brigade. Apollo Moon Shot." He chuckled.

She gritted her teeth and turned around on her stool. Moving the wastepaper basket out of the way, she turned her back to him and positioned one of his huge feet on her lap. Miss Finney held her breath, cut the first toenail, and then as she exhaled, she began to retch as the odor of old sweat and dead skin accumulated beneath the nail rose to meet her nostrils. She moved the wastepaper basket closer. She might have to vomit. It would be unprofessional but this was an unusual case. She realized she should have put a towel on her lap to protect her new uniform.

She held her breath again and looked at the claw-like toes on her lap. She thought of prehistoric lizards, bums in bus terminals, feral children. The taste of tuna fish from midnight supper bubbled up as she bent her head over the thick reptilian foot and cut the four remaining nails. Under the vice-like jaws of the ronguers the toenails split and fell apart like mica onto her lap. She brushed the thick opaque flakes quickly into the wastebasket.

As she finished the first foot, Dude spoke up. "Do I pay you for this, honey?"

Miss Finney gagged. "No sir." She paused. "The hospital pays me."

She retched quietly, smelling the sour odor from the soft underside of the nails. She put his foot down on the floor, brushed her lap, and lifted the other foot onto her knee, careful to keep her back turned toward him so he couldn't see her face. She tucked her chin in three or four times as she swallowed the tuna fish again.

Her ears were scarlet, she knew.

"Tell me something," Dude said in a hoarse, sleepy voice.

"Yes, sir?" she said keeping her back to him.

"Do you like to screw after you do this?"

Miss Finney felt a new wave of color flood her face and neck. "No, sir," she said.

She pressed her lips together in a trembling tight line and two of the nails bled where she clipped too close.

She thought of vomiting into the wastepaper basket in front of him. She wondered how she would react if this man were her relative, her uncle. She'd cut his toenails remembering childhood things, like evening walks with him while the sun lie on its back above the river, or crawling together on green hands and knees on sun dappled summer mornings looking for four leaf clover, and be blind to the yellowback feet, almost oblivious to the odor. But never deaf to the things he said. Never deaf to them. She put his foot down. He had fallen asleep in the chair and his snores were like the faint rumble of thunder on a distant mountain.

She shoved the wastepaper basket into the corner. Let him fend for himself, she thought. Let him sit in that chair all night. She stormed out of the room without seeing the big grin on skinny Mr. Serle's face as he turned toward the wall to sleep.

Cuatro Casas

The sun hung above the rocky point in front of them as Jiggs and Ken drove past a roughly lettered sign that said, "Pack Your Trash." They pulled into a glass-littered campsite at the edge of the sandstone bluff. The water below them had changed to gun metal gray and a hundred feet out a lone surfer was sitting astride his board near a dark kelp bed and a cluster of black rocks that rose out of the surf. To their left Jiggs noticed a white pickup, with a steel pipe frame above the bed, parked parallel to the bluff, a tent trailer hitched behind it. A plastic magnetic sign on the truck's door said, "Buel Snyder, San Jose, CA, 'Celestial Plumbing.'"

Jiggs brought the Bronco to a stop. As he yanked on the hand brake, Ken jumped out leaving the door hanging open.

"That's Buel out there," Ken said nodding toward the water. Still watching the surfer, he released the bungee cords on the roof rack and pulled down his surfboard.

As Ken watched, the surfer paddled ahead of a slow wave, leaped to a stand as the wave began to lift the board, and knees bent, angled across the face of the wave with the grace of a city kid on a skateboard.

"Whoo-eee!" Ken whistled. "Look at him, would you?" Ken leaned his yellow long board against the Bronco and rummaged under the seat for the board wax.

Jiggs climbed out of the driver's side, slammed the door, quickly glanced out at the surfer, then did a few squats on his stiff knees.

"Voila!" Ken held the wax can above his head. He watched as the surfer paddled back to the outside of the shore break. "Buel's got stamina for an old guy, I'll say that."

Jiggs yanked at his cutoffs and did another knee bend. He glanced around at the littered ground of a half dozen campsites along the ridge and noted the rusty fifty-gallon oil drums that were placed at intervals along the bluff. "He's not so old by the looks of him."

"Well, everybody's got a different schedule then," Ken said. He glanced at his watch. "They made some improvements on the house." He nodded across the road.

On the other side of the dirt road Jiggs saw a white Spanish style house, flanked by what looked like outhouses—a couple painted hot pink, a couple pastel blue. The screened-in porch on the side of the big house was obviously new. "Who lives there anyway?" Jiggs asked.

"Some Mexican guy named Guillermo. You'll see him later when he wants the two bucks.

"Two bucks?" Jiggs said. "For these crummy campsites?"

"Why not?" Ken said. "For all us aging California surfer hippies two bucks is nothing."

"Come on," Jiggs said, "a laborer here makes eight bucks a day."

Ken shrugged. "So that's four campsites. Doubt you'll see four in use."

"So, if the surf's so great here, why no more people?"

"This place isn't here for everybody."

"Huh?"

"Hard to find."

"Oh."

"Near impossible. You got the guided tour."

"Okay, Jiggs said, "it's no big deal." He slammed the car door. "Are they the *cuatro casas?*" He cocked his head to the left at the weather-beaten sheds down the bluff which seemed to be collapsing into each other for support. "They the four houses?"

"Nah," Ken chuckled, "that's the fishing camp."

Ken stood the surfboard upright beside the Bronco and ran his palm along its fiberglass surface.

"The launch ramp's behind the shacks," Ken said. "They keep the boats in them." Ken applied more board wax with an athletic sock he had found under the seat. He swirled the surfboard on its skeg and began waxing the back.

Jiggs turned to look back at the buildings across the road. "Ken," he said slowly, "you mean to tell me this place is named after four outhouses?"

"Yep, kind of poetic, ain't it?" Ken pulled his wet suit from the back of the Bronco and threw it over the open door.

"Look Ken," Jiggs turned to watch the slow curl of a listless wave halfway out to the point. "Is this place really worth the trouble? The surf looks dead."

"Would Buel be out there if this place weren't magic?"

"Who knows? I never met Buel."

"Jiggles, you haven't lived until you've seen this place at midtide," Ken said. "You wait and wait and suddenly it's there. All those southern swells, those water pussys just bursting at your back. You know how it is."

"Don't remind me." Jiggs stepped on a rusted can and then flung the flattened tin and some shards of glass into the blackened stone circle in the middle of the campsite. "Big fire tonight," he said.

Ken yanked his wet suit off the open Bronco door. "Sure," he said. "Sure. Knock yourself out."

Ken turned to the water and watched the blond surfer leap to his feet, executing quick roller coaster turns on his short board to increase his speed as he rode the wave.

"Oh hoo, Jiggs my boy," Ken whooped. He yanked on his black wet suit. "I'm off." He grabbed the yellow board and swung it over his head.

Jiggs followed and watched Ken run down the littered ravine to the beach, his yellow board balanced over his head. "No leash?" Jiggs yelled down after him as he watched Ken head for the water.

Ken grinned up from the white rock ledge below. "Some people don't need one," he shouted. "Come on."

"Where's this Cal you told me about?"

"Don't know," Ken yelled back. "He always meets us here."

Ken waded out into the water pushing the surfboard in front of him. When he was knee deep, he hopped onto the board and started paddling out—his legs bent up out of the water—depending only on the power of his thinly muscular upper body.

Jiggs walked back to the campsite. He leaned against the Bronco and folded his arms above his belly. The surf was coming in, wide rolling swells in sets of five with a four to five minute wait between sets. Jiggs noted again that Buel was a good conventional surfer who grabbed a right and just hung in there. Ken was a goofeyfooter who took the lefts facing shore, his back to the wave, his arm in the tube. Ken had told him that he, Buel and Cal had surfed together every June since they first met at *Cuatro Casas* five years before, glad for each other's company away from the brash young surfers at Trestles and Malibu who competed mercilessly for every wave, snaking out other surfers, dropping in without warning, every wave a battle of wills and egos. Jiggs could understand this. It was part of his recent displeasure with the sport. Jiggs supposed they had all been merciless once, but as Ken said yesterday as they drove down 101, they'd done it all eighteen years ago at Topanga.

Jiggs went to the back of the Bronco to unload. Even though there was still a fair amount of light he suspected it would get dark suddenly, as soon as the sun plunged behind the *Punta*. He pulled the cooler out from behind the seat and placed it near the fire circle, then returned to the Bronco to get Ken's tent, a folding camp chair, the Coleman lantern, the sleeping bags and water jugs. Feeling as if someone were watching him, he glanced over to the white house across the road.

There was a yellow bicycle leaning into the tall fence-row of organ pipe cactus in front of the house. Inside the screened porch a dark-haired man sat in a wheelchair. A young Mexican man stood not far from him, leaning against the screen wall and gesturing to the other man. Strange to see a wheelchair out here, Jiggs thought as he set one of the water jugs up on the Bronco's fender. No problems on the Baja he'd been told, just don't drink the water.

After he finished setting up the campsite, Jiggs climbed down the steep ravine path Ken had used. The sun was dragging a blanket of purple behind it and he knew he would have to hurry before it got dark. From the rocky beach the surfers looked like birds bobbing on the water's surface, their boards distant from each other, the black kelp bed between them. Jiggs wandered along the water's edge periodically disturbing preening gulls in the rock pools who squawked and flapped their wings as he passed. When he came upon a large collection of grey, lightweight driftwood in the cup of a boulder, he gathered an armload of the largest pieces.

When Jiggs got back to the campsite after several trips, his arms full of sandy driftwood, he saw the young Mexican zigzagging away along the edge of the bluff on the yellow bicycle. Jiggs glanced across the dirt road. The porch was deserted but he could see a small flickering light within the house. He stacked the wood beside the fire circle and collapsed on the folding chair with a beer. After about ten minutes, the sea breeze picking up, the Mexican came back on his bicycle along the same path at the edge of the bluff. He dropped the bike to the ground in front of the house and went in the screen door to the porch. The dark-haired man in the wheelchair rolled back out, and as Jiggs watched the man pulled himself up to a stand in front of the wheelchair. Under the young Mexican's scrutiny, he brought one stiff leg forward and then moved the other up to meet it. In this manner he slowly made his way across the porch.

Jiggs was still squinting in the deepening twilight, watching the man on the porch, when Ken and a fit-looking blond fellow in a bright blue wet suit came climbing up the bluff from the beach, their surfboards balanced over their heads.

"Jiggs O!" Ken said, "here's Buel."

Jiggs stood, nodded at the blond man and sat down again.

"Not bad, not bad at all," Jiggs said as he settled himself back into the folding chair. "I'd give you old surfer types a B+."

"Jiggs here is a tweedy college professor," Ken said offhandedly as he stood his board on end beside him.

"See any tweeds?" Jiggs lifted his beer and looked down at his cutoffs. "I was a damn adjunct lecturer, Ken," Jiggs said, "it hardly counts for anything."

Buel laid his board on the ground carefully, unzipped his wet suit at the neck and extended his hand. "Glad you could make it." He smiled. "Do much surfing?"

"No," Jiggs said. He half stood to shake Buel's offered hand. "Went skiing at A. Basin at Christmas and the knees still aren't the same—torqued them bad."

Ken looked down at his feet.

"Got to do a lot of swimming then," Buel said.

"So they tell me." Jiggs nodded toward the house. "What's the story with that guy over there?"

Buel turned around and gazed at the house for a long time. The man on the porch had changed his direction and was slowly making his way back to his chair. His right arm hung at his side. "That's Cal," Buel said.

"Cal?" Jiggs turned to Ken who was staring out to the black rocks of the *punta*.

Buel told Jiggs that Cal had stayed for a few extra days last year after he and Ken had left. One night Cal and Guillermo, the young Mexican man on the porch, had gone to Rosario, gotten blind drunk, and on the way back had driven off the bluff. Guillermo had been driving Cal's car. Nothing much happened to him. But Cal's head injury had resulted in moderate brain damage and severe weakness on one side. Cal had never left *Cuatro Casas*. Guillermo was taking care of him.

⌁

Orange flames leaped ten feet into the blackness above the bonfire and sparks flashed like sequins into the flounced skirt of the sky. Around the fire Ken and Jiggs had arranged the Bronco front seats and the bench seat from Buel's truck, covering them with bright striped serapes Guillermo provided as protection against the damp sea air. Ken's and Buel's wet suits were thrown over the open doors of Buel's truck to dry. Around the fire, their faces were glistening from the heat of the blaze.

"You've outdone yourself, Jiggs," Ken said. "So when are you going to hit the water?"

"We're going to have to cool that fire or move the seats back about five feet soon." Jiggs said. He glanced over at Ken who was rolling a joint from a stash Guillermo had just given him.

"*Gracias*, old buddy," Ken said to the swarthy young man who sat on a log next to his seat, the Mexican's soiled baseball cap and blue satin Royals jacket a strange contrast to his dark Indian face.

"*Con mucho gusto*," Guillermo said to Ken with a shy smile. He snapped his fingers and quickly turned back to the fire.

Ken turned to Jiggs. "Guillermo here doesn't speak much English, but he knows what's good."

Jiggs nodded and pulled his bucket seat back a couple feet from the fire.

Buel came out of the darkness behind them. "Good blaze," he said. "I've been walking along the bluff." He dropped into one of the car seats. "The cosmic mother's out wooing tonight for sure."

"Wooing?" Jiggs said.

Ken looked up from his methodical activity, rolled his eyes and went back to work.

"What took you guys so long?" Buel asked as he stretched his legs out toward the fire. "I've been meaning to ask all afternoon. I made *Cuatro Casas* two days ago." He noticed the row of carefully rolled joints growing on Ken's knee. "Never mind," he said with a smile, "I don't need to ask."

"We stopped at K38," Jiggs said. He jumped up to throw a few pieces of driftwood on the fire.

"Wasn't any good was it?" Buel looked up at the sky. A star or two shone through holes in the dark clouds. "Hey," Buel paused a minute, "did you hear about the guy who fell off the bluff at K38 not too long ago?"

"No," Ken said. He tossed some marijuana stems over his shoulder.

"Amazing," Buel said, "this guy was camping there in the parking lot next to the kilometer marker with his girl. Fell off at night and nobody knew. She did a lot of screaming and they finally went and found him. He was okay, though."

"The world's a dangerous place," said Ken.

"Yeah, isn't it," said Jiggs.

"I don't know about you guys." Buel glanced in the direction of the house. "Lately I've been trying not to put anything that isn't pure into my body."

"You always were strange, Buel," Ken said.

"It's important." Buel's tanned face was outlined in the firelight.

Ken waved a thin, tight joint in the air. "Well, this is pure unadulterated—" He pulled a burning stick from the fire, lit the joint and took a drag. "Talking about adultery," he said after a moment, staring down at the glowing joint he held cupped into his palm, "I've given up on women."

"*El amor es un bico*," Guillermo murmured. He was sitting on a stump facing the fire.

"Yeah, well Guillermo's the real lover round here." Ken elbowed Guillermo off the log. "Love's a bug, he says, a real bug. But I tell you women are too loony on their moony days. Avoid. Avoid."

Guillermo sat back down on the log and said nothing.

"I don't know about that," Buel said, "some of my best friends—" Buel smiled. "I thought you liked loons, Ken."

Ken flicked an ash toward the fire. "You forgot," he said, "I don't practice anymore." A burning stick popped and sparked. "Worked in a surf shop in Laguna Beach for a while this year, Buel. Met Jiggs again there, in fact. Hadn't seen him in years."

Ken took another drag from the joint and offered it to Jiggs who shook his head. "'I'm so tense!'" Ken pounded his feet on the ground in front of him, "I need a Xanax!"

"Sounds like you caught something from your patients," Buel said.

"Nah."

"'*Qué cuando pica*,'" Guillermo sang, staring into the fire, his hands hanging between his knees, "'*no se encuentra remidio*.'"

"Sure, sure, Guillermo," Ken said, "there's not a thing you can do for it."

"Surf it through," Buel said.

"Yeah, sure." Ken passed the joint to Guillermo who had stopped singing and was staring again at his hands. Guillermo took a drag, walked the joint over to Buel and padded back to his place in front of the fire. Jiggs noticed he was wearing soft moccasin-like shoes.

"It's been a long time since I smoked," Buel said after accepting the joint from Guillermo with a nod and a smile. "Last year, I guess. As I said, I've been trying to keep my body pure."

"Since Cal—" Ken said.

"You got it."

Guillermo glanced up when Cal's name was mentioned. He

quickly looked back down into the fire. In the darkening night they could hear the rising tide rolling onto the rocks below.

"I've been overextending myself," Buel said, "those contractors are after me all the time."

Jiggs got up. He pulled some driftwood from the stack and tossed it into the fire. A column of sparks rose into the dark sky.

"Yeah," Ken said above the crackle of the fire. "Can you imagine—" he chuckled, "Buel, the surfing plumber."

"Why not?" Buel asked. He took a long drag from the joint, extended it to Jiggs who shook his head and then passed it on to Ken who put the joint out in the dirt in front of him. They all sat quietly for a few minutes, leaning forward, staring into the orange and blue flames of the driftwood fire, the night still and beginning to cool around them.

Jiggs thought he heard something move in the pile of driftwood at his right. He listened closely. Nothing. He stared out into the dark desert beyond the flickering circle of light from the fire. Only an hour ago he had watched the twisted shapes of the cactus fade into the dark. By now small animals would be coming out of their cooling burrows, eyes luminous in the moonlight as they stalked the trembling prey that would sustain them. Creatures that in daylight froze in their tracks in adaptive invisibility could not use this ploy at night when predators, like bad dreams, sought them out by odor and intuition. Jiggs strained to listen for other sounds from the dark beyond them, but heard nothing more than the crackle and hiss of the fire. A heavy scent hung in the air.

"That's Queen of Night cactus you smell." Jiggs jumped as Buel spoke out of the dark behind him. "Okay," Buel said as he moved into the firelight, "I have a question for you, doctor."

"Me?" Ken asked.

"Yep," Buel said as he sat down again and stretched his legs out before him on the serape-covered seat. "This is a good one. What is the first level of consciousness?"

Ken laughed. "Guilt," he said with only a moment's hesitation.

"Movement," Buel said with a smile.

"Movement?"

"Yeah," Buel said, "but I can't explain it." He leaned forward and stared into the fire for a long minute. "But did you ever notice—" He sat back in the seat. "—if you turn in your sleep, your dream changes?"

"I feel a little like that now." Ken laughed. "It's just cell memory, old buddy."

"No, I never noticed," Jiggs said shaking his head. "Movement."

Guillermo glanced up from the fire. "Where you been?"

Jiggs looked at Guillermo as surprised as if he had suddenly taken off in awkward flight.

"Don't worry about it, Jiggs," Ken said. "Buel's been teaching our friend a little English."

"I'm serious," Buel said. "Movement."

Buel gestured to Ken who gave him another joint and the plastic lighter. "My wife's into metaphysics," Buel said. "Did I tell you?" The joint glowed in the darkness in front of him as he lit it. "She's off to England." Buel's voice was high and strained as he held in the smoke. "—wants to study one of those haunted castles."

Ken's laugh ended in a bout of coughing. "Do tell," he choked out. "Do you believe this guy, Jiggs?"

Jiggs shrugged. "I'm suspending judgement—"

"Geez," Ken said. He turned to Buel. "So who's going to take care of you while she's away? Any little honeys?"

Buel smiled. "The cosmic mother," he said slowly.

"Are plumbers supposed to talk like this?" Jiggs asked.

"In California they do." Ken threw the roach into the coals.

They sat in silence for a few minutes, staring into the flames of the sputtering fire, the night settling in upon them.

"My father died this winter," Jiggs said barely above a whisper. He cleared his throat. "Just got purple in his chair one night watching the tube. Late show. My mother found him in the morning."

"Too bad," Ken said glancing at Jiggs quickly and then back into the fire.

Buel and Guillermo were silent.

"Indian television." Ken pointed to the fire.

"Yeah," Jiggs said. "Yeah."

Suddenly Ken got up and galloped around the bonfire, slapping his sides. "'Oh, I'm so nervous!'" He stopped at Guillermo, pulled the baseball cap off the Mexican's dark head, put it on his own, and ran around the fire circle again. "Wait, wait," Ken said as he came to a halt again in front of Guillermo. Ken took the baseball cap off and peered down into it.

"Guillermo wants to tell me something." Ken bent down so the Mexican could speak into his ear. "Oh," Ken said, "Guillermo says he has to go check his goats."

"Those goats we saw by that shack coming in?" Jiggs asked.

"Sure," Buel said from the bench seat, his eyes closed. "Guillermo goes off on his bicycle to visit them all the time."

"In the dark?" Jiggs asked.

"Sure," Buel said. "He sees in the dark."

"What?"

"So to speak."

"What?"

"Reflex. He just knows the place."

Guillermo touched Ken's arm and spoke to him quietly for a moment. Jiggs could hear the rapid lilt of his Spanish.

"Here's one for you guys," Ken said. "Guillermo says his goats are stoned all the time. That's right," Ken said as he shook his head. "Stoned." He grinned. "Guillermo says he puts his head next to the goat's skull and he can feel the stillness in there. Feel the goat just being."

"They eat all that prickly pear," Jiggs said.

"No," Ken replied. "I swear that's what he said—just being a goat. Besides, cactus is good to eat. Isn't that right, Guillermo?"

"Sí."

"I swear that's what he said. Stillness. At least," Ken said, "that's as close as I can understand him. Guillermo's pretty messed up himself. But he says he lines his head up next to this goat's so maybe he can catch onto how it is—to just be—natural like."

"Okay," Jiggs said, "maybe like those country people who sit on their porches and watch traffic."

"Sure" Ken laughed, "they put their heads up next to cars,"

"Listen to the fenders, maybe." Jiggs chuckled.

"Those goats down there may be into stillness," Buel said, looking up at the dark sky, "but the hogs there are a whole different story."

"Exceptional beings," Ken said. He sat down on the car seat next to Jiggs. "Hey, I had a friend who had a pig so smart he named it 'Number One.'" He poked Jiggs in the side. "It looked like that big black one we saw, Jiggs. Liked to chase cars. Can you imagine a pig galloping after you as you drive down the road?"

Ken jumped up, blew out his cheeks and ran around the fire circle. After a couple more circular gallops he sat down. "Just like— that," he said winded. "But Guillermo has no respect for pigs. He just told me. Well, his hat told me."

Guillermo shrugged his shoulders and smiled.

"Guillermo, did I tell you that goats and pigs have a fine intelligence?"

"Too much of the weed," Buel said.

Ken grinned into the fire. "Buel would call it a 'first order consciousness.'"

Jiggs laughed. "Completely gone."

"Sure," Ken continued, "pigs can climb ladders, go get the mail, bring in the newspaper, and if properly outfitted can get a beer out of the fridge."

"What do you mean by 'properly outfitted'?" Jiggs asked.

"Oh, if you have a can dispenser," Ken said. "You wouldn't expect a decent pig to nose around in a six pack would you?"

"No, no, no." Guillermo said. He rose from his place on the log and gazed out over the dark expanse of the desert. *"Buenas noches,"* he said turning to them. *"Yo tengo dolor."*

"Dolor?" asked Ken.

"Sí, tristeza de estomago."

"What did he say?" Jiggs asked.

"Oh—sorrow in his belly," Ken replied. "Stomach ache."

Jiggs rose and threw several light grey sticks of driftwood into the fire.

Guillermo went quietly to the edge of the bluff to pick up his bicycle. He stood there and seemed to be listening to the sound of the water lapping against the rocks below. After a few minutes he hopped on his yellow bicycle and wobbled off.

"So what does he do now?" Jiggs asked.

"Puts Cal to bed, I guess," Ken said.

"No cosmic mother for Cal," Buel said from his place on the car seat.

"What's going to happen to him?" Jiggs asked.

"Guillermo?"

"Cal."

"Maybe you should ask about Guillermo," Buel said.

"Look, it's like this," Ken said throwing a glowing stick back into the fire. "With a brain injury there's rapid recovery in the first five to ten days, significant recovery by six months. After a year, not much more. If he were a kid he could recover almost completely. But he's not a kid."

"So how old is he?" Jiggs asked. "He must have been in good shape."

"He was the best," Buel said.

"About our age," Ken said. "Thirties, forties—I'm not sure."

"Age isn't important," Buel said. "Courage is important. Doing is important. Take Viet Nam for instance. It didn't take courage to go there. Just bravery, just withstanding. Going to Canada would have taken courage. What did you do, Jiggs?"

"So Guillermo's been taking care of him for a year?"

"Yeah, Jiggs, a year," Buel said. "Why do you ask? Why didn't you answer my question?"

Jiggs was silent. He went to the Bronco and came back wearing a faded flannel shirt over his T-shirt, and carrying a fifth of Jose Quervo. "Tequila?" He asked as he offered the bottle.

"That stuff makes me crazy," Buel said. He got up and threw a dry bush into the fire. It blazed and smelled like burning sage. "I want to get out early." Buel shook his head. "Look," he said, "I've got it straight from God, Herman Hesse, and T.S. Eliot."

"That's quite a crew," Jiggs said.

"Only the best," piped up Ken.

"You know the Sanskrit, *da, dattaim, dattyamin?*"

"No," Jiggs said.

"It's from *The Wasteland*, what the thunder said, man, where've you been?" Buel smiled. "My wife and I talk about it a lot. Anyway, at first I thought the words meant 'to care,' 'to sympathize,' and 'to discipline.' Now I know it's first 'to give.'"

"I have no idea what you are talking about," Jiggs said.

"That's what I'd guess," Buel said. "It's not convenient, hey? To step out of your own dreary conformity for even a moment?"

"Come on, Buel." Ken reached over to take the bottle from Jiggs. "Shit," Ken said. He took a swig, and then handed the bottle back to Jiggs. Ken nodded over to Buel who, in that short time, had fallen asleep in his chair.

Jiggs stared into the fire, the bottle of tequila between his knees. After a few minutes Buel got up slowly. He pointed to his tent trailer at the edge of the bluff. "See you both in the morning," he said and he slipped away from the fire.

Ken jumped up. "Yeah. Yeah. Me too." He gave a brief wave of his arm, crossed the campsite and disappeared into the dome tent at the edge of the road.

Jiggs tossed another piece of wood on the fire and then sat down on the ground in front of it, his back against the Bronco seat. He smelled the salty spray of the water behind him, now at high tide lapping against the rocks. He could feel the dark of the desert creep in upon the dying fire.

Jiggs wondered how he had been talked into this trip. He hadn't surfed in years. Ken had called it his annual "geographic cure," and claimed he was tired of driving all the way down to the Baja alone. Ken could be pretty persuasive when he wanted to be, and Jiggs wasn't doing much anyway. Sometimes, Jiggs thought, when you go a long way you learn something, and sometimes you don't. He hadn't learned anything so far, but he had had plenty of time to remember things he would have preferred to have left behind.

≈

It had been raining for several days after the funeral and restless, Jiggs had been wandering through the house. His mother found him downstairs in the small tidy workshop under the kitchen.

"What are you doing, James?" she asked him.

"Nothing much." He picked a power drill off its hanging bracket on the pegboard, turned it in his hands, and put it down on the workbench. "Just looking around."

"So many things crowd in around you in a lifetime," she said, looking at the orderly arrangement of tools hanging on the walls. "Why don't you take the tools back East with you? That's something he would have liked."

"I doubt it," Jiggs said. "I don't have any use for them."

"Maybe someday you will."

"You know I'm not handy," Jiggs said. He glanced out the casement window. "Where's all this California sun you brag about?"

"I saved the tools for you, James." She looked down at her hands. "Your Uncle Harry wanted them. I love your Uncle Harry you know, but I told him they were for you."

"Why didn't you consult me first?" he said. You make a thing poorly, he thought, and it falls apart, use it some more, and it's broken again. "Why bother?" he said aloud.

"He liked to keep busy, James." She turned away. "Switch off the light when you're through." He had heard her slow footsteps on the wooden stairs and then the click of the latch as the door closed.

&

Jiggs took a sip of the tequila. A small grey lizard scurried out of the pile of driftwood, skittered across the sand in front of the fire, stopped for a moment as if listening, then turned toward Jiggs. The lizard side-stepped up to Jiggs' hand that was resting on the sand beside him, paused, and then climbed on top of it. Jiggs studied the creature. It was about nine inches in length including the thin iridescent blue tail, the rest of it the soft grey color of kid gloves. Its narrow, ribbon like tongue flicked in and out several times. Its eyes were small black beads with glints of yellow that reflected the fire.

Jiggs didn't move. He had never been fond of animals. He'd

ignored the dog when he was a boy, let the fish tank become a stagnant pool in which dead moths floated on the surface and bewildered mollies slowly succumbed long before he noticed, becoming rigid monuments to his neglect.

The lizard crawled up his arm, stopped at the elbow, then proceeded to his shoulder and across his chest. It hung there, little claws caught in the threads of the flannel shirt.

There is nothing wrong with this creature, Jiggs thought. In fact, everything right with it resting on him as it was, unafraid, curious, taking a risk that he would not fling it into the fire.

Jiggs looked out into the desert. Clouds were visible in the night sky, and in front of him he saw the outline of a saguaro cactus in the pale moonlight. The cactus looked like a man poised, waiting. It was too late, he thought, he could never please him.

The lizard inched up his chest and flicked its tongue at the juncture of his neck and chin. Jiggs felt it as a dry caress, something like the kisses his mother had given him as a child. He sat up abruptly. The lizard fell to the ground and scurried back into the woodpile.

Jiggs stared back into the dark of the desert. He couldn't see the cactus anymore but he felt the wind begin to stir, and he imagined the frozen windmill he had seen near the vegetable farm they drove through to get there begin to turn with a rusty creak in the dark. Nothing real. Nothing real. He heard the surf wringing its hands wavelet upon wavelet all the way to the *punta*, and it came to him suddenly that Buel's cosmic mother guided each wave along with the palm of her hand.

Jiggs stood up on his stiff knees and walked over to the edge of the bluff. He thought of Cal being clumsily lifted into bed by Guillermo after waiting in his chair a long time in the dark.

Jiggs crossed the glass-littered campsite and crawled into the back of the Bronco to sleep.

～

It was six in the morning. The sun had just dealt its first cards over the lagoon behind the white house. Buel, in shorts and a T-shirt, stumbled out of his trailer. He looked up at the brightening sky and then down over the bluff to the surf below. The tide was low, pulled back from the rocks with haze hanging near shore, but beyond it, in the pale morning light, the water was spread out like a blue satin cloth. No wind. The waves were coming in in threes with a long wait between sets. It looked good. Or good enough. Calm. Buel went back into his trailer and emerged with a red and blue bundle under his arm. He crossed the dirt road still moist with morning.

In ten minutes Buel banged out the screen door wearing his blue wet suit, pushing Cal in the wheelchair ahead of him. Cal was wearing a red wet suit and a dazed expression. When they reached the edge of the bluff Buel stopped.

"Now just look at it," Buel said.

Cal gazed out over the water, his dark hair standing up like an accidental punk hairstyle. He rubbed the side of his thumb along the padded arm of the chair. "I haven't been here," he said, his voice halting and low, "—long time."

"That's what I thought," Buel said standing beside the wheelchair, his arms folded across his chest. "Take a good look."

Cal glanced down at his wasted legs and then out at the water. Buel waited a minute, and then knelt alongside the wheelchair. Under his knee the low-lying succulent cactus on the edge of the bluff split and bled. They studied the water silently for a few minutes.

"What do you think?" Buel asked finally.

"Good—enough," Cal said, his head tilted to one side, his face expressionless.

"I'll take the boards down." Buel jumped up and headed for his truck. "wait here," he called over his shoulder.

Cal nodded.

Buel came back from the truck with two long boards, one orange, one white, under either arm.

"Still a— logger?" Cal said.

Buel looked at Cal in surprise, then chuckled. He disappeared over the side of the bluff and down the ravine to the white rock beach below.

Cal watched the small, gray-winged white gulls ride the updraft that swooped up the side of the bluff. When they reached eye-level, they tucked their black heads and feet for a drop to the water. The red berry cactus beneath his chair had an odor both sweet and salty.

In a few minutes Buel reappeared over the rise.

"Here we go," he said. He swung Cal up out of the wheelchair, which fell to its side and collapsed with the movement. Buel carried Cal high in his arms over the bluff and down the trash-strewn gully to the beach.

"You ought to be glad you're not walking on this stuff," Buel said when they got below. "Broken bottles, wet paper. No respect. Just no respect for the earth that is alive, after all."

The surfboards were at the edge of the dark water, propped up on their skegs on the white rock, their noses wet.

"This is—crazy," Cal said as Buel set him down beside the boards.

"Doing anything at all is crazy if you think about it," Buel said taking a deep breath and bending to touch his toes. "Anything at all."

Buel stretched his arms out behind his back and glanced at Cal. "Put your feet in for a while," he said. "Let me figure this out."

Buel surveyed the surf in front of them. To the right large rocks rose from the water halfway out to the surf break. The dark *punta* jutted into the water at an angle in front of them and to the left, calmer water was dark with kelp. The waves were coming in like an arm sweeping across the surface, occasionally rolling under the black-green patches of seaweed to lift it out of its path.

"How do you feel about kelp?" Buel asked Cal who was sitting awkwardly on the rock shore, leaning on his left arm, the pale flesh of his forehead knotted into deep ridges.

"Kelp," Cal said squinting up at him. "A little's okay."

"Right," Buel said as he zipped up his wet suit at the back of the neck and waded into the water in front of Cal. He grabbed the man under the arms and pulled him up to a stand in the cold water. "Can you do that for a minute?"

Cal nodded.

With one hand under Cal's shoulder, Buel pulled the orange long board out and steadied it in the water in front of Cal. "Get on," he said.

Cal hesitated.

"Do it," Buel said, his stance wide, his hands on either side of the orange board.

Cal grabbed the board with one hand and fell onto it, belly down.

"All right," Buel said. He leaned over, still holding the board steady and attached its leash to Cal's thin ankle. "You don't need to lose this thing," Buel said as he adjusted the velcro anklet.

Cal nodded, his thin body stiff and crooked on the board. He raised his head to watch the surf forming at the *punta*.

Buel fastened his own leash, quickly hopped on his board and reached over again to steady Cal's. "How's your paddling arm?" he asked.

"Fine." Cal strained to pull the slack half of his face into a smile.

"Okay," Buel said, and he pointed to the surf break.

They paddled out slowly, lazy swells moving under them like a fat man in a hammock rolling over in his sleep. When they got to the kelp beds, the glistening seaweed on long tangled roots—as disturbing as water snakes—caught on their boards and entangled their feet which they hung behind them as rudders. Each time they got tangled they quickly kicked the slick seaweed off and went on.

When they reached an area of calm, Buel asked if Cal could get himself into a sitting position. Cal nodded and with his left arm—his face determined, then suddenly relaxed—Cal pushed himself up on the board.

"Now just think how we look from the bluff," Buel said.

Cal shook his dark hair back out of his eyes. "Pelicans," he said in a husky voice.

"Sure Cal, bobbing on the water." Astride his board, Buel faced the red sandstone bluff, his back to the *punta*. He could see the wheelchair lying on its side, the sun rising behind it, and to the left of it Ken's dome tent and the still-smoking fire.

Cal braced himself with his left arm and adjusted his position on the board. The swells were gentle beneath them. After a few minutes Cal's shoulders dropped and his expression softened.

They rode the swells without speaking, Buel thinking about the first time they met when Cal was still a surfer with a California reputation who had taken to him, and had shown him with not much more than a grunt or two how to walk the board. Cal did spinners on his orange long board and then offhandedly gave the board to Buel saying he just had a new one made. Later Buel had tried a short board and found it more to his liking, but he never forgot Cal's cool instruction, which had given him permission to surf badly in the beginning. Just do it was all.

Buel remembered those first runs, the excitement of the avalanche of water moving under him and catching up, always at his back. The pure energy moving through water and driving him ahead of it, a wall of water rising behind him. He felt within it, part of it, yet separate and powerful, full of grace in that element that at once bathed and stung. Often the water threw him against rock, often it lapped gently at his feet as he knelt on his board, the sun rising each morning beside him like a woman elegant in public and passionate alone. He was often tumbled by the power of a hot wave, then soon soothed by the lapping caress of the sea mother who entangled in the rooty snare of her kelp beds. Buel knew there was nothing he could say as he rode the board beside Cal, each of them staring out to sea with the dazed look of fishermen.

After a few minutes Cal lifted his chin several times toward the bluff. "Guillermo," he said.

Buel shaded his eyes and scanned the campsite. The sun had now risen above the tent. "I don't think he's there. Nope, I don't see anyone up yet."

"Guillermo," Cal said, "is there."

"Do you see—" Buel asked. "Oh, yeah," Buel turned to look at an oncoming wave, "he's standing by you, all right." Buel yanked at his wet suit sleeves. "Now look," he said, "it's starting to set up. When the first one breaks, I'll take it. You grab the second."

Cal gave him a startled look.

"Well, do you think we're going to sit here all day? I've watched you walk on the porch." Buel said. "I know you can do it ."

Cal shook his head.

"You outsurfed everybody here for years. You know the *punta* and you know what kind of stuff comes through here. Do what you've always done. Tumble a little maybe, you can always pull your board back with the leash and just plain hang on."

Cal nodded. "Yeah," he said with a crack in his voice, "smoking along."

"Forget it. The surf's setting up. Get ready."

A wave swelled before them. "Now!" Buel yelled. He paddled before the curl, leaped to a stand and rode across the face of the wave at the front of his board. He turned on the wave to watch Cal who was frantically paddling one-armed in front of the second wave.

"Now!" Buel shouted. "Do it now."

Cal hesitated, then pushed against the board with his stronger arm, a wobbly lead foot beneath him. He got to a half stand before the white water caught up with him. Standing precariously for a moment, on one leg and the weak toes of his trail foot, he lost his balance and fell.

Buel unleashed his board, dove in the water and went after him. For a moment he could see Cal's dark head in the surging white water and then it was gone. Buel could see nothing but a mad sweep of foam going toward the rocks.

Buel swam toward the spot where he had last seen Cal's head bobbing above the surface. He swam to the rocks beyond it and found Cal, his arm around a green, moss-covered rock, the orange surfboard a short distance away. Cal's wet hair hung in his eyes and a thin river of red flowed down his cheek form a cut above his left eye.

"Are you all right?" Buel was breathless. He let his legs drop and found the water was only waist deep.

Cal nodded. "All right." He was moving one arm in a modified side stroke.

"You can stand here," Buel said. "It's not deep." He waded over and touched Cal lightly on the arm. "Cal, pull in your board."

Cal yanked his leg to himself and the surfboard came bouncing toward him. He lay his left arm across it and rested his face against the smooth surface.

Buel rescued his own board from the surf and hopped on. "Let's go," he said.

Cal pulled himself onto his board and they paddled slowly back to the calm kelp-filled area where they had lined up before.

"What did you tell me years ago?" Buel said when they reached their destination. "'Rely on your board,' you said, 'I'm here but the board's better.'"

Cal wiped a hand across his forehead, looked at it, and smiled. The bleeding had slowed. "No," he said slowly, "not me."

"Yes," Buel said. "You. You gave me that hideous orange board you're riding. And there's still some of your magic in it."

"Magic," Cal said flatly. He glanced down at his thin arms and then over at the seagulls that were riding the swells a few yards away, their wings tucked, like trim little boats. Cal shook his dark head and then slipped off the board into the water.

He came up on the other side of his board. "Underwater," Cal said, "is easier."

"Kick, you turkey," Buel said. "Hold on to the board and kick your legs." Buel hopped off his board and swam behind Cal. He stood and grabbed Cal's thin legs in the water and began moving them in a rhythmic scissors kick. "Okay," he said, "keep it up."

While Buel watched, Cal maintained a slow kick, his left arm across the surfboard, he cheek resting on its wet surface.

"All right," Buel said when Cal slipped off the board again and came up shaking his head. "Okay, friend."

Cal moved his arms unevenly in front of him. The surfboard, still attached to his ankle leash, bobbed beside him with each movement of his legs. "Not good—enough," Cal said. He leaned across his board and lay there for a few minutes, his ribs retracting, his breath coming in rhythmic whistles. He slowly pulled himself onto the board and up into a sitting position. Cal rested a minute, his dark head down, his chin on his chest. He slowly turned to watch the water behind him.

"Not good enough," Cal mumbled as he stared at the flat line of the horizon to the left of the *punta*.

"Okay, so it's not the Banzai Pipeline," Buel slapped at the water. "So you're not Duke Kahanamoku, and it's not the ultimate wave. Damn it Cal, you've done enough surfing to know that three fourths of the time what you're really doing is fishing. Fishing for a wave. Just being there."

Cal stared at the long horizon that had been gradually brightening into a clear morning sky. His breath came in gasps. "It's something," he said at last. "At least," he threw his head back and shook out his dark hair. His face was pale. "—something."

～

About half past six that morning Jiggs climbed out of the back of the Bronco where he had been sleeping, stretched and looked over the water. He saw two surfers out riding their boards. When he turned the sun had just cleared the roof of the white house. Jiggs went back to the Bronco and pulled out his sleeping bag.

Ken emerged from his tent scratching his lean belly.

"Oh," Jiggs said nodding toward the bluff. "I thought it was you out there."

"Me?"

Jiggs gestured toward the water and continued rolling up his sleeping bag on the Bronco's hood. "Take a look."

Yawning, Ken went to the edge of the bluff.

"That's Buel," he said. "And—what the hell? Cal's out there with him."

"Buel must have taken him down," Jiggs said. "Early."

"Wonder how he talked him into it," Ken said. "How'd he talk Guillermo into it?" Ken wandered toward his tent.

"How come Cal hasn't drowned yet? " Jiggs shouted after him.

"Damned if I know," Ken said shaking his head. "Archimedes, maybe. Ever heard of him?"

"Of course, but what?" Jiggs watched the dark figures bobbing out on the water beyond the kelp beds. "That's crazy out there."

"Buel's got it under control," Ken said. He squinted up at the sun. "Good surfing day on the Baja."

Jiggs looked up and saw Guillermo coming along the bluff path toward them on his bicycle, a milk pail hanging from the handlebars. Goat's milk sloshed from the pail as Guillermo jumped off the bike beside them and stared out over the water. "*Madre de Dios,*" he said.

"Heap big mathematician," Ken yawned. He turned to Guillermo.

Balancing the bike and the milk pail on its handlebars, Guillermo pointed to the wheelchair that was lying on its side further down the edge of the bluff. "Cal?" Guillermo said.

"Geez," Jiggs said walking up to them, "I didn't even see that chair."

"A body in fluid," Ken said, stretching. "I need some coffee."

"How can he do this?" Jiggs squinted at the surfers who were riding their boards near the rocks.

"Is buoyed by a force—" Ken continued, "—equal to the weight displaced."

"Ken, cut it out," Jiggs said.

Guillermo lifted the milk pail off the bicycle handlebar, set it on the ground, then lowered the bicycle into the cactus berries at his feet. He squatted beside the milk pail at the edge of the bluff and watched the bobbing surfers out on the water.

"Looks okay to me out there," Ken said. "Come on, get up Guillermo. We can have coffee now that you've brought the milk."

"Look," Jiggs said, "how can he do this? It's just plain stupid to have Cal out there."

"Why?" Ken turned to go back to his tent. "Buel would say Echidna the sea mother has it covered."

"*Verdad*," Guillermo said, his gaze still fixed on the two figures out on the water.

"All right, Ken," Jiggs said, "I don't mean how can he do it scientifically, or even mythically, I mean—well, humanly."

"Ah, there it is, Jiggs. When there's nothing else—" Ken turned away. "You figure it out." Ken turned to Guillermo. "I saw a stump down the road that will be perfect for the bonfire tonight. Mind if I borrow your vehicle, Guillermo? Think I'll check it out."

Guillermo nodded and turned back to watch the water.

Ken moved the milk pail aside and picked up the bicycle by its rusty handlebars. "'After I roam up and down—'" he shouted. He hopped on the bike and rode in a circle in front of Jiggs and Guillermo, "'o'er the waste as a wanderer.'" He kept the bike wobbling in place, "'and lay my head in the bowels of the earth.'" He rode close to Jiggs and then wobbled out beyond the fire circle. "'Let mine eyes see the sun.'" He glanced up at the sun which was over his tent now, and then back to Jiggs. "'When will the man who is dead ever look on the light of the Sunshine?'" Ken turned and rode off toward the bluff path. "Gilgamesh," he said. "The best thing about this bicycle," he announced over his shoulder, "is—no brakes."

Jiggs and Guillermo watched Ken ride off, zigzagging along the edge of the bluff.

"He's truly crazy," Jiggs said.

Guillermo said something in Spanish. Something about *aqua*, water, Jiggs thought, but he couldn't make it out. The young man shrugged.

Jiggs walked to the edge of the bluff and watched the two men, one blond in a bright blue wet suit, one dark-haired in red, ride the calm between sets.

After a few minutes Guillermo nodded to Jiggs and sauntered away along the ridge path. Several yards down Jiggs saw him cut across the road past the small pink and blue houses and head toward the lagoon.

Maybe the goats were still gathered at the shed for their milking, Jiggs thought, or maybe Guillermo was going there simply to put his head against the skull of his favorite goat. Jiggs squatted down on his stiff knees and picked one of the cactus berries. The sticky pink-tinged juice stained his fingers. He glanced up to see Cal on the water, standing on his orange board. He was leaning to one side in an awkward, unnatural stance, but he was surfing, nevertheless, all the way to shore. Jiggs heard a whoop from below.

Jiggs dropped the cactus bloom. He jumped up and ran to the Bronco. He pulled out his wet suit which was stuffed under the driver's seat and put it on quickly. Moving to the rear of the Bronco he released his old green long board from the roof rack and with the heavy board under his arm, he charged down the gully to the beach.

When he got there he found Buel at the edge of the water pulling in the boards. Cal sat on the rocks, his head down.

"What are you risking his life for?" Jiggs demanded.

"What?" Buel said glancing up at Jiggs in surprise.

"You heard what I said." Jiggs dropped his board at the water's edge and waded over to Buel. "He's been battered on the rocks. Look at him."

"Haven't you ever gone against rocks?" Buel stood. "It's part of it. Jiggs, sometimes you have to do something."

"Do something? You mean you couldn't think of anything else? He could have died."

Buel looked down at the water at his feet. He shook his head. "He could have died before, but he didn't." Buel reached back to unzip the neck of his wet suit. "We got the cosmic mother looking out."

Cal shifted his position on the rocks. He looked from one to the other. "Hey." Cal had a lopsided grin on his face. "Water—'s fine."

Jiggs watched Buel pull the boards further up on the rocky beach. Then Buel went over to Cal and lifted him in his arms. He steadied himself, and started the climb up the soft side of the bluff.

Jiggs turned back and stared over the water. The black rocks of the *punta* were covered with the white dots of gulls, and pelicans rode the morning glass near the horizon. Movement, Jiggs thought. He grabbed his surfboard and with it under his arm waded out into the blue-black water.

Sportin' Life

lthough it wasn't light yet, Amy had been up for an hour and was sitting in the nurses' station waiting for report. She wondered if she would ever get used to this, ever get over early-morning-dreads she had each day walking to work.

The night nurse came in looking tired and frazzled. Nights wasn't a shift for anyone without a large ration of masochism and Amy suspected Gaylord, with her large sad eyes and shapeless body, suffered in her profession more than most.

"Madden had the radical neck yesterday afternoon," said Miss Gaylord as she plopped down on the stool, "and she's bonkers already."

"What do you mean?" Amy asked. She knew she was being assigned Mrs. Madden today. All first year nursing students eventually had to work with radical neck dissections. She knew it was just a matter of time, and her luck had run out. Gross, that was all you could say about them.

"Oh, she's started to squirrel," Gaylord said.

"Squirrel?"

"Save everything. She's insisting nothing be thrown away in her cubicle. Even the dirty Kleenexes she's used. Disgusting."

Amy sighed. Here it comes.

"Okay," said Miss Gaylord, "let me get this over with so I can get out of here." She flipped open the Kardex.

"Madden, Lizzie C. Carcinoma right mandible. Hemimandibilectomy 11/24/61. Vital signs stable at 138/90, 88, 20. Low grade temp at 100.2. Swelling moderate. Slept fitfully. Had to be suctioned times four. A looney tune. Jones, Ethel B. Appendectomy, 11/20/ 61...."

Amy took notes. She prepared herself for the worse. Madden had been pretty hard to look at even before surgery with that large dense body, frizzy dyed black hair, and that eight centimeter tumor under her jaw. She'd tried to distract ooglers with that purple lipstick Amy guessed, but it had certainly caught Amy's attention.

On admission Lizzie Madden had talked fondly in a gravelly voice about "her girls Niecey and Jo" and Amy had thought she meant her daughters. But after reading the intern's note on the History & Physical Amy knew what kind of girls they were and what kind of business Lizzie Madden had down on Race Street.

They get all kinds in here, Amy mused, but you try to treat them the same. Try. She'd found it hard to be pleasant after being raised strictly by a family traditionally Lutheran and only marginally joyful. Lizzie Madden had been spreading her legs for decades, then directing those who did the same, cajoling, comforting, cavorting with them until they had forgotten, or—the less intelligent ones—never known, where they had left their shame behind. But yesterday Lizzie Madden had sat in the doctor's office as a bright spring day pounded light through the small windows of the waiting room, the thing on her jaw protruding firm and hard like a new orange before picking. Amy imagined a few people stared at her, but she suspected most buried themselves in their recurrent privacies.

Amy pulled at her tight apron, shoved her notes in her pocket and hurried down the ward to the cubicles at the back. Ward K was small, tucked into a tower of the old Ravner building, but the Head Nurse, Miss Bendix, had a reputation for strict control over the nursing care and a well run unit, so the surgeons usually recommended that their most "interesting" cases be admitted there. When Amy saw her name posted—A. Vogel, Ward K, 11/1/61-12/1/61—she wasn't sure whether she was being rewarded or punished. The gossip was that Miss Bendix was so obsessive-compulsive she'd follow student nurses and close cabinet doors before they could get their hands out.

Amy pulled back the curtain to the cubicle, went directly to the white metal bedside cabinet and lifted out the stainless steel washbasin without looking at Mrs. Madden. She heard gurgling snores arising from the bed. Needs suctioning. Had that night nurse really suctioned her four times? Amy stood with the basin against her starched bib and steeled herself to glance at the person in the bed.

She was lying on her side, a big mound of a woman, an IV bottle hanging over her, the tubing wrapped around her arm. The woman's face was partially obscured by the puckered white bedspread. Amy placed the basin on the straight chair and tiptoed over to the bed. She pulled down the spread and gazed into a swollen purple face, a frightened blue eye open and regarding her as the wet snore-like sounds bubbled at the opening of the metal tracheostomy at her throat.

Amy jumped back, but quickly composed herself. Forced composure was the first lesson she had learned in nursing school. She was seventeen when she began her training and no one had told her, but this was the first informal lesson everyone learned: how not to show in one's face the horror felt daily.

"Good morning, Mrs. Madden," Amy said pleasantly.

The woman in the bed tugged at the intravenous tubing that circled her arm and tried to speak. When she could not, her eyes got huge in the kind of look Amy had seen only on calves before the mallet knocked them into senselessness. It was the moment they knew instinctively what was to befall them. Mrs. Madden wore the same look in her eyes.

"Oh," said Amy quickly, "don't worry, you can't talk now because of the trach—the tracheostomy—this thing in your windpipe." She pointed to her own throat and then to the woman's. "This is just temporary. 'Til the swelling goes down. Didn't anyone tell you? You won't be able to talk until it is removed——or even before that—you can talk when you learn how to cover it."

Mrs. Madden pulled her free hand up to her neck and jerked at the neck dressing. Amy leaped toward the bed and grabbed her fingers. "Oh, not yet. Have to keep the area sterile." The woman looked puzzled.

"'Til you heal some. Don't worry."

Mrs. Madden shook her huge swollen head and then with quick

panicky motions pointed to her throat. Her breathing was noisy, whistling.

"I'll be right back," Amy said ducking out with the washbasin. "I'll take care of that," she said. "Don't worry."

Amid the startled glances of other patients and nurses Amy ran down the ward to the nurses' station.

"She needs suctioning," Amy stage whispered to the Head Nurse, Miss Bendix, who was sitting at the desk, her head with the wide-winged cap bent over the telephone receiver, another phone ringing beside her.

Miss Bendix put her hand over the mouthpiece. "Then do it!" she spit out and returned to the phone. She covered the receiver again. "Vogel, we've got an emergency lap coming in bleeding," she said. "You've been trained to suction."

"But I've never done it."

"Now's the time to learn." Miss Bendix returned to the phone and waved her on.

Amy rushed back down to the cubicle, took a deep breath and went in. Mrs. Madden's breathing was louder and the look face was of someone now wide awake, and terrified.

"Back in a jiffy," Amy said, "just like I told you."

Amy hurried to the bedside and found the kidney basin with a suction catheter lying like a red rubber snake in the bottom, and beside it the steel cups of peroxide and saline. Next to the bedside table the dusty suction machine was perched upon its wheeled stand, the glass, black-rubber corked collection bottle half full of foamy pink liquid. Amy breathed deeply and remembered lesson number one. If the procedure was done in accordance with all the steps she had memorized it should go perfectly fine.

She flipped the toggle switch at the side of the suction machine motor, pulled on some sterile gloves from the folded paper wrapping, picked up the tubing and ran some saline through the red rubber catheter tube. She leaned over Mrs. Madden who by now was lying on her back propped with pillows, her eyes closed, her breathing noisy and wet sounding above the hum of the suction motor.

With her gloved free hand Amy turned the metal lever of the trachesotomy tube at Mrs. Madden's throat and pulled out the inner canula. She dropped the slimy curved metal tube into the kidney basin, inserted the rubber tube into the metal tracheostomy, and suctioned out the thick mucus that was blocking Mrs. Madden's windpipe. Immediately the sound of her breathing through the metal airway was quieter. Mrs. Madden raised a weak hand to Amy and turned in the bed.

~

When Amy came back with the filled wash basin Mrs. Madden motioned her away. Amy stood there with the basin in her arms and glanced around the littered cubicle. There were dirty Kleenexes and crumpled paper all over the floor and Mrs. Madden was hugging two tissue boxes to her chest. Mrs. Madden's eyes were closed, the swollen mouth on her discolored face fixed.

Amy set the basin down on the chair and hurried down the ward to the nurses' bathroom. She barricaded herself inside for five minutes, ignoring the periodic knocks on the door. She leaned over the small sink. Somehow, she thought, I'll get over this.

~

The next morning Amy arrived at work ten minutes early. She had willed herself not to sleep past her wakeup time and in consequence had hardly slept at all. Worried that she would come up with a reason not to go to Ward K, she went early knowing that if she kept moving the situation would somehow not seen as awful. She dreaded seeing Mrs. Madden this morning because she had heard that on the second morning radical necks appear much worse. The bruised and incredibly swollen facial tissue takes on outrageous new colors and there is usually even more mucus, which is likely to be thick and yellow. Amy was not looking forward to this at all.

~

Mrs. Madden raised her head when Amy entered the cubicle. They had been right. She looked much worse this morning. The night nurse said she was getting even more squirrelly. Could that be only at night, Amy wondered? Surely night must be particularly frightening if one can't talk and can't breathe.

Miss Gaylord had a theory: Lizzie Madden's past was haunting her at night. She was being suffocated with her past sins. Miss Bendix said "piffle" to that. Amy thought Miss Bendix was really a kindly little woman, evident if she imagined her out of uniform. Amy had even heard that Miss Bendix had a trained mezzo soprano voice and sang at weddings and in local light opera, though Amy found it hard to believe. Gaylord had raised her eyebrows at Miss Bendix's comment, but said no more.

"Are you ready for this, Amy?" Miss Bendix had asked her as they got out of report.

"Yes, Ma'am," Amy said. "I'll try."

"Don't try," said Miss Bendix. "Do."

∾

Amy had a large brown bag in her hand for the trash. She began at the windowsill and hastily threw in all the old hospital menus Mrs. Madden had stacked on the sill and several boxes stuffed with used Kleenex. She found a soiled towel behind the chair and stuffed it in the bag as well. When she tripped on the chair leg it scraped against the floor and Mrs. Madden woke up.

Mrs. Madden jumped up in the bed and Amy fell back at the sight of her. Her dry black hair fanned up from behind her face, which seemed to have expanded to the size of a side of beef. The pressure dressing that had filled in the right side of her face had been changed and the new one, smaller, revealed the loss of half of her jawbone. What chin remained was distorted and misplaced sideward; the steady mysterious eyes gazed at her while the face seemed to turn away. Amy held herself taut and worked so she would not reveal in her facial expression just what a horror Mrs. Madden's face now presented. She willed upon herself a mask of reasonable interest, a pleasant nonjudgmental face that did not reveal what she saw.

Imagine the woman as a fresh-faced child, she told herself. Superimpose upon this face the image of Lizzie Madden as a young woman. Do not remember the thick lipstick like an audacious purple-red bruise, reminiscent of those bruised mouths and black eyes she may have sported. Work on your imagination, Amy told herself, work on your will.

"Good morning, Mrs. Madden, I didn't know you were awake."

The woman pointed to the windowsill and then to the brown bag Amy was hiding behind her starched apron. Mrs. Madden waved her hands in frantic gestures repeatedly pointing to the bag and to the window. Amy knew what she wanted but pretended she didn't. She had to clean up the cubicle. That was her assignment. The cubicle was cluttered and unhealthful. She shook her head no.

Lizzie Madden's eyes flared. She moved her hand rapidly through the air as if she were writing. Amy pulled a ballpoint pen out of her pocket and a scrap of paper and gave it to her.

"I must clean this up," Amy said. "Infection."

"DON'T YOU DARE TAKE AWAY A THING!" Lizzie wrote in large block letters on the scrap of paper and handed it back to Amy. She waved the ballpoint in the air.

"But my Head Nurse told me—"

Lizzie Madden shook her swollen head vigorously, leaped out of the bed and grabbed the paper bag out of Amy's hand. She pulled the bag close to her chest and standing in her flimsy patient gown turned her open back on Amy, who ducked out of the cubicle.

∾

"Well," said Miss Bendix to Amy that afternoon, "how's your favorite patient?"

"Do you mean Mrs. Madden?"

"Of course, who else?"

"Vitals okay, secretions down, won't do a thing for herself."

"And the hoarding?"

"Well—"

"Come up with something."

"Yes, ma'am."

∾

Amy entered the cubicle carrying a child's lift-up plastic slate. Lizzie Madden turned over when she entered. This morning the woman's face had lost some of the swelling, which had made her look like someone who had been severely beaten. Now the unsettling look of a permanently distorted facial structure was becoming more obvious. To her dismay, Amy discovered that the beaten-about-the-face look was more acceptable to her than the new malformed face that was surfacing as the swelling went down. She wondered if Mrs. Madden had the courage to raise the overbed table lid and peer into the mirror which was attached there. It would have to be done soon, but first a magic slate to communicate.

Lizzie immediately understood when she saw the child's plaything in Amy's hand. She reached for the magic slate and Amy gave it over.

"GOOD MORNING!" Mrs. Madden wrote on the slate with its wooden pick.

"Good morning." Amy smiled. Now what?

"I WANT TO SEE MYSELF," Mrs. Madden wrote.

"No," Amy said, "it's too early. Tomorrow is time enough."

"NOW!"

"We never do that until the fifth day," Amy said as she moved around the bed to the windowsill. "Time to clean up a little."

"NO!" Lizzie held up the slate so Amy could see the letters that filled the entire surface.

"Yes, Mrs. Madden. I know you're sore all over, and cleaning up is exhausting, but yes."

∽

When Amy came back into the cubicle with the paper bag, Mrs. Madden was sitting up in the bed looking into the mirror inside the overbed table. Amy rushed up to her and took hold of her hand. Mrs. Madden's body was shaking with silent sobs.

"Now don't you worry," Amy said. "It's not all healed yet and the swelling's not all down. That discoloration will fade away. You know about bruises. And you can use all kinds of scarves, and there are even some facial prostheses—"

Mrs. Madden squeezed Amy's hand and continued her silent crying. Amy handed her the slate. She took it in her free hand and continued staring into the mirror.

∽

"Serves her right," Miss Gaylord the night nurse said the next morning after report. "She looks like she should. All those years spreading her legs in sin."

"That's sufficient," Miss Bendix said. "Miss Vogel here has done a very nice job with Mrs. Madden. You'll notice the cubicle is cleaned up, some too. Something that you haven't been able to do."

"The old witch stays awake all night and threatens me," Miss Gaylord said.

"That's enough," said Miss Bendix. "We have enough problems here with the patients. I'd suggest you curb your tongue."

"Well, all I can say is I'm glad I have fours days off."

Okay, Amy thought, she's just worked ten. Gaylord stomped out of the nurses' station.

∽

Amy walked into Mrs. Madden's cubicle and found two young women sitting on the windowsill. They looked as if they had been up all night, their heavy makeup smudged around the eyes. When they saw Amy they got up and scurried out without saying goodbye to Lizzie who was curled up in her bed, her face to the wall.

"Good morning," Amy said, "was that Niecey and Jo?"

Mrs. Madden remained motionless.

"Bet you're glad to see some visitors."

Lizzie gestured toward the slate that was lying face down on the chair. Amy handed it to her. She sat up in the bed and began to write in small, deliberate letters.

"THEY ARE TWO OF MY GIRLS. THEY SAID THEY COULD NO LONGER WORK FOR SOMEONE WHO LOOKED LIKE ME. SAID I'D SCARE EVERYBODY AWAY. IN SHORT, EVEN THEM."

Amy read the note slowly. She kept her head down and let the moisture form and then pushed it back. She read the note a second time and then handed the slate back to Lizzie. She went to the bedside cabinet and got out the wash basin.

"I'll be right back," she said.

Amy came back with the basin full of hot, soapy water, carrying a fresh washcloth and towel. Under her arm she clasped a canister of baby powder. She put the basin and powder on the overbed table and rooted in the bedside cabinet for a hairbrush. When she found it, she directed Mrs. Madden to turn on her side and she began brushing the tangled mass of dark hair at the back of her head.

She brushed the hair carefully, gently holding the locks over her palm as she eased the tangles out of each portion of hair separately. As she brushed, Amy began to sing, almost under her breath, a German song her grandmother had taught her. She didn't know what the words meant, only the sound of them as she sang.

Du, Du, liegst mir im Herzen,
Du, Du, liegst mir im Sinn.

As she sang, Amy watched Lizzie Madden's shoulders relax.

Lizzie grabbed the magic slate from the bedside table and wrote "I KNOW THAT SONG" in large letters. Then she lay down on her side again and Amy picked up a handful of her black hair.

Du, Du, machst mir viel Schmerzen,
weisst nicht wie gut ich Dir bin.

The hair was brittle from many dyings, and desperately in need of washing. It had the odor of wet dog and biscuits, but to Amy the scent was not unpleasant.

Ja, ja, ja, ja,
weisst nicht wie gut ich Dir bin.

When Amy finished the hair—she had managed to untangle all but a matted clump at the very back of Lizzie's head—she put the hairbrush back in the cabinet and dropped the washcloth into the soapy water that was no longer scalding, but pleasantly warm. She turned open the back of Mrs. Madden's gown and washed her back with long firm strokes. The small knobs of her spine pushed at her skin, like the backs of young children bent over the beach.

When Amy had rinsed Lizzie's back she reached for the towel and

At his cue, the children began shrieking with laughter.

Uncle Walter paced up and down the opposite bank. "Klaus, you okay?" He called over above the noise of the children.

"Shut up, you guys," Flora said. She whispered between her teeth. "I said shut up." She turned to Klaus. "Want to use my car?"

"I'm okay." Klaus held his thumb out from his body, squeezing his arm at the wrist. "Just bleeds a lot," he said. He chuckled. "But most of that's just beer."

Bass waded in from the middle of the creek with the pole still in his hands. "I'm really sorry," he said to Klaus.

"Shit, Bass," Klaus said, "we're not half done here. Look at all those critters." He made a sweep of the creekbed with his good hand. He turned to Bass and winked. "Now Dolly can take my place with the pliers. She's real good at it, did you notice?"

"I was watching," Bass said.

Klaus picked up the turtle sack with one hand, slung it over his shoulder, and headed for the farmhouse. The kids jumped up around him saying they never saw a turtle bite before, and could they look at it, while Flora tried to pull them away, promising them rides in her car, a good seat up front, and maybe even a beer if they'd just leave Klaus alone. After a few minutes the children came back, sat down and turned their attention back to the creek.

Bass waded into the middle of the stream again, swinging himself in the waders against the slow constant flow of the water. When he got to the middle he shook out each hand like a pitcher, transferring the pole from one hand to the other as he did it. He stooped in his waders, and whacked his glasses back against his head with his free hand. "I'm ready," he shouted.

Uncle Walter called Homer over to the far side of the creek. By now Walter's bump had gotten so large it looked as if his head was coming to a point in front of him. After a short conference with Homer, Walter waded across the creek to help Klaus back to the house. Homer took Walter's place on the far bank.

"We'll make a sample pot of soup with that guy," Walter shouted back to us, waving Klaus' turtle sack. I decided not to tell him that Brenda had already beat them to it.

rubbed in a circular motion so that all the areas of her back would be pinkened, the blood running there to protect the skin from this gentle manipulation.

Amy washed Lizzie's arms, lifting them to wash the bristle of black hairs that grew there. She washed the back of her thighs, her calves, her feet, all the time singing her grandmother's song, so that she might impart something more to the woman than simple cleanliness.

She asked Mrs. Madden to turn over, and lifting aside the hand that Lizzie had raised to her face, Amy moved the washcloth over her forehead—then rinsed—then down her cheek and the left side of her nose. Amy rinsed the cloth and then carefully washed the intricate channels of both her ears. She washed the top of her cheekbone above the dressing, careful not to allow any wetness to invade the gauze. Mrs. Madden kept her eyes closed.

Still singing, Amy rinsed the washcloth, then stroked Lizzie Madden's chest. She gently lifted her breasts and washed under them, then washed the tops of her legs and feet. Then, when she had finished, she rinsed the washcloth, and handed it to Lizzie

In Praise of What Persists

Leaving Gibraltar, we headed west across
the Atlantic for Savannah. On this course, we
crossed part of the Sargasso Sea. The area is
loaded with seaweed at a depth of two to six
feet, and the seaweed has little black seeds,
about the size of holly berries. The old sailing
ships avoided the place, as they would get stuck
and only the strongest winds could free them.
*   Sea snakes migrate here for mating;*
the Sea is full of them.

As Jesse rounded the corner into the hot dusty backyard of the apartment building that early summer afternoon he heard laughter coming from the fire escape. He looked up and saw Lonnie Keyes and his younger brother, Sparkle Tab, on the third floor landing.

"Get out of there," the old man yelled up at them. "What do you think you're doing?"

"Seeing what all you have in there," Lonnie shouted down at him. "Seeing what stinks!"

He spit down at Jesse over the metal railing and then poked his brother in the ribs.

"Yeah, stinks!" Sparkle Tab mimicked, glancing up at Lonnie for approval. Sparkle Tab, unlike his flabby, pimple-faced older brother, was dark and small for his age.

"Get out." Jesse shook the loose rail of the fire escape from below. "Get out, get out!"

The boys clambered down the steps and ran past the old man, each jostling him as they went by.

Jesse sat down on the bottom step after the boys had gone screeching out of the yard. He heard them shouting to each other as they ran down the alley. Rude kids, he thought. Perverse.

From his seat on the metal stairs Jesse saw something brown peeking through the dry soil under one of the rose bushes along the fence. He quickly got up to scrape dirt over it with the side of his shoe.

As he packed down the earth he decided to plant another rose bush, though not because roses were more beautiful than other flowers, in the beginning Jesse did not particularly like roses; he distrusted their beauty, felt uncomfortable with their reputation for loveliness while alive with thorns. Yet, he had made them part of his intrigue and he knew they were—in the same way he was—both prickly and resolute. Although hybrid rosegrowers might not agree, Jesse considered roses to be inexpensive and hardy. He knew that as soon as one branch would grow brown and brittle in despair at that depleted ground, another would come green and throw out buds. He rather liked seeing them scratch for existence in the barren backyard of the apartment building, eking moisture from that dead earth and surviving. Last evening the "Black Swans" had surprised him with buds like tight, purple-black fists.

Jesse climbed the fire escape and with difficulty pulled himself through the third floor window into his sparely furnished room. He noticed his place still smelled of dog. He could see the single bed and the white-painted table and chair, and as his eyes got accustomed to the dim light he saw an object on the linoleum floor. He pushed the empty dog bowl aside and pulled a glass jar out from under the sink. A cockroach the size of a medallion skittered across the linoleum. He crushed the insect beneath his shoe, listening for the pop, and then watched the soft stuff ooze out on either side of the parchment-like shell.

He dumped the contents of the jar on the table. A dollar forty-one cents. If he checked the cans on the way to the A&P he could probably find enough empties for deposit to make up the difference. He would buy the "Queen of Heaven" rose he saw yesterday for $1.89 in the quick sale bin.

Jesse picked up the dog bowl and put it back under the sink, and seeing the small soiled rug in the corner he rolled it up and put it under his arm. He would dispose of this too on the way to the store.

Jesse's neighbors had become accustomed to seeing the old man walk the same route each day along River Street, then up a cobblestone alley crossing several streets to the A&P, his wild white hair standing out around his wrinkled face, his faded oversize clothing hanging on him like the hand-me-downs of some gigantic older brother. But in the neighborhood they gave him no more than cool avoidance.

The A&P was only a few blocks up from the river and occasionally Jesse would run into someone he had known in his days on the ocean-going freighters. His last job had been as mate on the river tug, "Julia C.," and some of the men who hung around the docks still remembered him. By the time he retired, the river had silted up and trucks and trains had more business than the tugmen. He'd taken this room in order to stay near the river, but it was hard for him to accept the port's new image. Instead of the honest working tugs and functional drab warehouses, the riverfront now sported fancy shops and tugs gaily painted for the tourists. Classy freighters with foreign names and flags moved through the newly-dug channel.

Avoiding the littered apartment hallway, Jesse stuffed the rug under his arm and climbed out the window onto the fire escape landing. As he started down the steps a window flew open above him. Mrs. Keyes poked her head out between the swinging chains of soda can tabs her son Sparkle Tab had hung in the windows like curtains.

"What'd you say to my boys?" she boomed.

Jesse squinted up at her. The big black woman had a handsome face in spite of the puffy scar across her neck that always made Jesse wonder how and when she had been slashed. He knew she watched him often from her window, but he didn't think she suspected anything.

"Just told them to stop looking in my window. Man needs his privacy."

"Well, that's no cause to yell." She pulled her bulky self back into the window.

> *After passing the White Cliffs of Dover,*
> *we started to feel "channel fever," as we had*
> *been at sea a long time. But as we were entering*
> *the channel, we looked back out to sea and saw*
> *two full-rigged ships—a most beautiful sight—*
> *running beside each other before the wind. We*
> *later learned they were in a grain race from*
> *Australia to England, the last grain race by sail.*

Jesse got halfway down the fire escape when he remembered he had left his money inside. He climbed back into his room and turned to check that Mrs. Keyes had not come down the fire escape to spy on him. One day he had looked out his window and found Sparkle Tab standing on the fire escape staring wide-eyed into the darkened room. For once Lonnie wasn't with him. Jesse wasn't sure if Sparkle Tab had seen the dog lying on the small rug on the floor. "You can come in and see him if you don't tell," Jesse said. But the boy had quickly turned on the fire escape landing and disappeared.

Animals weren't allowed in the building, but Jesse had been sure the rare sound of the dog's yelps would be lost in the commotion created by the Keyes brothers upstairs. From the dog's relative silence people might have thought he was one of those soundless African dogs Jesse had heard of who were devoid of vocal cords, or at least the ability to use them. The old dog and Sparkle Tab became the silent partners in Jesse's stealth of caretaking.

Jesse picked up the handful of change from the counter, tied it into his handkerchief and shoved the ball of coins into his pocket. As he went down the fire escape a second time he heard a phone ringing. It must be Mrs. Keyes'. His phone was disconnected. She was always on the phone—talk, talk, talk. Her pimple-faced son Lonnie was the same. As Jesse reached the bottom of the fire escape, the phone rang again.

With a screech Lonnie Keyes came running through the alley and reappeared in the yard with Sparkle Tab following closely behind. They rushed toward Jesse who quickly sat down on one of the narrow metal steps.

"Out of the way, old man," Lonnie growled as he squeezed by.

"Lonnie," Mrs. Keyes shrieked out the window above them,"Answer the phone. Right—now."

Jesse tried not to listen. Chaos, they live in chaos, he thought. They had lived above him for two years now, continually crashing and banging into each other, dragging their furniture across the bare floors. Jesse had never said anything about it, although sometimes he would walk down to the corner liquor store on hot summer nights and buy a pint of Ripple or Thunderbird to put him asleep. He didn't do it often. Most of the time he would stay out in the back yard, sit on the bottom step, and study the roses while the sky faded from blue to mauve. Studying roses had become a form of meditation. He marveled at the bushes blooming over and over again like lives, each rose—each generation—perfect in itself, but soon obscured by the incredible number of blooms. He had become overwhelmed by their fecundity. He told himself again he didn't like roses themselves, but he liked their persistence. He would sit on the steps noting each new bloom in a pursuit of peace away from the raucous banging of his upstairs neighbors.

Jesse got up after the boy had passed and readjusted the rug under his arm. Even at that distance he could hear Lonnie yelling into the phone through the open window.

"Okay, Dayton, what do you want?"

Jesse started down the alley. The only phone calls he had received recently had been on the hall phone from Mr. Lawson, the landlord. Jesse had tried to explain that his check hadn't come.

"Sure, sure," Lawson had said.

"Wait," Jesse said, "it comes at the end of the month and somebody knows. I fix my mailbox and it's busted again."

"I've heard that lame story before. Find a new place to live."

This conversation had been repeated weekly for the last three months. Lawson said the same thing, Jesse said the same thing. Time went by. Nothing happened. Jesse tried to think of other things to say to Mr. Lawson: his son Tim would send him the money any day. He'd pay up.

Jesse stopped walking to rest for a moment. The A&P was six blocks away. In each trashcan he passed he looked for bottles to make up the forty-eight cents he'd need to buy the "Queen of Heaven." At the first dumpster a block away from his building he threw away the soiled rug and pulled out a few soda bottles and a brown paper bag. When he was halfway to the store it started to rain, a fine, misty rain off the river that felt good on his face and hands. He realized he was very warm. It was early June and he still had on his dark grey sweater in the habit of winter and a cold rainy spring. He looked up from the sidewalk and thought he saw Mr. Lawson's car speed by, then another. Each time he considered waving, but by then the car was gone.

The rain was coming down harder and Jesse's white hair was in wet, dripping corkscrews to his shoulders. As he walked he shifted the soaked brown bag of bottles to the other arm.

> *The sea was very rough and it was cold and*
> *raining at the entrance to the Columbia River going*
> *into Portland. We passed a ship aground on a shoal,*
> *with its cargo of lumber listing off its deck.*
> *I liked Portland because it smelled so good.*
> *We sailed under green bridges and everywhere there*
> *was the smell of spruce trees and fresh cut wood*
> *from the sawmills. Portland is also the home of the*
> *best Delicious apples. I ate a lot of them as I walked*
> *around, as I had bought a bag of them with my shore*
> *allotment. When I got back to the ship, the crew*
> *stole what I had left, but I didn't mind.*

The store smelled of dust and coffee. It was one of the original supermarkets, bypassed in numerous remodelings by a company, which was always on the verge of closing it, then seemed to forget. Rain slanted heavily outside the plateglass window. As Jesse made his way down the aisle he left a trail of water behind him. The clerks had seen him many times before and seemed not to notice as he stopped in the dog food aisle to look at the cod liver oil and finger the dog collars.

Jesse found himself thinking again about the day the old dog Eli began regaining his strength after a week of dragging his haunches behind him. He had lived two more months after that while Jesse stewed in a subtle agony of guilt. Perhaps the neighbors had noticed the wet newspapers and brown bags of dog waste he had buried each evening beneath the rose bushes. He had tried to escape detection by planting the cheapest rose bushes he could find, giving himself an excuse to be digging in the yard. Perhaps caring for the dog was merely prolonging his pain. Jesse sensed the dog's inherent weakness and saw, before anyone else might have noticed, when Eli's tail began to get limp again and his legs began to stiffen.

The morning two weeks ago when Jesse found the dog motionless at the foot of his bed he was glad his check had arrived for once. It had given him enough money to buy the "White Swans" that camouflaged the grave.

Earlier that morning in the time of half-waking he had seen something dark looming in the doorway of his room. At first he thought that massive bulk was one of his sons, or his landlord Mr. Lawson, or maybe a Georgia State Trooper. But it was just a shadow that had moved away by the time he woke again, the sunlight now bright into the corners of the room. Yet the memory of that shadow had left him restless. As his son Tim had said, or maybe it was Jack—he wasn't sure, it was so long ago, and they weren't really his sons, not blood, just boys he had taken under his wing during his sea years—but anyway, one of them had said it: "We live in our minds." Jesse believed he had to pay attention to certain things that would suddenly linger at the tip of his mind. Jesse had even tried to call a priest about this shadow, from the hall phone in the middle of the night. He got a recording.

He wondered who might call back: God in soothing tones or a secretary demanding a credit card number. Surely a priest would come, and he would be fat and Irish, and he would yawn and stand sleepy through the rite. It wouldn't take long. Kiss the purple and you're through. Life could flicker out then, Jesse thought. Officially.

In Calcutta, there was a nude body of a dead man
in the gutter by the road, because there was no money to
bury it. The Burning Ghat was a place alongside the river
where bodies could be cremated and the ashes thrown into
the river. But it cost about $1.80 American, a high price
for these people

He left the dog food aisle, skirted the meat counter, and entered the garden and produce aisle. Under the slanted shelf of fresh peaches he found a few scrawny-looking rose bushes. There was a bland pink "Charlotte Amalie," a "White Swan" that was absolutely dead, and a limp but still viable "Queen of Heaven." Jesse smiled. He had known it would be there. We live in our minds.

Jesse took the rose bush to the checkout counter and then went outside in the rain to bring in the bottles he had left by the entrance. He knew he had enough of them, along with his change, to buy the rose bush and the woman at the register, having dealt with Jesse before, rang it up without bothering to figure the deposits. He looked down at his wet shoes and told himself the rain would be good for the roses.

The Kalighat Temple in Calcutta was very
beautiful, but did not have the garden of the Jain
Temple. What it had was a wooden yoke with a steel
pin in it, where a goat's neck could be held, so the
large curved knife that hung beside it could be used
to cut the goat's head off before it was offered to
the temple. There were thousands of flies in this place.
Nearby, there was a fruitful tree and a barren
tree, and the women would tie locks of their baby's
hair on these trees. I never found out why.

As Jesse walked back to his building along River Street he kept his head down and avoided the dock and the bustling people on the cobblestone sidewalk as best he could. He recalled that late afternoon when he had found the black setter caked with mud standing sick and wobbly-legged at the bottom of the steep incline that separated the river from the upper street. There seemed to be an instant understanding, a common anxiety between dog and man, and Jesse had half-carried, half-dragged him in the early dark, taking the alleys to avoid being seen. Finally, with difficulty, Jesse carried the large bony dog up the fire escape to his room.

He had named the setter "Eli" thinking that even with such a pathetic creature names were important. Jesse had often reflected on the sad perversity of Mrs. Keyes upstairs who allowed Lonnie to continue to call his brother Sparkle Tab.

As Jesse approached the apartment building he saw a few people out front in the light rain milling among some furniture that was sitting at the curb. He walked closer wondering who was being evicted, but soon recognized both the things and the people. Lonnie, his buddy Dayton, and a few other people were laughing and throwing cardboard boxes over into the street. Jesse saw that his brown sofa, a few worn books, the white-painted kitchen table and his mattress were all soaking wet.

When Jesse got close, Lonnie grinned at him and gave him a shove. "Well, look who's here," Lonnie said.

Jesse fell back onto the slick pavement, dropping the rose bush. He looked up at the people who were rummaging through his belongings. He knew them, most of them, but today they looked like caricatures of themselves as they leered down at him through the rain. A couple had walked away as he approached, taking his coffee pot as they left; a young man snatched a mariner's chart from a wet pile in front of him and laughed as he fled.

Jesse got up and grabbed his pillow from a stout woman who had appeared from across the street. He threw the pillow onto the wet sofa. Another woman, with a wrinkled brown face, picked up the rain-spattered paper bag with the rose bush, grinned at him with a mouth full of rotting yellow teeth and carried it away.

Jesse glared at her. "Take it, take it," he said. His legs rubbery and he sat down on the couch.

Lonnie leaned down in front of him and shouted into his face, "Dirty old man stinks." Lonnie pulled a navy blue wool blanket from a cardboard box and lifted it to his nose. "Yeah stinks," he said and he threw the damp blanket into the gutter.

"Stop this, Lonnie," Jesse said.

"I told you, Dayton," Lonnie shouted. He turned around and laughed at Dayton who had moved away and was standing against the building with his arms folded across his broad chest. "Stinks." Lonnie turned back to Jesse. "Ain't that right old man?"

Jesse got up from the couch and stood in the littered gutter. The rain fell steadily. He felt people staring at him and he turned around. More people were there gaping at his things.

Lonnie tapped Jesse on the shoulder. "All this stuff stinks."

Jesse shook his head. "What are you doing this for, Lonnie?"

"You a stinking man. Spoil the neighborhood."

Jesse shook his head again and moved away from the boy. He could see that most of the things that mattered to him were broken or gone already, all except the marble-patterned notebook still in a box beside the couch. He picked it up and held it against his chest. Inside, thin red pencil lines marked his voyages on maps he had pasted in, and in darker ink was his account of his trips on the Merchant Marine freighters when he was hardly older than Lonnie himself.

With a whoop, the boy with rosy acne lunged at Jesse.

"You don't need this, old man." Lonnie grabbed for the notebook.

Jesse pulled back clasping the book tightly to his chest. He searched the crowd. Not one soft face. The rain was teeming now, warmly and persistently, and lightning flashed from behind the apartment building. Jesse felt the damp of his shirt and sweater, and the water seeping through the soles of his shoes.

> *Halfway down the Red Sea, we anchored the ship and waited for a change of pilots. The gangway was lowered and the floodlight was turned on as I stood watch. Not long after, a large sea turtle—maybe eight feet in diameter—came up into the lighted area.*
>
> *He just hung there, so I thought I'd get a closer look, but when I got-down to the bottom step of the gangway, he suddenly sank away.*

"Honkey," the boy laughed. "Ghost." Lonnie jumped at Jesse, ripped the notebook from his hands, and threw it into the gutter.

The book fell open. Lonnie saw the writing inside and retrieved it. He flipped through the pages, then he held the book up and began to read in a singsong voice.

"'January 10, 1936,'" he read. "Hey, look at this, Sparkle Tab, my man." He beckoned to his brother. The younger came around the side of the red brick apartment building, grinning and fiercely chewing gum.

Jesse was silent. The rain was falling hard on the top of his head and little streams of rainwater came off his bushy eyebrows and down the sides of his nose.

A woman shouted down from her fourth floor window above them. "Lonnie, you give that back. Right now."

Lonnie grinned over the faces of the small crowd of onlookers that remained on the sidewalk. "No way." He turned back to Jesse and shook the book. Scraps of paper fell to the sidewalk.

"Look at this, Sparkle Tab." Lonnie began to rip pages out of the yellowed notebook and let them flutter down to the wet cement.

Sparkle Tab threw away his gum and put his fingers to his mouth, whistling shrilly amid the hoots from the small crowd.

Jesse watched as the pages fell into the street. His face, which had been wet and flushed moments before, became pale, then grey like the face of someone who had been overcome by a sudden illness.

The boy shoved Jesse away from the couch, the flat of both his palms against the old man's shoulders. "I don't believe this shit, old man," he said as he shoved Jesse a second time. "You live in my town," he shoved Jesse again, "and won't even look at nobody."

Sweating, Jesse pulled the boy's hands off his shoulders and reached for the notebook. "It's important to me, Lonnie."

"No, no, no." Lonnie said as he shoved Jesse repeatedly, backing him into the brick wall of the alleyway.

Pressed against the building, Jesse felt suddenly cold. He shook his arm. His left hand was numb. He looked directly into the boy's wide blemished face and decided to try a new tactic. "Lonnie Keyes, I know you. I know your mother and I know your brother, Sparkle Tab."

Lonnie dropped his head back to get a mouthful of rainwater but he did not back away. Sparkle Tab, who had followed behind Lonnie, watched Jesse for a moment and then turned away.

"Why do you call him that?" Jesse asked watching as the younger boy slipped away through the crowd. "What's his real name, Lonnie?"

Jesse searched the crowd again for Sparkle Tab but in what had seemed like only a moment he had disappeared. Mrs. Keyes stood there in the midst of the crowd, as large and grim as a wall of black marble. He turned back to confront Lonnie but the boy avoided his gaze.

Jesse was getting indigestion, a slow burning under the breast-bone, and he was perspiring profusely. He pulled off his sweater and threw it toward the pile of wet boxes. It fell short and landed in the middle of the sidewalk. He stood back against the building to rest. Silly to be wearing a sweater in this muggy rain anyway, he thought, but he'd have to watch to be sure nobody went off with it. "It's only a notebook, Lonnie," he said in a low voice.

"No man, this is getting interesting." Lonnie tapped Jesse under the chin with his forefinger. "Why the big deal?"

Jesse mumbled something as he rubbed his left arm.

"Eh? Eh?" Lonnie taunted. He put the notebook behind his back and danced in front of Jesse. "I can't hear you."

Jesse's arm was pins and needles to the elbow and he was breath-less. He tried to shout. "That book's only—" He felt a sharp jab under his armpit— "important to me." Jesse turned quickly to see if some-one had sneaked up in the alley behind him. No one. He turned back painfully. "It means nothing to you, Lonnie. It's a travel diary. You don't travel much, do you?"

Lonnie was dancing on his toes in front of Jesse, a grin on his face. "Now you never can tell. Never can tell." Lonnie glanced over into the mumbling crowd, looking for his friend. "Old Dayton made it all the way to Nicaragua. Didn't you, Date?"

A huge dark man raised a fist.

Jesse moved out of the alley and sat down heavily on the curb. He was breathing hard. His feet rested in a puddle in the gutter but he didn't seem to notice. Hair plastered to his head, his wet shirt was transparent. There was a great weight on his chest and the pain would not lessen.

"Ghost, ghost, ghost," rose from the small crowd in a chant.

Thunder rumbled, and from the curb Jesse saw a bolt of lightning touch down on an old blue Chevy in the used car lot across the street. The flash illuminated the scene.

Sitting on the curb, Jesse saw a blackness in the corner of his vision that had nothing to do with rain. He looked up into the dark sky and caught, for a moment, a whiff of the river.

> *Once, in the Indian ocean, we found phosphorus*
> *given off by sea animals glowing so brightly that*
> *the night sea seemed to be filled with stars.*

Sparkle Tab, as breathless as if he had been running, clawed his way forward from his hiding place in the crowd. He pointed at Jesse, a wild look in his eyes Jesse could not interpret. "You really got him scared Lonnie, look at his face."

Lonnie had turned to watch a powerful young man punch the man next to him after a loud shouting match, and in the confusion the crowd fell against them like a collapsing wall. Sparkle Tab ran off, and Lonnie danced back on his toes, but Jesse fell flat onto the sidewalk. He fought for breath. They were too close, falling over him and getting up, leaning over him and grinning, pointing.

Lonnie danced over to Jesse, bent down, and spit in his face. "You look pale, Mr. Ghost."

Jesse tried to wipe the saliva from his cheek with his sleeve but he felt so weak he couldn't lift his arm. The weight on his chest was crushing his ribs back to his spine. He grasped, tried to get up, but fell back with a stabbing pain in his jaw. "Call somebody," he said.

Lonnie watched the sparring crowd for a moment then turned leaned down and shouted into Jesse's face. "You think I want the pigs down here?"

"Call." Jesse broke into a cold sweat. After a moment he propped himself up on one elbow and squinted into the crowd. "Call."

"What for?" Lonnie danced away.

Mrs. Keyes pushed through the noisy crowd swinging a pillow. "Let me through," she growled at them. "Let me through!" She studied her son sadly for a moment.

The boy scowled. "Momma, you stay out of this."

Mrs. Keyes put her hand on Lonnie's arm. "He's not a bad man."

"Woman," Lonnie shoved her away, "you don't know."

"Lonnie," she said, "look at him. What you doing to him?"

"Doing nothing." Lonnie said. "What did he do to me? Never talked to me like I was a human being."

"You ain't a human being." She pulled on his arm. "Come on, Lonnie. Lord Jesus come on home."

> On the west coast of Mexico, we saw an abundance of sea life during our watches—sharks, whales, dolphins—and a display of heat lightning from the horizon up to the top of the sky that filled night after night with fireworks.
>
> One time, a giant ray—a good ten feet from tip to tip—surfaced near our ship, and just as we all became aware of him, gave one great beat of his wings and was gone from sight.

There was a shout from the crowd and a patrol car pulled to a stop halfway up the block. The red light, revolving slowly, pierced the rain. The crowd scattered.

A van stopped a few feet from the spot where Jesse lay and a uniformed man climbed out from the driver's side and peered up into the rain.

"Nothing like a summer storm to stir things up," he said. He put on his hat, then took it off and threw it back inside the vehicle. He looked over at his partner who had gotten out of the other side of the van and was kneeling, bareheaded, over Jesse. "What'd they do this time, Jake?"

His partner looked up. "Just rolled an old drunk, looks like."

"I've seen that guy before." The tall man walked over to look more closely. "Yeah, looks familiar."

The first man stood up. "Let's get him off the street."

"Whoa, whoa." The tall man stared down at the old man's chest. "Not breathing."

"What?"

"He's not breathing."

"Oh shit." Jake looked down at the old man, and then back up to his partner. "What do you think?"

The tall man bent down and put two fingers on the side of Jesse's neck and felt for a pulse. He looked at his partner. "Want to do the heroics?"

Jake rubbed his sleeve across his mouth. "Me?" He frowned. "Look at him. I don't want to put my mouth over that ungodly spit-tle—get an ambu bag."

"All right, all right. Looks a little stiff, doesn't he? Must've been out here a long time."

Jake squinted up at his partner and then quickly looked away, down the littered street. "What's all this stuff?" he said as he stood.

"Eviction. Another coroner's case too, looks like." The tall man glanced at the rain-darkened sofa and the wet boxes that were scat-tered over the street, disintegrating in the downpour. "Dispatcher said some young kid called."

Jake glanced over at the used car lot across the street and then spat down into the gutter. "All the luck. Bet he watched them take it away."

"Petty larceny, my boy." The tall man slapped his pockets looking for his cigarette pack. "I wonder how long he had all that junk. Got it from the bell-ringers, I bet, the blue bonnet army."

"Yeah, but people stealing your stuff from under your nose." Jake stopped. He was looking down at Jesse and he thought he saw the old man's chest move. But it was only a whip of rain that had gotten under his shirt.

The tall man glanced at his partner. "You'll get used to it." He waved on the patrol car that was still parked further down the block. The driver raised a finger and then drove off.

The tall man found his cigarettes, lit one, took a long drag and then sat down on the wet curb. "Ah, come on Jake," he said, "cool it. It's not as if this was a major crime."

"No? Maybe we should—" Jake wiped his face with his sleeve and looked back down at Jesse "—tell that to a priest."

"What priest?"

"Any priest. Any goddamned priest."

The tall man glanced down the street at the paper being swept away by the fast-moving rainwater. "God," he said as he dropped his cigarette into the gutter. "God."

> *It seemed, to my surprise, that the ocean was as flat as a lake during my first days at sea.*
>
> *The Polish Bo'sun worked us very hard, I guess because we were working so cheap—one cent a day. We had deck scrapers we used from dawn to dusk. I had twenty-five water blisters on my hands and the one on each palm was as large as a quarter because we had no gloves to use. We had the title of workaway.*
>
> *In 1934, the food was so poor on most ships that sometimes, when it just couldn't be eaten, the A.B.'s would call the Steward out to watch them dump it over the side into the ocean. But nothing changed.*

Cane

"Cane cane I want my cane."
    "Just a minute, Mr. Cohen."
    "Cain and Abel, Cain and Abel. Are you able to get me my cane?"
    "Be right there, Mr. Cohen."
    "Cane you. Get me my cane."
    "Yes, just a minute."
    "Cane you! In my way, girlie, and so help me, I'll cane you."

≈

"Who's that?"
    "Just Mr. Cohen."
    "Why doesn't somebody get him his cane?"
    "He has it in his hand."
    "Oh."
    "See what I mean?"
    "You think I'll get used to it?"
    "Probably not."
    "Shall we go out there?"
    "Guess so. It's time."

≈

"Cane, cane. I want my cane."
    "Check your left hand, Mr. Cohen."
    "How can I? I'm looking for my cane."
    "Don't shout Mr. Cohen. I'll help you."

"I'll complain! My cane! How can a man live here without his cane?"

"You have your cane, Mr. Cohen."

"I do not."

"But you do, it's in your hand."

"Lies, lies. How can you lie to a man about his cane? Maybe you could lie about other things, but not about a man's cane."

∾

"What about his cane?"

"You go in there and deal with him. I'm tired of it."

∾

"Mr. Cohen, here I come."

"Cane, girlie. Take that, and that. How dare you take my cane?"

"I'm just putting it in your other hand."

"Take that, you slut. Where's my cane?"

"Your cane is in your left hand, Mr. Cohen."

"All right. And leave it there, retrieve it there. Cane. "

"Nothing I'd like better."

"A skein, a crane, a plane, and my cane. Cane. Cane. Are you able to find my cane?"

"In your hand."

"Cane, cane. I want my cane."

"Just a moment, Mr. Cohen."

∾

"I've got to do something about him. He's driving me nuts."

"How about moving him down the hall? With his room next to the nurses' station you hear every word he says.

"All right. A good idea."

∾

"Mr. Cohen. Mr. Cohen, we have a new room for you."

"What for? You just want to steal from me."

"No, I don't Mr. Cohen. Your cane is in your hand. Let me roll you down to the end of the hall. You can have a new room, and the nurses won't bother you."

"Good. And get my cane."

"Yes. Here it is, in your hand."

"My hand? My cane in my hand?"

"Yes."

"Cane. Cane. My cane in my hand."

∾

"Have you heard Mr. Cohen lately?"

"No, I haven't. Have you?"

"No. What a relief."

"Have you checked on Mr. Cohen?"

"Yes, I peeked in. He's sleeping in his chair."

"Have you heard Mr. Cohen recently?"

"No, but I checked on him and he's sleeping in his bed."

∾

"Mr. Cohen."

"He refuses to answer. I've tried."

"Mr. Cohen. How are you?"

"As I told you before, he refuses to answer."

"Is he all right?"

"I think so. But weaker."

"Mr. Cohen, Mr. Cohen. Where's your cane?"

"He doesn't answer. I told you."

"Here, Mr. Cohen. Let me put you in a wheelchair. You've been in bed all day."

∾

"Where's Mr. Cohen? I couldn't find him."

"I moved him back to his old room."

∾

"Mr. Cohen, how are you?"

"Cane."

"What did you say?"

"Cane, cane."

"How are you doing, Mr. Cohen?"

"Cane, cane, are you deaf?"

"No, Mr. Cohen."

"Cane, cane, I want my cane."

"It's in your hand, Mr. Cohen."

"Cain and Abel. Cain and Abel. Cain and Abel setting the table. Are you able to get me my cane?"

"Yes, Mr. Cohen."

"My cane, my cane, my kingdom for my cane. Leave it there, reprieve it there."

"The cane's in your hand, Mr. Cohen."

The Man Who Loved Chekhov

(for Paul)

The mountain air was alive with mosquitoes. Janet brushed a cloud of them away from her face. Each evening she and Angelo sat together in the Adirondack chairs behind the fieldstone wall and watched the sun go down. They shared this evening ritual after their long day at class and jobs, the Virginia earth green beneath their feet, the buzzing air resplendent with the dusty smells of sun-baked weeds and grasses from the hayfield in front of them. This evening the sunset evolved slowly. The huge orange ball inched into the trees beyond the strip of lawn and field, pulling behind it a fan of rosy color.

"He spent all afternoon with me again today, Ange," she said flicking a mosquito from her arm.

"How is he doing?"

"The same."

"Does he have family?" Angelo asked. "He seems to have a penchant for solitude. What does he do when we're not around?"

"I don't think there's a family," Janet said squinting in the sunlight, "he spends a lot of his time in the community. Sponsors the symphony. Things like that."

"Keeps busy."

She nodded. "That's one way to alleviate the pressure," Angelo said, "temporarily."

He pulled himself up from his slouch in the wooden lawn chair as if preparing to leave. They could hear the shouts from the after-dinner volleyball game on the lawn across the road behind them.

"I'm done in," Janet said. "Let me direct him to you for a day or two. Okay?"

"All right." He stood and dug his fists deep into the pockets of his khaki slacks. Dark and lean-faced he looked down at her then turned back to watch the sky. "Is he still—?"

"Yes. You may be valedictorian at this graduate school, Ange, and the only undercover priest, but he's certainly the valetudinarian. He makes a career of helplessness." She grimaced and pushed her wiry hair out of her face. "Today at lunch, in the middle of the dining hall, I saw him literally sob into his soup. Nobody could look at him."

"Okay, I'll carry the ball for a while."

Angelo walked off around the corner of the Infirmary cottage. Janet turned back to the sunset. Each evening this summer she and Angelo watched the sky and devised their strategies as nurse and priest co-combatants in a war against Walt Hedenberg's despair. Walt had learned of his illness only the year before. It had begun subtly: a cold, a sore under the tongue, a suspicious node in his neck. Despite his diagnosis, Walt had come back to the summer campus for classes again this year. For a while he pretended nothing was wrong, even though his skin was sensitive from the radiation treatments, and shaving was frightful.

Janet knew to the casual observer Walt's beard was the only thing different about him this year. But he clung to her and to Angelo like a man frantic for life who was dying of thirst. He sucked them dry with quiet but insistent demands. All summer Walt crossed back and forth across the road, talking to Janet in the Infirmary, then to Angelo in the men's dorm across the road, then back to Janet again. Neither state-of-the-art medicine nor religion was acceptable solace for Walt.

Students would squirm in their seats when Walt sat across from them at breakfast at one of the long tables in the dining hall which hummed with gossip, talk of the Chekhov play in rehearsal, papers due, and the daily threats of romantic assignation. Surrounded by the sounds of voices, clanking silverware, and the morning smell of bacon and freshly baked biscuits, Walt would listen to the other students for a while before the tears began to slide down his reddened cheeks and catch in the blond stubble of his beard. Soon the dining hall would grow silent, and one by one people would leave.

Someone threw open the screen door of the Infirmary cottage. "Janet, phone!" The door banged shut.

From the rear porch where she had been flipping from *To the Lighthouse* to a book on medicinal herbs, Janet hurried inside and picked up the black earpiece of the ancient phone.

"Look Janet," Ana was calling from the college switchboard. "I've got a medical supply company on the other line. The truck with the oxygen tanks can't make it today. They're coming tomorrow."

"Oxygen tanks, What oxygen tanks?"

"They said Walt Hedenberg ordered them. He's been using oxygen at home."

"Oh, no." Janet glanced at the cracked ceiling of the Infirmary hallway. "Sorry, Ana. We don't have the equipment to handle somebody who plans to be that sick. Besides, the tanks are a fire hazard. One cigarette, and pow!"

"That's all I know, Janet, honey. They'll deliver four, they said."

"Thanks, Ana." She hung up the phone.

Janet looked out the window to the front porch, which served as the Infirmary's waiting room. She glanced at her watch. Afternoon clinic time already. Two students sat in the porch rockers. Neither seemed to be short of breath or bleeding profusely. As she rushed past them toward the administrative offices across the road, Janet told them she'd be back soon.

Angelo was standing on the shoulder of the road in his jogging shorts and T-shirt, shaking out his arms and stretching in preparation for his late afternoon run. Each day Janet watched him lean and pull at the steps of the men's dorm across the road from the one-person infirmary she ran for the summer college. He hadn't run yet.

"Walt's ordered four tanks of oxygen," she said. "Four oxygen tanks, Ange. To put in his room. Now what?"

He lifted his head and looked at her. "I'll think it over while I run off the doubt and inclinations."

"Doubt and inclinations." She grinned at him, glanced at the administration building, then turned back to the Infirmary to treat the students sitting on the front porch she could feel watching her.

The girl had black fly bites on the back of her neck at the hairline, which Janet smeared with antihistamine cream, the guy, a suspicious-looking turned ankle. She called down the mountain to the town hospital twenty miles away for x-ray stress films to see if there was a hairline fracture. She wrapped the student's ankle in an ace bandage, and supplied him with crutches and a plastic bag for ice. After calling Riley, the campus caretaker, to give the fellow a ride to town, there was a knock at the screen door.

Walt Hedenberg stood outside the door on the porch, his nose touching the dark screen.

"Hi, Janet."

She squinted at the door. "Oh, Walt, come on in."

She nodded toward the antique high-backed chair with the purple cushion she used as a patient's seat. She sat down at her desk opposite the chair and the narrow bed she used for students who needed a rest from the noisy dorms.

"Looks like the start of sprained ankle season," she said, and finished jotting her note into the Infirmary logbook. It was time to bring more crutches and ace bandages up from the College Infirmary in town. "Back woods medicine," she said. She looked at Walt and laughed. "Or at least that is what Father Angelo calls it."

Walt smiled a little, pulled the chair closer toward her, and sat down.

"Janet, my oxygen hasn't arrived yet."

She studied him, looking for a change that might make the oxygen necessary. A tall, blond man in his early forties, with a handsome face augmented by a beard, his color was pink, and he was breathing easily. He appeared in no acute distress. She picked up her stethoscope from the side table and standing behind him, moved the disk over his back, under his thin shirt.

After a minute of intent listening, she spoke, "Sibilant rhonchi."

"What did you say?"

"Wheezing. But it's faint. You have asthma, Walt?"

"Used to. I mean, what if I can't breathe in the middle of the night and nobody's there? " Tears welled up in his eyes.

"Okay, Walt. You can sleep here in the Infirmary front room if you want to."

"Thanks. At home if I can't breathe I just turn on the tank. Two liters a minute, and I'm fine."

"Well, you look fine to me, Walt. Don't make yourself too sick, too soon."

After he left she picked up the Infirmary log, checked her watch, and wrote a note documenting date, time, and nature of his visit.

~

Janet and Angelo sprawled again in the wooden chairs, waited for the sun to take its final plunge. There were no mosquitoes tonight, only the incessant moan of a dove.

"Ange, I'm a broken record. What should I do'"'"

"Why don't you call the doc and ask him?"

"It's not a doc question I'm asking here. I don't have patience with Walt anymore. I don't like myself this way." She shook her head. "I have trouble being civil to a very sick man. But he's such a baby about it—a baby."

"Okay, Janet, I'll pull out my Jesuit education, a little Vatican two-step."

"Well, I guess the timing is right."

"We just came through field mouse week—when anyone who can break, will break."

"Field mouse week?"

"Yes," she said with a long breath. "Don't you know about this?"

He shook his head.

"From back in the 20's, I guess." She laughed. "Some woman wandered off in the next to last week of the semester when the stress level is highest. Three days later she was found crawling around on her hands and knees in the hayfield looking for field mice. 'Here little mousie, here little mousie.'"

"Guess you could say she lost it," Angelo said dryly.

Janet laughed. "Guess so. Thanks, Ange."

"For what?"

"For reminding me." She touched his arm. "One thing Walt did do was call the medical supply company and cancel the oxygen."

"Is that good?" He turned to her alarmed.

"I got Riley to bring a portable oxygen canister down from the ski area for him.

Even if the worst should happen it's enough to get him down the mountain to the hospital. Not so dramatic as those five-foot tanks that Walt ordered. Can you imagine lugging those monsters up three flights of narrow wooden stairs to his room? We would have to be all muscle. Plus, I couldn't check what was going on. I told him he could stay in the Infirmary. Walt scares himself."

"Maybe he scares you?"

"Nah." She shook her head. The sun hovered above the treeline. "Well, maybe, I've gotten attached to him. You know me."

He looked into the trees. "I had a good run last night, but I didn't come up with any new ideas for Walt. I've been preoccupied."

"I've noticed."

He pointed to the sun. "Look."

She glanced at the sky beginning to pinken, and then quickly back to him. A purple barn swallow swooped low over the stretch of lawn in front of them.

"Okay." Janet tapped the arm of his chair. "What's going on?"

"Nothing."

"Look, I've been watching you. You've been stinking around all summer. Your body language, if you'll pardon the expression—come on, don't smile—says trouble."

"It's just that time is up for everyone," his eyes studied a hayfield which in the evening breeze was a lake of moving grass.

"How do you mean?" she asked.

"Graduation tomorrow, the Chekhov play. All the brothers, my friends at the residence—told you where I live, didn't I?"

She started to say he hadn't. They'd met the first summer she worked at the college when he came to the Infirmary with a bad case of poison ivy. At first she didn't know he was a priest because he wore clothes like the rest of the students. In the three summers she had known him he hadn't told her anything about himself, anything about being a Jesuit.

He went on without waiting for a reply. "All the lay brothers from the residence where I live in the winter have new assignments.

They're moving, scattering. Nothing will be the same. And I won't be back here."

He turned toward the hayfield as he spoke, his profile, against the low sun. She could see the pockmarks on his cheeks in this light. She studied the narrow face, the plain, functional features. How ordinary his appearance was except for his amused eyes. She watched the fan of his lashes blink at the refracted sunlight, the hairs at the top of his ear, fine as rays of light, and the ridges running from his nose to mouth.

"How old are you now, Angelo?"

"Thirty-eight."

She nodded. Somehow she never thought of a priest having a specific age. She and Angelo were born the same year. His long body rested in the old-fashioned lawn chair, muscles firm from jogging, with only a little softness around his middle. She wondered if he had ever made love, but she could never ask. She noted the stiff slope of his shoulders, the tightness of his back as he leaned forward in the heat of her scrutiny.

"Damn it, Janet, this place is made for mating." He stared down at the ground. "I've been watching all summer. Birds, animals, people. Even the grasses multiply here."

He raised his head to view the narrow lawn, the moving hayfield. The roar of chainsaw erupted from the copse of trees.

"I've just realized," he glanced toward the disruptive sound, "can you imagine—just realized—I'll never have my own children. I've known it of course, intellectually. But it came home to me this summer."

"It didn't occur to you before?"

She thought of her own son at home being cared for by his father as part of the divorce agreement. He was secure in a little brass case in her heart she rarely opened to others. Like a priest, no one wanted a nurse to have a private life. It was hard to be silent, to stay in the Infirmary on her side of the road, to be content in the still pool of her life.

She remembered one day last winter walking down the hospital hall. A woman had called her into her hospital room. "You probably don't remember me," the drab, middle-aged woman had said, and

Janet had indeed not remembered her. "Three years ago you said something that turned my life around. And I've been looking for you ever since."

"I've been here," Janet said. "What was that?" She sat down beside the woman's bed. "What did I say?"

"I was really depressed, and you asked me if my dog loved me."

"I did?"

"Yes, and then you said, 'Well, if your dog loves you, then you must be lovable, don't you think?' And I've thought about that. And you know it's true."

I need to get a dog, Janet thought. We all need to get a dog.

After a few minutes, Angelo turned in his chair to face her. "You know," he said, "I was so busy with scholarship and teaching, a family didn't occur to me."

∼

The next day Janet grabbed Walter by the arm as they came out of the dining hall after lunch and pulled him toward her red Jeep parked in front of the building.

"Walter," she said, "get in."

"But I have a rehearsal."

"You're early. Rehearsal starts at two. This won't take long."

Janet climbed into the driver's seat and slammed the door. She tossed an empty Coke can into the back seat. The sharp edge of the opening caught her hand. Muttering to herself, she sucked on her thumb as started the Jeep. Walt sat in the passenger seat, his back stiff. He coughed a couple of times and looked at her.

She took off staring straight ahead, and drove a mile down the narrow mountain road. At the first picnic area she screeched off onto the shoulder and turned to him.

"Walt, have you talked to Angelo, Father Ciresi?"

"A couple times."

"Well, talk to him again."

"Where are you taking me?"

"It's a surprise."

They drove another mile down the mountain at breakneck speed, negotiating between the thinly-treed rock wall on their left, and the drop-off to the river on the right. At an overlook, Janet pulled the jeep close to the guard railing facing the valley below and turned off the ignition. A red-tailed hawk soared in front of them, then dropped to the river far below.

"Have you ever been soaring, Walt?"

"No."

They looked over the valley for a few minutes in silence. The air was fragrant and dry; the midday sun beat down on their heads.

"Look at that hawk, would you?"

"I see it."

"And the river rushing along down there over the rocks."

"I see the river."

"Walt, come on," Janet said. "Spill it. Something."

"Okay," Walt turned to face her. He shaded his face with a hand. "You're so smart. Tell me what kind of sappy god would create this," he threw his hand in the air, "and then give me a karate chop in the throat? Throat, chest—wop! You're dead."

"You're not dead," she said. "That's the point."

"Pretty cruel, I'd say."

"Because you can name your disease, and the rest of us pretend we have nine lives?"

"Something like that."

"Look." Janet gazed up at the milk blue sky for a moment. "Your crying frightens everybody, Walt. That's the problem. Everybody feels too much here." Her voice softened. "Maybe this is happening to you too. The city armor falls away after we're here a week and everybody's defenses tumble." Janet turned to face him. "You're not being ignored, Walter. Believe me." She looked at him until he returned her gaze. "Lift your head, man. You get us so scared we can't talk to you. Even me, Walt, and I'm supposed to be immune to this stuff." She gazed down to the river. The wet rocks far below glistened gray and brown. The hawk was gone.

Walt stared down the valley, his face set, expressionless. A cloud of white butterflies flitted over the weeds on the other side of the guardrail.

Janet watched their casual flight. The butterflies reminded her of a summer day she and the man she would eventually marry had taken a ride in the country and stopped beside a lake. Overcome by the day and each other, they had made love in the dry lakeside grasses. Clouds of white butterflies had flitted over them as they sighed, turned, and rolled into the water.

"Okay," Walt said after a moment. "Now take me back to rehearsal."

"Walt, talk to me."

"You know," he turned to her, "I do love Chekhov."

"Do you understand what I'm saying?"

"Very well. Do you?"

"Enjoy each day, can you?"

"Sure, Janet." He pointed to a butterfly posed on the top of the guard rail.

"The Chinese say white butterflies are good luck. The souls of their ancestors."

"And enjoy the next day too."

"Okay," he said.

She put her hand on his arm. "Thank you, Walt. I had to say it."

~

Janet was working late at her desk when a knock came on the Infirmary door. She opened it and lamplight fanned out onto the dark lawn. Angelo was there. He looked as if he had been running.

"Janet, can we talk?"

"Ange, sure. Come in."

She tucked her shirt into her jeans and let him into the small front room. "What time is it?" she asked.

"I don't know—"

"It doesn't matter." She smiled. He was in the same jogging shorts and T-shirt he had on earlier in the day. "Sit down. You want some instant coffee?"

She walked toward the kettle warming on a hot plate in the corner of the room.

"No thanks," he said, still breathing hard from the run, "I'm swearing off the stuff."

He sprawled in the chair opposite the small bed and the desk.

"What am I thinking of?" she said, the kettle in her hand, "coffee for insomnia? What is it?"

He stretched his arms and, as if he had not heard her question, sat for a long time staring at his knees as his breathing calmed. She observed him from where she had perched on the edge of the bed.

"Angelo, I can talk you asleep."

"There are some things I can't say."

"Then we'll go back to our favorite topic."

She sighed and looked out into the dark. "I took Walt for a ride today. To the overlook. I tried to reason with him. I guess I sounded heartless, telling him to take one day at a time." She shook her head. "Sounds like A.A. But you know, Ange, there's an organization by that name for cancer patients, One Day At A Time. I was trying to tell him not to waste his energy worrying about a future that isn't here yet. At least that was what I wanted to say. Basically, I told him to stop crying."

She looked down at her lap. "Maybe I shouldn't have said that."

"We say what we can." Angelo opened and closed his hands in front of him. "Did Walt get it?"

"He said yes, but no, he didn't get it."

"I'm not surprised. He's resistant, all right." Angelo pulled himself upright in the chair.

"Ange, do you have any comforting words? I'm fresh out."

"I don't even have words for myself." He paused. "Maybe not wearing clerics—"

She slid off the bed, walked over to him and touched his shoulder. "You don't need a black suit."

"What do you see now?" He held his hands out in front of him. They were quivering. "Look at me. I'm drowning in the priesthood. I'm up half the night aching for the kind of life a part of me wants."

She turned away. After a moment she went behind him and ran her hand over his shoulders.

"Just as I thought," she said. "Your muscles are tight as sinners in a confessional."

"That's pretty good," he said. "Right on the money, Janet."

She smoothed the white spread on the examining room bed.

"Okay," she said, "lie down." She patted the mattress.

He stood and paced around the room. "Maybe I shouldn't."

"Well, maybe you should."

He stopped, paused a moment, then lowered himself face down onto the bed. The clock on the shelf above them ticked steadily. Janet rubbed her moist hands dry on her jeans.

She leaned over him, hair hanging in her face. She reached under his shirt and began massaging his bank, moving her palms upward from the base of his spine to his neck, then pressing down along his sides and back again in firm, oval strokes.

"Angelo," she said, "take off your shirt."

After a pause, he sat and pulled the T-shirt over his head and lay down again on his belly, head toward the wall.

She kneaded the muscles over his ribs, working up from his waist, one flank and then the other. "This is called petrosage," she said as she slid her fingers to his midback and made little circles up and down the fleshy paths on either side of his spine.

His breathing eased, and the spasmed muscles that had been knotted fists beneath his skin became flexible beneath her hands.

She leap-frogged her palms in rapid strokes along the muscles of his shoulder blades to his upper arms. His shoulders seemed to relax with her touch.

"You have good strong trapezius muscles," she said.

She turned down the navy cotton waist band of his jogging shorts and pressed circles on either side of his tailbone. She felt him tense and moved away.

"Just a minute." She turned to rummage in a corner cabinet and came back with a bottle of lotion.

"Hope you don't mind the perfume smell," she said. "Pretty sweet. Hard to tell what it's supposed to be. Maybe honeysuckle. Lotion reduces friction, makes a better massage."

"Janet."

"Yes?"

"I went into the God business early. I never had a back rub before. I've missed a lot, haven't I?"

"Not so much," she said.

"I've tried prayer with Walt, words of comfort, philosophy, ethics, theology. Everything from Aquinas to. . . But what do you say to someone who is mourning his own life? If I could say something, I would, but everything goes flat. I'm not adequate."

She stroked his back, now fragrant from the lotion. How lovely a man this is, she thought, and she couldn't tell him. He's like a butterfly. A doubtful face, but beautiful wings.

"At least," Janet said after a few minutes, "Walt is going to the rehearsals. He's interested in this play. Something by Chekhov." She looked down at her hands resting on his shoulders, then lifted them. "You'll be fine, Ange. You know that. Maybe pray?"

He rolled over and sat on the edge of the bed. For a moment he cradled his head in his hands. "Thanks for the rub," he said, getting up. "You're good."

She returned his look and then sat in the straight-backed chair at her desk.

"I gathered this bouquet today," she said. "I put a note on the door so anyone wanting me would know where I was, and walked up the road gathering flowers."

She pointed to the large bunch of purple flowers in an aluminum pitcher on the table by the window. "I decided to pick only purple ones." Her voice gained volume. "All the purple wildflowers I could find.

"See that?" She pointed to a square stemmed stalk with spikes of small flowers that looked like a ruffled lavender torch. "I've been trying to look that one up in a plant book. I think it's Heal-All, good for throat ailments. I'm ready to try that on Walt. Anything. Make tea from it."

"Don't get reckless. Why purple flowers?"

Angelo stared at the bouquet in the circle of lamplight.

"Purple for passion?" he asked.

She turned to him. In the three years she had known him, this was the first time Angelo had come to the Infirmary at night. In her mind she touched again the tense muscles of his shoulders. She imagined kissing the back of his neck.

"I've thought of passion," she said.

He studied her face. She watched his expression transform, like evening sky. One moment flushed, expectant, the next at rest. In that moment she acknowledged the thick dark hair of his forearms, the muscles of his thighs, the angles of his knees.

She turned to her desk and focused on her logbook. "Passion in our work," she said. She ran her finger down the closed book's cover. "*The Seagull* opens tomorrow."

"Yes," he said, "Chekhov."

He walked toward the door. "What do you say, shall we see our friend Walt at dress rehearsal tomorrow?"

She nodded.

"God bless," he said without turning around.

The door clicked shut.

Janet picked up the log, then put the book down again without making an entry. After a moment, she rose from the chair. She switched off the table lamp, and carried the pitcher of wildflowers with her through the dark Infirmary into her bedroom at the back of the cottage. The silver pitcher glinted in the light from the window as she set the flowers on her nightstand. Without undressing, she lay on the bed.

In the pale moonlight she stared at the ceiling, with a kind of breathless pain in her chest. The flowers smelled woodsy and pungent, and out the open window lay the hayfield, a motionless lake of grass in the shadowed blue light.

In a moment she would get up and undress. She would leave a pair of jeans and a shirt laid out on the chair with her flashlight, in case she had to get up for an emergency in the middle of the night. With a kind of fierce pride she knew she could throw on her clothes and be there in a run.

～

When Janet arrived, dress rehearsal for *The Seagull* was in progress. Several students were on the stage of the small dimly lit theater dressed in stiff nineteenth century garb, looks of misery on their faces. Jay Duering, the director, paced the stage in front of them.

"No, no, no, no," he shouted as Janet sat down at the back on a wooden folding chair.

"Performance tonight," the director shouted, "and none of you are living your roles. Concentrate." He gave them a withering glance. "You've heard this before. Have you no imaginations?"

"We don't have Russian souls," a pale young woman called out. There was a titter of laughter behind her.

The director scowled. "You must have souls, period. Forget the Russian business. Chekhov is talking about living human beings."

He paced in front of them. "The play within the play comments on embracing death. Think about it, children! Think—dead seagull. How about *that!*"

"But Jay, we're trying."

He wheeled around. "I realize a few of you aren't alive. Remember we are acting here. Acting! Forget your precious selves."

Walter appeared on stage from behind the curtain. His face was ashen and he moved slowly.

Jay looked at him sharply. "Walt. You going to be all right for this?"

Walter nodded. "Fine," he said.

"Okay, let's do it."

⁓

That evening the graduation dinner was held in the dining hall and Angelo Ciresi, as valedictorian, moved to the lectern to give his address. Angelo wore his clerics. For many of the students, this was the first time they had seen him as Father Ciresi, in his black suit and turned collar. The common vision of him was in class in a T-shirt and running shorts, a little sweaty from a run.

Angelo adjusted the microphone. "I've come to talk about passion," he said. He caught Janet's eye. His composed face had the look of a boy. "Passion in our work."

Janet listened as he spoke of community and dedication, but during the speech she drifted into her own thoughts. She remembered when she had just left nursing school, and had her first job in a little hospital near the Blue Ridge. They were short-handed, and she had worked the first month without a weekend off. When she was finally free, she took a wiry, tanned carpenter she had just met camping with her in the mountains. It was June, and they had filled the inside of their tent with armloads of green, yellow and white honeysuckle, making a foot high mattress of the sweet smelling vines.

When his speech was over, Angelo was surrounded by fellow students. Several young men clapped him on the back, a few others shook his hand, and many of the young women delighted at the opportunity, kissed him. He accepted their affection with a look of surprise and gradually, a slow smile.

"Well," Janet whispered to Angelo later as they sat together at the back of the theater, "this is Walter's big act. Wish him luck."

On the stage of the little theater, Walter, as the old man Sorin, wheeled himself in a high-back wooden invalid chair into center spotlight for the last act. He climbed out of the chair, and standing beside it, motioned his head toward the stiff Victorian sofa on left stage.

"*Is that bed for me?*"

Angelo nodded to Janet.

"*I want to give Kostya a subject for a story.*" Walt said in the enfeebled voice of Sorin. "*It ought to be called 'The Man Who Wished'—L'homme qui a voulu.*"

Several minutes later a young girl leaned down into the darkened seats and beckoned to Janet. "You're needed at the Infirmary," she whispered.

From the stage Janet heard Walter, speaking as Sorin.

"*What a persistent fellow he is!*" *Walter's* voice rang out. "*You might understand that one wants to live!*"

Janet glanced at the stage, then squeezed past Angelo. "Sprained ankle," she whispered in his ear. "What do you bet?"

"I don't." He smiled and put a finger to his lips.

On stage, Dorn, the doctor, was speaking.

"*The dread of death is an animal fear.*" *He* spoke with authority. "*One must overcome it—*"

Janet left the theater and started across the moonlit lawn. She heard Sorin's laugh behind her.

⟡

After treating the student for an ankle sprained at volleyball, Janet stood in the doorway of the darkened theater. Moths flitted at the outside light above her head. It was too late to return to her seat.

On stage, as the cast took their bows, Walter stood beside the empty wheelchair, his head up, eyes bright, back straight, a feverish flush on his cheeks. The other actors fell away, retreating to the wings. At Jay's direction, Walter remained standing.

Janet moved back into the shadows as the audience clapped in prolonged applause. One after another, they rose to their feet applauding as the house lights swelled. She watched Angelo smile broadly as he stood among them. Janet ran a knuckle along her cheeks and turned away.

~

She made her way down the wooden path to the stone filled river bed. It was midnight by then, and she had left a note on her door saying that she was going to the river. If anyone needed her she would be at the end of the path behind the Infirmary, where the path met water.

The trail was steep and soft, but she had traveled it so often during the day she had no trouble distinguishing the turns. The logs fallen across the path were illuminated by moonlight. She had her flashlight, but switched it off and put it in her jacket pocket, preferring to slide down the dewy banks in the half dark. Above her was the brilliant dusting of the Milky Way, the sharp points of separate stars.

She could hear the cool water splashing over the rocks. Cool water, nearing cold. She reached the bank and paused to listen to the water and the stinging, creature-filled silence of the forest night.

On a smooth boulder at the water's edge, she slowly took off her clothes. She sat on the rock to untie her tennis shoes and remove her socks. The light night breeze stroked her shoulders. She unzipped her jeans, stepped out of them and her cotton underpants, rolled the clothing around her shoes and deposited the bundle at the foot of a tree.

In a moment she would be used to the night coolness. She smoothed the goose flesh on her arms. Janet knew she could take her time. No one would find her here, no one would come looking, despite the note on the Infirmary door.

She stepped off a large rock into the shallow water. The stream moved over the slick pebbled bottoms, reaching her ankles, licking her calves as she waded downstream. After a few minutes she turned and walked carefully back to the rock, the sharp slippery stones pressing into the soles of her feet, the moonlight dropping the shadows of pines in front of her. Back at the bank, she held on to the rock and settled into a cold shallow pool, extending her long body, her head pillowed on a flat outcropping of rock. She remembered seeing a Japanese headrest once in a museum, and understood now why resting one's head on a thing of the earth would bring on restful sleep.

The cool water flowed over her body as she lay pointed upstream. The water caressed her from toes to neck in recurrent strokes, like a mother, a masseuse who never grew weary. As she lay there, the river rippling over her, the moon moving behind the pines, the air was alive with the smells of pitch, the pungent richness of decay, and from somewhere honeysuckle. She thought of Walter, of Angelo, of her son, all the people she had earnestly ministered to, sometimes with an effect that radiated like rings in water into nothingness.

Where Are You Now, Ella Wade?

W e climb the tower of the Ravner Building and find Miss Bendix at the desk. She's gray and thin as grass. No cap. No crisp uniform as we remember. She wears a lab coat over street clothes and on her name pin, a long meaningless title.

She smiles. "Today you have our Ella." Miss Bendix is still head nurse.

Ella's in the corner bed. Our nerves jangled, we find comfort in the Zen-like sameness of her care. We escape to her as threatened children might escape to a bedroom corner with the dolls, or up a backyard tree.

Ella has been comatose for years. The early portions of her chart are off the floor in the caverns of Medical Records or maybe lost. We do not know her age.

"Ella." We call her name to humanize her body. "Ella. Ella Wade."

Her eyes are open, unblinking.

In surgery, while she sat upright in a chair, they hinged a bony trapdoor in her skull, and someone peered inside to hear the hollow echoes of her mind. Then they closed the door. Her head was shaved before the craniotomy. Somehow her hair follicles were persuaded to shut down as well. She remains forever bald. She's our dusky Nefertiti, her bare head wrapped in cotton. Dark lashes kohl her eyes. Her egg-shaped head is covered by stockinet, a hat made from a sleeve of clinging cotton. It's gathered at the crown with rubber bands, and at her forehead rolled, a ski-cap diadem.

"Hello, Ella." We stroke her hand. "How are you?" In her silence, she is an infant without cry, without want, without future. "Can you hear us, Ella?"

We turn our Nefertiti in the bulrushes of her bed. On the rivulets of her sheets she is like a log bobbing in our minds. Outside the hospital window, birds cling to the trees like fruit.

"Ella," we call her. "Ella." She is a mirror in which our fantasies play. In the air of our imaginations we hear a whispered response.

If we left Ella in the tower in a lonely room, would she awaken, sit up in bed, and wonder? Or is there still upon her lips the poison taste of bitter almond, or sweetness crystallized to coma long ago? Did a tumor eat her mind? An auto shock her with such impact she didn't want to know?

Her easy breathing says she's lost in there. She does not fight our good intentions. Her body is neither stiff nor heavy. One person can position her. Without the weight of consciousness—as innocent as dawn before the wires fused forever left with right—she's light. So light we think sometimes she seeps from her trapdoor into the air above us. She has a fondness for us, we imagine, as baby loves the breast or as a lover, for a moment, loves the loved.

We stand by her bed and watch the intern dig a house key up the soles of her feet. The response to the Babinski test says, no malingering. She's really gone. We are wordless wind in the bare room of her mind. We do not ask each other what private dream sustains us in her care.

"She's blind," the intern says. But we think no. We insist that Ella sees us. She records her view on film, in a golden box in her head she'll one day open. The intern strides away.

Ella must do nothing but keep intact her flawless skin. Stroked, bathed, lubricated around the clock by generations of nurses, protected from sun and padded against injury, her skin's integrity is unbroken.

She breathes without assistance. No supplemental oxygen, no airway, her ribs retract, flesh out, retract, flesh out, like bony gills. Her lips are buds of flesh above a toothless mouth. Her teeth have been removed for "ease of care," and yet in our minds we return them: broad, strong, slightly yellow. Why, we ask, no dignity of teeth?

We help her modest swimming in her Nile of air. We take her

through her strokes—crawl and back and breast. We exercise her long thin arms, slim legs. We bathe her. We call her name again, again, massaging her buttocks and along her spine. We feed her through a tube coiled at her belly.

"Ella," we say. "Ella Wade. How does it feel to have a belly full?"

We move Ella's limbs in the directions they should go. We circle around the clock-face of Ella's body; the range-of-motion exercises are as orderly as a clock tower that works. First the right arm at nine o'clock, left arm at three. Left leg at five o'clock, the right at seven. We flex her wrists, her elbows, her knees. We circle her extremities, like chopsticks in dry bowls, in the sockets of her shoulders and her hips.

We name the bones as mantra as we go: humerus—radius—ulna—carpals—metacarpals—phalanges, then femur—tibia—fibula—tarsals—metatarsals, phalanges again. Again, and more. Sometimes we speak of nursery rhymes or saints. Sometimes we name the angels that we know: Gabriel, Michael, Aziel, Raziel, Arios. We spread her fingers wide and lift each phalange toward the ceiling, to stretch against the always stronger muscles of contraction. We know this uneven muscle strength, this natural move toward closure, keeps us neat. Like a door upon a spring, the loose limbs stow themselves along the body.

Miss Bendix comes around and helps us flip Ella on her side, more a gesture of bonhomie, we know, than a response to some real need. We wonder if Miss Bendix still has the heart to sing.

"Is Ella as you remember her?" she asks. She smiles.

"Yes, Miss Bendix. Quite the same."

"We change." Miss Bendix flits a finger through her graying hair. "But Ella stays the same."

Miss Bendix turns, is gone.

We place a pillow between our Ella's knees to keep them free of chafing, to air our Ella's private parts, to keep her sweet. We've put a footboard on the bed, a wooden earth beneath her for when she's stretched full length. And when she's turned every other hour for sprinting in the air, sandbags keep her feet from curling. Her easy breathing says she's lost in there.

Those feet are slim and arched, the ankles thin. Her toes overlap upon each other. Her first toes ride upon her great toes. Her smallest toes seek their sisters to claim less space upon earth, we guess. But still, we keep her foot soles flat against a surface, careful that her toes don't drop, or she'll be hobbling to eternity on pointe—or three-inch heels—the ball joints of her hips and shoulders frozen too.

Left alone, a body curls into itself like cold-shocked leaves. We who stretch Ella to extension six times a day have kept flexible enough to dream without deformity. But still, we know our efforts will not heal her.

Her mouth opens and we wait. There is no sound. In a moment, her eyes squint into a yawn.

We listen for the voice that never comes, an ancient chant perhaps, a song. We know after a stroke, the smash-up of a cerebral vascular accident, those mute to spoken words can often sing—a different portion of the brain engages song—and in our mind's ear we hear our Ella singing scat, or Billie Holiday, or Billy Swan, or rap.

Her hands rest at her sides now, where we've placed them. She can do anything with these hands in our imaginations. We see her grip the throttle of a plane, towing training targets above the trees. Steady, steady. Finished, she pulls the plane into a climb. She climbs, climbs more, and then the twisting curl away of her chandelle.

Her fingers are square-ended, the moons distinct, pale yellow on the oblong nails. We tuck into her palms the taped white washcloth rolls we make for her. She holds them loosely like batons for a relay race she never runs. We make them to protect her from the moist dark of her own hands. The nails of her contracted fingers would pierce her palms. We marvel how her nails grow and get dirty. Ella digs potatoes in her dreams.

Our lives make noise, we know, and wounds. We scan her body to look for proof of her participation, and find not scar, but evidence. On her long body for the first time we focus on a faint dark line from umbilicus to mons. How could we have missed it, the unfaded *linea negra* of a pregnancy. She is not pregnant now. What's left is just a shadow. Oh, we say, our mouths circular wounds upon our faces. She ran eclamptic into coma with a child. And now she's caught in a refusal, forever stuck in the body that will slow, slow, and one day stop.

If we peer out of the corners of our eyes, a subtle light still comes from Ella's body, a pale light most people take note of only when it's gone. What is there in us, we ask, that keeps believing our Ella will someday emerge into the world, like a small fox, its eyes newly opened, clawing out of its burrow. How startling will be the sun that day, how blue the sky. We know we keep believing this because we must.

She yawns, our Nefertiti. We think she needs some space, some air.

"Ella," we ask whispering, "would you wake if we no longer needed you?"

We see her, bewigged and dentured, standing on a street corner at a bus stop. Her brown doll eyes are lined in black. She's squinting in the sun. She clutches fare coins tightly to her chest and sings out to us.

"My bus is coming." She waves. "Here it is."

Turtle Soup

In September the creekbed down from our farmhouse teemed with snapping turtles. The night before the turtle hunt, when I was sure my parents, Homer and Brenda, were asleep, I crawled out my bedroom window and sat on the porch roof in the moonlight. I thought about healing for a while—one of my favorite subjects—and then had an abrupt conversation with God—we didn't agree—before I noticed how pleasant the cool air was on my bare arms as I braced myself on the pitched roof and listened to the night sounds. Whenever the hoarse rhythmic whistles of the young frogs were interrupted, I could hear the turtles under the willow trees that overhung the creek. Their sharply-pointed toenails scraped and clicked over the rocks, and the glide of their horny, dark-plated bodies over the muddy lip of the creek bank was almost soundless—then plop, into the water. Sometimes I heard a lumbering group of old snappers reach the creek bank at the same time, and when their heavy bodies hit the water together there was a sudden splash, as if a nighttime swimmer had plunged in quickly to challenge the cold.

We lived in a corner of southwestern Pennsylvania, where the hills roll headlong into West Virgina. To the north, the Back Mountain where my father Homer and his family always lived was protected and green, but the south face had been dug out to the core, the surface laid back and carted away by strip miners. The miners avoided the depleted south valley where coal vein fires had been smoldering below the surface for fifty years. My father was a young man when the residents first noticed snakes of black smoke rising from the fissures in the earth. Since no one was able to put the fires out, most people ignored them.

Whenever I would ask about the smoke rising from empty lots around town people would seem genuinely surprised and say to me, "What smoke?" or, "Oh, Dolly, that's nothing to worry about."

Boonetown had grown up beside the abandoned mineshafts, over the tunnels, which gave way periodically whenever the weight of the streets above overcame the rotting mine timbers. The town's old-timers seemed to know the old mine's underground structure. Many had worked the mines in their youth and often, while sitting on their unpainted porches, they would speculate about the next cave-in site. But, in the way of older country people, they usually kept their speculations among themselves. Many a new person, anxious to work in the new strip mine on the hillside above town, moved in not knowing about the mine tunnels beneath the streets. A new resident would buy a house surprisingly cheaply, or park his car on a deserted street, only to awaken one morning to find his house on a funhouse tilt, or his car disappearing into a black cavern below the asphalt.

"*Caveat emptor*," my father Homer would announce, smiling at the superior tone of his one Latin phrase, and speaking to any person, tree, cow, dog, or tractor near him when he heard this kind of news on the local radio station.

Homer rarely went down to town, and he refused to have anything to do with the mines. He proudly boasted that our family had homesteaded the Back Mountain when homes were heated by wood fires, not coal. The kitchen of our farmhouse was the original log cabin, and the rest of the sprawling house and outbuildings had been built gradually during those fortunate years when the mine was productive, people had money, and the corn crop was good. During this time I grew up on Back Mountain, listened to Homer's Latin, noticed my mother cooked a lot—as I flew through the kitchen—and except for one thing, I never wanted much I didn't get.

There was a stand of woods behind the farmhouse then, beyond the rhubarb patch, and at nighttime I'd listen for the bobcats to come down from the woods to fight over the garbage with our coon hound, George. The bobcats usually won, of course, but I liked to imagine the look on George's face when a bobcat came sneaking up behind him. I would look for paw prints in the morning whenever I thought

I had heard a skirmish the night before, and I'd check under the porch to be sure the dog was all right. He'd hide there usually until late afternoon, howling or growling quietly now and then if the defense of the garbage had been especially rigorous.

One morning when I was peering under the porch looking for the coon hound, I overheard my parents in the kitchen talking bout the "hell fire" underneath the town. After that overheard conversation I began questioning God. "Now why is *this* so?" I'd ask or, "Would you *please* explain this to me clearly?" I tried to be polite to God, but I did have a certain impatience.

For instance, I'd asked, "Why did the bobcat get George?" The hound was too slow one night when the bobcat came down from the woods. I found the dog in the morning, frightened and bleeding. I grabbed his front paws and dragged him out from under the porch. The bobcat had bitten George in the neck, and when I pulled the gash open I found a hole large enough for my fist. It looked as if the bobcat's teeth had severed the muscle that went from the dog's chin to his chest, and once severed, it had sprung back like a large rubber band, leaving a gigantic empty cavity.

Each evening for weeks I pounced on the dog. After slipping a noose over his muzzle I would cross my warm hands over his neck. The wound swelled, but eventually, miraculously, it healed. Whenever I put my knee on George's chest to hold him down to do the treatment, I would coo to the dog and concentrate on healing. I didn't have a clear idea about infection or circulation, but after the first day or two the hound was cooperative. He'd whimper a little and then get quiet, trusting, his big brown eyes rolled back in his head. Once healed, the coon hound always held his head to one side as if questioning how I'd done it.

Convinced that I had the power to heal, I began to worry about my strange effect on machinery. I preferred not to go to town, imagining that my mysterious power was in some way demonically connected with the town's own black smoke from Hell. Why then did every car or truck break down whenever I got in to ride down the mountain? My mother Brenda would shake her head, climb into the pickup and drive down into town without me.

On shopping days, when Brenda was gone, I usually wandered down to the creek. Once I spent half the morning pushing and shoving a huge snapping turtle into my wagon.

I proudly dragged it up the hill toward the house. The monstrous snapper's clawed feet and rubbery tail hung over the sides of the wagon, and he rolled his yellow eyes at me whenever I forgot and looked at him directly.

My father was standing under the buttonwood tree in the side yard, briefly resting out of the sun. He watched me struggling up the embankment with the heavy turtle-laden wagon.

Homer, small, bony and tanned, leaned further back against the tree trunk. "Glad to see you put a stick in his mouth," he said as he wiped a hand on his thigh. "We don't have time for turtle hunts now, Dolly. Klaus is here and we're doing the haying."

"Geez," I said. Sweating and caked with mud from my struggle at the creekbed, I stared down at the turtle.

The snapper looked tired. He rolled his yellow eyes at me.

"Geez," I said again.

My father wiped his forehead with his handkerchief and put it back into his pocket. "Got to get to work now," he said.

I went to the rear of the wagon and put one hand on either side of the turtle's grey-green tail. Easing the wagon across the short stretch of yard and down the steep grassy bank, I leaned back to balance the turtle's weight. Halfway down the slope I slipped on a slick patch of mud and the wagon pulled away from me. It went careening crazily toward the water, crashed into a large rock at the water's edge, and catapulted the monstrous snapper back into the creek.

I looked down at the sprawled wagon and decided I would be patient. I knew once a year the family gathered to drink beer and cook turtle soup all day if one of my uncles, usually Klaus, would agree to be the turtle catcher.

I was fifteen that September, tall and embarrassingly over-developed, and so plain by the townspeople's standards I wasn't even considered worth idle gossip. After all, how could a person as stout and serious-faced as I was ever hope to win herself a man? But I knew the snappers at my father's Back Mountain farm were a notorious topic of conversation. What does Homer Sweet do, the town folks wondered, to persuade those turtles to take over his creek? Does he haul down his garbage? Could there be enough succulent weeds at that particular place, fat flies or frogs, enough sick water birds and sluggish fish to support this teeming population? Most of the townspeople felt there was a mysterious aura around our farm. Our family kept to themselves, and the only daughter, me, walked everywhere day and night, never rode in a car like normal people, and was always mooning over the health of some animal in a way which was far beyond reason as far as they were concerned. The townspeople looked upon us with suspicion except for the single time each year when the turtle hunt was held. If Homer had sold tickets, most of them would have come.

~

Early the next morning I watched my father walk out to the mailbox to wait for his brothers and their families to arrive. Homer insisted that the annual turtle hunt was exclusively a family function so my mother Brenda always instructed my Uncles Klaus and Walter to skirt the town by taking the side road over the ridge to Back Mountain. There used to be a horde of cousins and great uncles that came too, but that was before the mine closed. By the time the mineshafts were half-filled with debris these men were gone forever and Homer's brothers and families were the only relatives left.

Although it had rained earlier that morning, it was a clear September day and the nip in the air had not yet shocked the trees into color. Brenda told me to go out to Homer to see how he was faring after he had been waiting at the mailbox for over an hour.

"Why don't you invite Joe Beebe, or some of those other fellows in town?" I asked my father when I joined him. I hitched my skirt up at the waist. "They're real interested."

"Too interested, I'd say." Homer had his hands in his overall pockets and was staring down the deserted road. "No thanks."

"All right," I said squinting at him. "I'm supposed to tell you that Uncle Walter just called. They're late. Leaving now."

"Sure they didn't call from some speakeasy?" Homer stared off into the blue-tinted hills. "It takes them forever to get anywhere. Always having to stop for refreshments."

I shrugged. "Don't know. They don't call them speakeasy's anymore. Just cause you aren't a real drinker doesn't mean you can't have patience."

"Patience!"

"Well, see you later," I said to my father, "I have something to do."

I was halfway up the road to the house when a dusty mint-green and white Bel Aire Chevrolet came roaring up. It screeched to a stop just beyond the mailbox. Uncle Klaus jumped out of the car, waved to me, and ran back to give Homer one of his bonecrushing handshakes. I walked back down to the road.

Homer grinned at his younger brother. "You had me worried for a while, Klaus," he said shaking his head, "we have to get these numbers down." He leaned closer to Klaus and I heard him whisper, "Abundance."

"Lots of critters this year, huh Homer?" Klaus bellowed.

"Hundreds." Homer ducked down and peered into the car. "Oh, hi there, Ruth." Klaus' tiny, red-haired wife was sitting in the passenger seat fidgeting with her purse. "Well, what do you know?" Homer said, looking at my fat headed twin cousins who were staring at him from the back seat. "Edith and Evelyn sure are pretty."

Ruth smiled at Homer but those fat twin babies regarded him blandly.

"Say hello to your Uncle Homer," Ruth growled into the back seat.

"Llo, 'Omer," one of the twins said. She covered her face with both hands. The other twin stared out the window.

Like his brother Homer, my Uncle Klaus was a farmer, but so sunburned, wind-burned, and booze-burned his face had a perennial flush. With his redheaded wife and daughters, I thought they looked like a carload of soft tomatoes. I smiled and backed away, pointing first to myself and then the farmhouse behind me.

I backed away but kept watching. Klaus and Homer talked while Ruth waited impatiently in the car. Every once in a while she'd yell

something into the back seat. In a few minutes a quiet black Ford
rolled up behind the Chevrolet.

It was Uncle Walter, the middle brother, who lived only a few
miles away from Klaus, two hours away from us. I knew that although
Klaus and Walter traveled in separate cars, they shared jokes and a
bottle of Schnapps at rest stops along the way and by the time they
got to the Back Mountain Klaus would be jovial, Walter somber, and
Ruth ready to join the Women's Christian Temperance Union.

In the black Ford, Walter's German wife Mae would have no
comment, at least not in English. Although my Uncle Walter was a
bookkeeper—a skinny, dark, bony man unlike his bulky blond brother Klaus—up close I'd noticed the blue, red-lined eyes were the same.
Except for the day of the turtle hunt when Homer would drink a beer
or two, Homer was the only sober brother most of the time. And since
it was turtle hunt day Homer, grinning in a way I rarely saw on other
occasions, even walked back to grunt hello to Aunt Mae—who sat
sharp-nosed in the passenger side of the Ford in her flat green hat—
someone he usually had no use for.

I knew Ruth would be bringing the huge speckled blue soup kettle and Mae some of the ingredients since Homer provided the turtles. Aunt Mae rarely forgot the sherry, schooled as she was in
Prussian precision, and I suspected that my mother easily drowned
redheaded Aunt Ruth's W.T.C.U. ambitions by inducing her to nip a
little in the kitchen while the men were down at the creek, just to
"shake off the road dust."

At the start of the day Aunt Ruth and Aunt Mae were usually anxious to talk to Brenda and they'd shoo me away at every opportunity.
I supposed it was because they wanted to talk about something "unfit
for young ears" but I knew they were being silly because I had heard
most of it already from other sources.

"Poor dear, you go out and get some air," Aunt Ruth would say to
me each time I appeared in the kitchen. Now that I was almost grown,
and had been shooed out of the kitchen repeatedly, I'd lost interest.
My mother and aunts assumed I preferred to be outside, I guess, and
in the way of traditions born of individual circumstance, I had begun
to believe it myself. In fact, I was convinced of it.

I watched Homer jump into the back of Klaus' Bel Aire behind Ruth. The twins scrambled away from him. They huddled together in the corner of the back seat and eyed him suspiciously. "That's just your Uncle," Ruth said. The redheaded twins began to cry.

Walter and Mae followed in the Ford. I could see Aunt Mae was shaking her head and talking at Walter in her heavy German accent. Walter had found her in Dusseldorf during the war. Homer always said he wished his brother had returned her too.

The cars followed slowly as I walked ahead of them up the dirt drive to the house. When they got to the creosoted log that marked the parking area, Aunt Mae emerged from the black Ford carrying a grocery bag on each bony hip. Ruth climbed out of the green and white Chevy carrying a screaming red-haired twin on each soft hip in a similar position, her carrot-red hair hastily tied back out of the way of the twins grasping fingers.

The screen door banged open and Brenda came out to greet them, wiping her hands on her flowered housedress. "Hello, Walter." She smiled at him as he got out of his car. "Hello, Klaus," she said as he slammed the Chevy's door. Brenda stuck out her tongue at Uncle Klaus and laughed. He always was her favorite. She got the kettle from the Chevrolet's back seat and ushered Ruth and Mae into the house. Before going in Brenda turned to Homer. "So nice of you fellows to help carry things."

"What did you say?" said Homer.

"Never mind." Brenda banged the screen door behind her.

While the men sat on the green porch rockers and cajoled and consoled each other over farm loans and the bowling league—Walter and Klaus offering advice in their respective areas of expertise—I slipped away.

I crossed the yard to the tool shed, turned the wood latch on its nail, and went inside. After moving a couple shovels, a hoe and several wooden boxes, I found the green canvas tarp folded in the corner. I rolled it under my arm after replacing the things as well as I could remember. I was going out of the shed when I saw the pliers suspended between two nails by the door. I dropped the pliers into my skirt pocket. Homer, Uncle Klaus and Uncle Walter, leaning back in the rockers with their beer bottles in hand never noticed when I passed under the buttonwood tree by the side of the house and crossed over the short stretch of yard.

~

The grassy bank was still wet from the morning's rain. I eased myself down the steep slope to the creek. The sun shining through the willows dappled the ground and the yellow-brown water with a camouflage palette. A row of mud turtles were lined up on a rotting log that had fallen half into the creek, and several large snappers were sunning themselves on flat rocks at the water's edge.

"Good morning, guys," I said.

The turtles looked up with indifference.

"Been enjoying the morning?" I pulled the tarp out from under my arm, rolled it tighter, and laid it in the crotch of an elm tree, which stood back from the water. The tarp was half hidden by the elm's leaves. A large snapper lying on a rock in the middle of the creek extended his head and opened his horny mouth in a yawn, his tongue pink and heart-shaped. Keeping an eye on him, I chose a stick from the scattering of water-washed sticks at my feet, leaned over the bank and held it out to the snapper. The turtle lurched its head forward as fast as a striking rattlesnake and snapped the thin stick in two. The severed end hung by a thread.

"Oh, ho," I said out loud, "feisty today, Percy?" I shook the stick until the end fell in the muddy water. "Well, I just came to warn you." I slung the remaining half of the stick into the bushes. Another large snapper crawled out of the brush.

"Today I'd advise stealth and nastiness."

The large green snapper on the rock retracted his head into his pleated neck and closed his eyes. A few smaller turtle plopped into the water and several scurried away through the wet leaves.

"Not you," I said to the monstrous snapper on the rock. I ducked through the willow branches the sun spotting my arms like freckles. "I heard you last night," I said to the turtle. "Feeling your oats, I'd say."

I surveyed the muddy, rain-filled creek. The other side of the stream was alive with mud turtles of all sizes crawling over the damp weeds at the water's edge. I looked back at the turtle luxuriating on the rock, sunning himself so peacefully. He had a smile on his face I'd swear. The pliers hung heavy in my pocket.

When I got back to the porch my father, Uncle Klaus and Uncle Walter were talking about a distant relative Klaus had just met and invited to the turtle hunt. Aunt Ruth was inside the house, leaning against the screen door, listening.

"What kind of hunt did you tell him it was, Klaus?" Aunt Ruth asked her brother-in-law through the screen door.

"You don't have to hunt for them," I said coming up onto the porch, "they're just lying there."

Aunt Ruth chuckled, but Homer frowned and turned back to his younger brother. "Where is he, Klaus?"

"Probably lost," Klaus laughed. "He's from Ohio. Just got early retired from a Coker out there. Says he fell from a rig and landed on his heels." Klaus stood up and bounced back on his heels to demonstrate. "Like this." He bounced again. "He's got jelly heels, no doubt about that."

"What do you mean by jelly heels?" I asked, interested. I sat down on the arm of my father's green rocker and he kind of shooed me away at first like I was a fly.

"He's not a bad looking man, otherwise." Klaus turned to his other brother. "That right, Walter?"

"Never met the man, Klaus." Walter was leaning back in the rocker, his legs braced against the log wall of the house, a beer bottle in his hand. He slid his legs off the wall and rocked forward. "Think you're making it up."

"Would I do that?" Klaus asked.

"Sure," Homer said. Walter agreed.

"I might." Klaus lifted his beer to each of his brothers.

Aunt Ruth pushed the screen door open. "Klaus," she said to her husband, "get that other kettle out of the trunk will you?" She looked at me. "How'd you get so wet already?"

I glanced down at my damp skirt and then at my reflection in the window next to the door. I had spent a lot of time in front of the mirror lately but it didn't seem to help. I was really like a blond baboon: built square with overly long arms. I tried to keep my elbows bent a lot so they wouldn't hang to my knees, but it didn't work. My dark blond hair was cut severely, straight across my forehead and blunt cut below the ears. Homer had set me in a chair and chopped it off this way with his big scissors ever since I could remember. I frowned again at my reflection.

"Don't you think I should go to the beauty shop and get my hair cut another way, Aunt Ruth?" I tilted my head to another angle so I could see my reflection better. Aunt Ruth had gone back into the house.

"Dolly, I don't want you in town under one of them infernal hairdryer things," Homer said. "Harmful rays."

Klaus peered at my father for a minute, shook his head, and then got up and went to the Chevrolet. Uncle Walter took a long look at his watch, shook his arm, and looked at it again, so I guess they weren't agreeing with him.

"Even your mother knows better than to have her brains fried that way," Homer said, warming to the topic. "Never mind what talk goes on there."

"*Caveat emptor*," I said,

"Don't mock," Homer said.

Walter nervously cleared his throat.

"What about barber shops?" I asked lazily, still looking at myself in the window. I was still sitting on the arm of Homer's rocker. I pushed my hair over to one side and studied my reflection. "Aren't they places just to sit and talk dirty?"

"Dolly." Homer stood up and I fell off the arm of his chair.

"Why can you say those things—" I picked myself up and brushed down my muddy skirt—"and then when I say something just like it, I have to keep quiet?"

Homer pulled himself up as tall as his five foot six and a half inches would allow. He looked up into my face. "The Good Book says—"

I gazed over his head. "Well, honor and agree with are two different things."

"Dolly," Homer waited a long moment, "why don't you go in and help your mother?"

"She's not doing anything."

Homer squinted over my shoulder into the sun. "You get my point?"

"I certainly do." I glanced down at my muddy shoes for a second. "But how about my point?" I mumbled.

"What did you say?"

"But there's a lot of dangerous talk that goes on in barber shops."

"Dolly, you ever been in a barber shop?"

"Well, Flora Beebe and I kind of listened outside her father's shop one day."

"One day?"

"Well, a few days."

"Did Joe Beebe catch you?"

"No. He's just hoping Flora'll drive away and never come back."

Uncle Walter cleared his throat. "Ah, remembered something in my car," he said. He jumped out of his chair and limped off the porch as if his foot were asleep.

"Well," I said, "that's what Flora told me when she got that new Fairlane for her eighteenth birthday. But she plans to fool him and hang around and exasperate him just as long as she can."

"That's a man who's in for a lot of exasperation," Homer said. "Why don't you ever help your mother? Watch the twins, why don't you?"

"They don't need watching—they're too fat to move." I looked out beyond the shed to the rhubarb patch that had been flattened by the rain.

"Get along," Homer said. "We have to get the turtle stuff together. This Bass Noble fellow should be along any time now."

"What's a bass noble fellow?"

"That's his name, Bass Noble. Mr. Noble to you."

"Oh."

I wandered into the farmhouse kitchen. It was the oldest part of the house, and to me a musty dark place that always made me feel as if my elbows had grown too large for my body. I kept side-swiping the door jam, scraping against the plastered over log walls, and hitting my head on open cabinet doors. I stumbled against chair legs, and anytime I got near a knife I cut myself. As I banged in the door, my mother Brenda glanced up from the cutting board and smiled, her wiry brown hair standing rebelliously away from her head.

"Onions and babies," she said. "They clear all the poisons out of your system." Brenda wiped her face with the back of her hand and sniffed. She looked down at the onions. "Want to cut some?"

"No, thanks." I went to the sink. "Purification through suffering, I'd say. I just came in to get a drink of water." I turned on the faucet and made a great fuss about getting a jelly glass out of the cupboard.

"Where'd you hear that 'purification' stuff?" Brenda asked me with one eyebrow raised.

"Oh, I just made it up."

"*Mein Liebling*," Aunt Mae called over from the kitchen table, "you must learn to cook someday."

I grunted.

Aunt Mae, still wearing her green hat, was feeding Aunt Ruth's twin daughters applesauce from a number two tin can. Edith and Evelyn were howling, sitting in the highchairs Brenda had put out next to the kitchen table, and banging the spoons they held in both hands against the tabletop. They kept up a persistent duet of howls that were only temporarily stifled when their mouths were full.

Aunt Mae smacked her lips as she shoved a spoonful of applesauce into one of the twins faces. I never could tell Edith and Evelyn apart. The little girl mushed the sauce around in her mouth, puffed her cheeks, then rolled her applesauce-coated tongue out of her mouth. Seeming to enjoy the applesauce's texture, she let it escape out of the corners of her mouth in a light yellow ooze down her chin. Oblivious to this, Mae dipped up another spoonful and shoved it into the voracious open mouth of the other twin. Aunt Mae leaned forward each time in turn while the other twin yelled, pursing her lips, and smacking them, and saying, "Ah, so good—*mein Liebling,—Apfelsauce—asselsauce*."

"The celery's done, so are the onions," Brenda told me over the din of the twin's lunch. "Want to do the carrots?"

I was leaning against the sink trying to be invisible. I shrugged.

"*Ja*," Aunt Mae said as she scraped the bottom of the can, her hat sitting crooked on her head, "Dooley, you should help your *Mutter.*"

I watched Aunt Mae lick her lips as she pushed the last spoonful of applesauce into the face of one of the twins. The other banged a sticky spoon on Mae's sleeve.

"Hush!" Aunt Mae frowned in the baby's direction. "Hush, hush, *mein Leibling.* The twin looked at her and howled. Soon her sister joined in.

"I figure if I have to learn to cook I will, Aunt Mae," I said, "but not today." One of the twins let out a shrill screech. "Ooh, do they have to scream like that?"

"You would scream too if there were one too many of you."

"Mae." Brenda called from the counter.

"Ask their mother," Aunt Mae said adjusting her hat with one hand. "Ask Ruth." A yellow ooze hung from Mae's hat veil just in front of her ear.

I ran some water into my glass. "I'm real good at doing the dishes."

"I'll remember that this evening," Brenda said as she leaned down and pulled a turtle from a brown bag that was on the floor next to the stove. I watched the snapper swim in the air, then Brenda dropped it into one of the large kettles that was boiling at the back of the stove. Using two large slotted spoons she lifted a limp turtle of similar size out of the steaming water in the other pot and carefully laid the snapper down on the counter. She pulled a white towel off the back of one of the wooden kitchen chairs at the table where Mae was busily cleaning dried applesauce out of the twins ears with spit and the ends of their bibs. Brenda paused, watched Mae for a moment, then shook out the Turkish towel and went back to rub the turtle with it.

"What you doing?" I asked my mother.

"Dolly Sweet, don't you play dumb with me, you know what I'm doing."

"No, I don't."

"You've seen me do this before. I'm just rubbing the skin off ."

"No, I haven't. How did you get that turtle? We haven't started the hunt yet. We're waiting for that Bass Noble fellow."

"Well, I can't wait around all day," Brenda said, "I had to get the pot seasoned. I went down to the creek while you all were hanging around the mailbox." Brenda plopped the turtle carcass back into the boiling water and lifted the other one out onto the counter with the slotted spoons. She rubbed the skin off the head and legs with the Turkish towel, humming to herself.

"Yuk, that's awful," I said as I peered over my mother's shoulder.

"Not so bad," Brenda replied. She dropped the turtle back into the water. When she pulled the turtle out a second time its legs had fallen off and the shell was cracked. "Fetch that knife will you, Dolly?"

I handed her the large butcher knife from the utility drawer. "Not that one, the little sharp one."

Brenda ladled the turtle legs out of the pot, pulled the nails off and threw the legs back into the water. She took the knife I handed her, cut under the snapper's shell, and removed the meat. She carefully separated out the gall bladder, the sandbags, the rope of large intestine and put them aside.

"What's *that?*" I said seeing the soft loop of the intestine in Brenda's hand.

"Don't ask, honey, and I won't have to tell you."

"But what is it?"

"Just innards. Quit making that face. Want to do a service and cut the turtle meat into little strips?"

"Nope."

"All right," Brenda sighed. She quickly cut the meat and chopped up the liver and small intestines. There were a couple turtle eggs she tossed in the pot with some broth and put all of it on the front burner over a low light. She threw in a slab of butter, shook some salt and pepper on top and then wiped her hands on her apron. "That's lunch," she said. "Did you bring the sherry, Mae?"

"Maderia, Brenda. Ruth did," Mae said with a smile. "*Sehr gut.*"

"Oh," Brenda said, "where did Ruth disappear to?"

"Haven't seen her in a while," I said. I filled the jelly glass with water and drank it down in one gulp.

Aunt Ruth emerged from the bathroom in the hall just off the kitchen. The toilet was roaring behind her, her face as red as her hair. She pulled me into a hug.

"Dolly," Aunt Ruth whispered into my ear still clasping me to her damp little body, "I've been in there for ten minutes jiggling the hopper handle and waiting, and jiggling, and waiting, and jiggling and—"

"I get the point, Aunt Ruth." I listened to the Niagara roaring inside the open bathroom door behind her. "There's a secret to it," I said trying to disentangle myself from Aunt Ruth's grasp.

The short, red-headed woman looked up at me. "You sweet child," she said, "such a grown up." She hugged me tighter. "I don't want your father to think I'm careless," she said.

I unwrapped myself from Aunt Ruth's moist embrace. "That's okay," I told her, "you just go over there and help with the dishes or something."

I disappeared into the bathroom and pulled the door shut behind me. "Geez."

I took the top off the toilet tank and peered in. There was a trap door, a chain, and a black rubber bulb on the end of a long arm. It didn't look too complicated. If the trap door was adequately closed the tank should fill with water until the bulb floats and shuts the thing off. Simple. I reached inside and pulled on the chain. The cover lifted and dropped down again. I listened to the gurgle and waited for the tank to fill. Someone was knocking on the bathroom door.

"Just a minute," I said.

"Dolly, is that you?" It was Uncle Walter.

"Yeah."

"Just let your Uncle Walter in there and I'll fix that bugger."

"Just a minute." I jiggled the toilet handle and gave it a good flush. "Almost got it, Uncle Walter. Are you in a hurry for some reason?"

"I'm fine, Dolly, fine. Let me in."

A sucking noise came from deep within the toilet bowl. I lifted the seat and peered inside. The water was swirling around like a mountain whirlpool after the ice floes.

There was a loud pounding on the door. I ignored it. "Come on now," I mumbled under my breath, "why this?" God didn't answer. I took off the tank cover again. Everything looked fine in there except the trap door was lifted slightly. As I leaned over the tank the pliers in my pocket clanked against the porcelain. I thought for a moment, took the pliers out of my pocket and used them to bend the bulb arm down. That ought to do it.

There was a softer knock at the door. "Dolly let me in," Aunt Ruth said. "I sent Walter to get the plunger."

"No need. I fixed it." I lifted the seat. Through the whirling water I saw something that looked like a small animal darting back into his hole. I looked again. Nothing.

Geez, I thought, those mud turtles are everywhere. They must be in the septic tank too. That's what my father calls "abundance."

I replaced the tank cover. There was a new roar, a splash, a plop, and a surge of water overflowed onto my shoes. I jiggled the handle several times but the water just kept flowing onto the floor.

"Dolly," Uncle Walter yelled, "I'm coming in."

"Uncle Walter, don't," I shouted back over the roar. I glanced around for a towel. I yanked one off the wall rack and braced myself against the door. There was a loud thud against the bathroom door. The door burst open, trapping me behind it flat against the wall. Uncle Walter came sliding in over the wet linoleum just like he was headed for home plate. He was waving the plumber's helper wildly above his head as he came to a sudden stop against the bathtub.

I grabbed the towel and leaped over Uncle Walter on my way out. When I got to the hall, Aunt Mae was storming toward me, one hand on her head holding down her hat.

"*Was ist los?*" Mae demanded. I ran by. Mae rushed into the bathroom, slid into a somersault on the wet floor and landed on top of Walter. As she came to a stop, her hat leaped into the air and came to rest on the bridge of her nose. Seeing this, I ran.

I was almost to the screen door with the wet towel still in my hand when I noticed my mother at the sink gesturing toward the bathroom with the chopping knife. We heard a loud groan and another flush.

"Better get lost fast, Dolly," she said in a stage whisper and she waved me on.

~

The men were in the tool shed. I could hear Uncle Klaus' gruff voice and my father's milder tones, and the sounds of things being moved around inside the shed—the clanking of garden implements, the scrape of heavy boxes being pulled over the rough floor. I went up to the door and glanced inside. Homer and Uncle Klaus looked up.

"I've done everything I could in the house," I said.

"You seen the pliers?" Homer asked.

Klaus was swinging burlap sacks from either hand. "Six flour sacks enough, Homer?" Klaus asked. His voice boomed in the small shed.

"Should be," Homer replied. "Dolly?"

I was looking off across the side yard toward the creek. The sun was high, near noon, I thought.

"You can do something for me, little lady," Klaus said to me as he stretched his arms over his head, sacks in hand. "I'm thirsty already."

I nodded as I pulled the pliers out of my skirt pocket. I held them up to Homer. "I'll get you one, Uncle Klaus," I said.

"I thought so," Homer said as he took the pliers. "Get Klaus' beer, and see what Walter is up to. He went charging out of here a minute ago with the plunger."

"Oh yes?" I said.

Homer handed the pliers to Klaus as he went to the back of the shed. He grabbed a couple of long poles that were leaning against the wall. "Get along, Dolly," he said without turning around.

I started walking back to the farmhouse.

"There's something strange about that girl," I heard Uncle Klaus say. I stopped and listened. "She's never going to find herself a man. You're going to be like that poor old Joe Beebee with that daughter of his, Flora, if you don't watch out." Klaus coughed again. "Homer, it's been on my mind a long time to say so."

"Well, you'd just better put it back in your mind, Klaus," Homer said. "Nothing to worry about. She'll be just fine. Wait until those redheaded twins of yours grow."

I saw Klaus come to the shed door and throw the burlap sacks onto the ground outside. He saw me and had a strange expression on his face. He turned around and looked up to the wood-beamed ceiling of the shed. "Had any trouble with bats this year, Homer?"

～

Uncle Walter was wearing a lipstick kiss, a brave smile and a goose egg between his dark eyebrows when he met us outside the shed a few minutes later. Homer decided not to wait any longer for Bass Noble. My father and Klaus shouldered the poles, and I dragged the rusted wagon out from under the porch. I loaded it with the burlap sacks and a washtub full of home-bottled beer that Brenda had put out on the porch. Walter stood by, looking confused, and rubbing his forehead. Then without explanation—I knew why he wasn't talking to me, of course—Uncle Walter left and went to his car.

Just as we were about to go down the slope to the creek a brown pickup roared up the drive and parked behind Walter's Ford.

"Must be Bass," Klaus said.

I watched a man get out of the truck. He stopped to say hello to Walter who had his head in the Ford's trunk, then the man limped over to the rest of us. To me he seemed much younger than Klaus or my father, probably in his thirties, and he had dark blond wavy hair, glasses and a prominent nose. The painful way he walked made me wonder if he had ever put his mind to healing.

"Hello," Homer said. He set down his pole and leaned over to shake the younger man's hand. "Good day for a turtle hunt. Just a little chill to the air," Homer said. "Ever been on one before?"

"Bass Noble." The man shook my father's hand and nodded to Uncle Klaus. "Can't say that I have." He smiled showing me some crooked teeth. "I'm willing to learn," he said.

"The only thing to remember," Homer said as he snuck a quick look at Bass Noble's ankles, "is those snappers are sweet as lambs in the water, vicious just as soon as they get dry."

"I'll remember that," Bass said. His glasses were sliding down his nose. He pushed them up with the side of his thumb. "Sorry to be late, but I came through town. What was all that black smoke I saw?"

"What smoke?" Homer replied.

"Here Bass, take this pole," Uncle Klaus said. He motioned Bass over. "Good to see you."

Bass willingly shouldered the pole, and Klaus, relieved of his burden hovered around the wagon. I handed him a beer and the opener. He winked at me as he handed the opener back. "Keep an eye on this one, Dolly," Klaus said.

"You gonna drink it fast?"

Klaus lifted an eyebrow at me, glanced over at Bass, and raised the bottle to his lips. "I'm not talking about the beer, honey."

When we got to the bottom of the hill the creekbed spread out in front of us like a teeming pond. More of the turtles had come out of hiding as the day got dryer and warmer. I saw a couple dozen snappers swimming slowly in the muddy water, oblivious to our noisy approach. Homer put his finger to his lips. He motioned to Bass to put down his pole as I rolled the wagon in under one of the willow trees near the water. Klaus was standing on the creek bank tossing the pliers from one hand to the other.

Walter brought up the rear. He was carrying an armload of black rubber waders that he must have remembered at the last minute and had gone back to his car to retrieve. After awkwardly sliding down the hill with his load Uncle Walter dropped the waders at Homer's feet.

"Have a beer, Walter," Homer said looking at the swelling lump on Walter's forehead.

Homer went to the wagon, opened a bottle and handed it to Bass who had been standing uncomfortably on the creek bank watching the turtles. Homer opened another beer for Walter and then one for Klaus and himself.

Homer turned to Bass, and swept his bottle in front of him. "Here it is, Bass, the best turtle hunting creek in all of Pennsylvania."

"Well," Bass said. He stooped, and peered downstream through the tree branches. There was a musky thick smell coming from the water. I watched the blond man squat there on his wobbly heels. His green shirt and trousers were tight against his back and legs in a way I found strangely appealing.

"There seem to be a few good ones over there," Bass said pointing out over the water, "on them rocks."

"Yes," Homer said with one of his big smiles, "and all this abundance because I have a genuine patented method to attract them turtles."

"Didn't I tell you, Bass?" Klaus piped up.

Walter frowned at his brother, the goose egg now Ping-Pong ball size above his eyes.

"What's that?" Bass asked as he stood. "How do you do it?"

"Who wants waders?" Walter called out.

"Consider it a secret," Homer replied.

"Oh, a secret." Bass hobbled over to a dead tree that was leaning over the water. "Much duck hunting in this part of the country?" he asked.

"What you waiting for, Homer?" Klaus asked. He winked at me.

I had been anxiously surveying the creekbed. Several large snappers were sunning themselves on rocks in the middle of the stream.

"A few good ones," Homer said. "A few real good ones."

Walter galumped up to me in his waders. He fished down inside them and brought up a small pair of pliers out of his pant's pocket. He held them up to me with two fingers. "Brought these from home," he said. "Things have a way of disappearing. You aren't going to cry again this year when we get those creatures bagged, are you Dolly?"

"No, Uncle Walter," I said. I peered at the enlarging knot on Uncle Walter's head. "Maybe you ought to put some ice on your forehead."

"Nope," he said, "don't have the time." He put the pliers back down into his waders. "For safe keeping," he said as they disappeared. Uncle Walter's smile was like a moon eclipsed by the mountain on his forehead.

"Uncle Walter, I am grown up whether you noticed it or not. I've even helped drag the road kills down here."

Bass looked up. He had been standing back from us leaning against the willow trunk. "Oh!" he said. "So that accounts for the size of that one over there." He pointed to a large green snapper that was swimming toward us.

"Dolly!" Now Homer was frowning. I ignored him.

A snapper the size of home plate pulled itself out of the water. It slid over the mud bank and after first turning away from Homer, lumbered over to me.

Bass rushed toward me swinging the pole in front of him. He shoved the long pole in front of the snapper's face. "Watch it," he said in alarm, "I've heard these fellows have a mean bite."

The turtle opened its toothless jaws. Its tongue was thick, light pink. The creature made a small clicking sound, then spit.

"Don't bother, Bass," I said. I motioned him back. "I know this one."

"Know it? Come on."

"No, it's true. Some of them are real smart."

The snapper crawled off in the direction of the wagon, its thick legs splayed out from its plated shell, its pointed thick tail hanging behind.

Bass whacked his glasses back up on his nose with one hand. "You sure about that?"

Klaus, Homer and Walter were chuckling.

"Bass," Klaus said, "now do you see what I mean?"

Bass shook his head.

I pulled the tarp down from the crotch of the elm tree where I had placed it earlier. Then I found a thick stick in the underbrush and held it out to lure the snapper from its hiding place. The turtle poked its big sharp head out from under the wagon. With a quick motion it snapped its jaws onto the stick.

"Bass," I said, "if you want to help, how about moving the wash tub out of the wagon and out of the way?"

"Anything you say." Bass lifted the tub filled with ice and beer, walked it on his thighs a few feet and set it down with a thud.

I grabbed hold of either end of the stick, the huge snapper hanging from it by his powerful jaws, and hoisted the fellow into the wagon. I pushed the turtle-laden wagon into the bushes.

"There, Percy," I whispered, "time to disappear." The snapper rolled its yellow eyes up at me as I covered it with the tarp. "Night night."

"What kind of turtle hunt is this?" Walter galumphed up to Homer in his waders. His goose egg had grown so large that he stopped every so often to look up at it.

"Walter, don't look at me like that," Homer said. "We've been doing it this way for years."

"You have?"

"Sure. Dolly gets her turtle out of the way before the serious stuff begins. You and Klaus are always so tardy getting here you miss it. I don't know why she did it so late this year."

Bass looked at them and then at me. He had this funny look on his face and then he put his hands on his hips and laughed.

"Oh, it gets better," said Klaus.

"Yes, I guess so." Bass rocked back on his wobbly heels and watched me hoist the wash tub onto my shoulder and carry it further back into the shade. "I bet it does," he said turning back to Klaus. He found the beer he had hastily put down a few minutes earlier. "I know it does," he said.

There was a screech of wheels on the road above the creek and the sound of a car motor being clicked off.

"Who wants to see Flora Beebe's new car?" I called over to Homer who was lifting the turtle to get the empty sacks that were in the wagon beneath it. My father was talking, maybe cursing, to himself and he didn't answer. Bass and Uncle Klaus, each clasping a pole, were laughing and Uncle Walter was sitting on a rock holding his head.

"It's a brand new 1956 Ford Fairlane, royal blue."

My friend Flora Beebe slid down the grassy bank with a half dozen of the town kids sliding and chattering behind her.

"It's a beauty," Flora said. She looked down at the creek that was swarming with snappers. "You haven't started yet, have you," she said. "I brought some friends."

Flora pulled her oversized man's shirt down over her jeans. I have to admit I was a little jealous of her slimness and her wild dark hair. I was even a little envious of her freckled face.

"Where'd you get all these kids?" I asked her.

"Found them out on the ridge road hitchhiking here. Bet their parents wish they could do the same thing. Think your dad will let them swing one of them poles? I sort of promised."

"I doubt it," I said. "He doesn't even let me do it."

Flora glanced over at the men as they were pulling on their waders down by the creek bank. "Who's that younger blond-headed man?" she asked.

"Name's Bass."

Flora laughed. "Bass, like the fish? This isn't another story of yours, is it?"

"No," I whispered, "that's what they said his name was, really. I called him that once and he didn't correct me."

"Well, you know me," Flora said, "kind of clumsy on land and water. But I can drive like hell. I'll just watch this. Think you can sneak me a beer?" She looked over at the men again. "Humm, that Bass is much nicer to look at than those ugly turtles."

I went over to the wash tub and threw her a beer. "Take this and shut up," I said. "He's *my* relative."

"Just making an observation. Did you hide Percy yet?"

"Sure. Under the tarp." I pointed to the distant tree where Homer had pulled the wagon.

"Look, Dolly," Flora said in a loud whisper, "these rowdy kids just might find Percy and if they do—beware." Flora raised her dark eyebrows several times and flicked an imaginary cigar.

"They won't," I said. "They'll be too busy trying to get a beer if they're anything like last year. And they'll get to the beer too," I said, "just as soon as Homer gets drunk. Klaus is halfway there already. And Walter—well, Aunt Mae will take care of him. He complains a lot but he won't do anything."

"Dolly." Homer was calling me with that tone of voice I knew meant he was getting really impatient.

"Okay, okay." I turned back to Flora. "You hit any opposums today?"

"No, I'm trying to keep the car spit-shined. Just waxed it this morning."

"Keep those kids under control, Flora. I'm warning you. I gotta go."

I joined the men and pulled on the remaining pair of waders.

"What are you doing?" Homer hissed at me.

"Helping."

Homer grunted. He turned to the new man. "Bass, you grab that pole and wade into the creek. Get in the middle."

"Homer—what's going on?" Uncle Klaus said, his face red.

"Klaus," Homer said, "you can hardly stand already. You collect in the sacks and see that the critters don't ooze out once you get them in there." Homer turned to Walter who was massaging his forehead. "Walter, why don't you do the pliers on that side of the creek." He pointed to the opposite bank.

"Pliers?" Walter asked.

"Oh, all right, I'll do it," Homer said. "Why don't you go back and feed the twins."

"No, no," Walter said. "Give me that other pair of pliers." He pulled the small pair out of his waders. "These aren't big enough."

"So what do I do this year?" I asked.

"Mind the beer," Homer said.

"But I do that every year."

"Keep those kids away. Flora too."

Bass had been looking nervously into the snapper-infested water as he waited to start. He leaned on the pole until I joined them. When I had settled myself cross-legged on the bank in my waders he lifted the long pole waist high like a pole vaulter and waded into the water. He kept his eye on the dark gray snapper that was sunning itself on a large flat rock in front of him. Other snappers swam around him placidly.

"Will these—these reptiles—attack me?" Bass asked as several turtles swam by on either side of him. He looked above his head and saw three or four of them on the dead tree trunk that was suspended over the creek.

"Don't think so. Then again," Homer said smiling, "there are always the independent thinkers."

Bass regarded him for a moment, then grinned. He positioned himself in the middle of the stream, widened his stance, and steadied the pole over the water. "Now what?" he asked.

Meanwhile, Uncle Walter was crossing the creek at the shallow area a little downstream. He leaped over the smooth stones in his large black waders carrying the pliers and a couple of empty sacks. Once across, he stationed himself on the shore opposite Bass. Klaus sat on a rock on the near side of the creek, a sack open at his feet. Homer went over next to the beer tub and sat near me. Flora paced behind us. I saw she had a big smile on her freckled face. Every once in a while she would lean down to talk to one of the excited children who were sitting on the grassy bank as attentively as if they were in a reviewing stand.

"Just flip that guy on the rock to one of us," Walter called over to Bass.

"Flip?" Bass said.

Bass hung the pole in front of a large gray snapper lying dormant on the rock in the middle of the creek. The turtle lunged for the pole and Bass whipped back on his soft heels. He swept the pole in an arc toward Uncle Walter. Walter jumped as the snapper landed at his feet.

"Go get 'em, Walter," Homer yelled.

With a swift action of the pliers, Walter pulled the head off the turtle, then the toenails. He dropped the heavy carcass into the sack and swept the horny remains toward the water with the side of his foot. He did it so fast the snapper didn't have time to bleed. Its hard beak still hung from the pole as Bass swung it in front of another turtle that was on a rock a little further downstream.

Cheers rose from the bank, first from Homer and me and then from the children who were on the grass behind us. Flora Beebe hovered behind the children. Every once in a while she chugged the beer she was hiding under her shirt.

I tossed Flora another bottle when Homer wasn't looking. Then I crept up behind Uncle Klaus and dropped a bottle down in front of his face. "I was just gonna ask," Klaus said, his voice thick.

Bass swung the pole toward Klaus and he quickly jumped to his feet, dropping the beer. "Put it on that rock, honey," he said to me as he readied his pliers. "Lookie at this one, Dolly, will you?"

"Nice one, Uncle Klaus."

There was as cheer from the bank as the turtle came swinging toward Uncle Klaus at the end of Bass' pole. One young boy jumped up so he could see better.

"Selby, you sit down," Flora commanded.

"Ah, gee, Flora," the boy said. "This is an event! Do you think they'll let me do it?"

"No, sit down."

A moderate size snapper flew through the air toward Klaus and me. The children squealed. The snapper let go its grip on the pole and fell at Klaus' feet. Uncle Klaus pounced on the turtle with the small pliers. The beast lunged back, clamping its jaws on his thumb. Klaus let out a bellow that was soon echoed in various pitches from the bank. Flora added her own imitative bellow that sounded remarkably like a Jersey in heat.

As Klaus stared down at his thumb I grabbed the pliers out of his hand and closed them around the snapper's neck. I squeezed the pliers tighter and tighter until the turtle loosened its hold.

Homer came running over, breathless and awkward, tripping in his waders. "You sure used to be faster than that, Klaus," he said. "Are you all right?"

"Fair to middling." Klaus rocked back on his haunches cradling his hand against his large belly. "What a dilly that one was."

A young boy with white-blond hair ran over to us and stood above Klaus. "What kind of marks did he make?" he asked Klaus. "You gonna have a scar?"

"Get back here Selby," Flora yelled from the bank.

"Oh," he said, "this is important information. A kid can't—"

"I'll kid you," Flora said. "Move it."

Meanwhile, I was holding the squirming turtle body, clamping the pliers around its decapitated neck. I looked down at the flopping turtle, reached for an open sack, and dropped it in.

Homer took Klaus' bloody hand and examined it carefully. "Klaus, you'd better get back to the house and have Brendie clean that. Pretty deep. Do you think turtles get rabies? You're always worried about those bats back at the shed."

"No!" Walter yelled from across the creek, "Needs tetanus. I mean Lockjaw." I could hear Walter laughing nervously.

The children, spurred on by Flora, cheered as I situated myself on the near shore, pliers in hand.

"Let her rip," Homer yelled.

From the middle of the creek Bass glanced at me. I nodded. He hoisted the long pole over the water and began swinging it in a wide arc. He started slowly, but got into a rhythm, and as the townkids and Flora cheered him on, he swung the pole to the left until a swimming snapper grabbed onto it out of pure irritation. Again and again he flipped the pole into the air with a turtle dangling from it, shook the pole a little to be sure the snapper's bite was firm, and then swung the turtle down in front of me on one side of the creek or in front of my father on the other. Wielding the pliers, we plopped the weighty headless shells into the sacks at our feet. The smaller mud turtles weighed up to five pounds, but every once in a while Bass would hook up with a granddaddy snapper that had been hiding in the brush, and he'd swing all twenty-five or thirty pounds of him up and over in front of me. Each time Bass got a big one the kids hooted and whistled. And perhaps in sadness at the loss of their weaker numbers, the old big fellows came crawling out of the brush and into the water to be swung to their fate.

After about twenty minutes Bass stopped and leaned wearily on the pole. "Dolly," he said looking at me with admiration as I yanked the nails out of an unusually large specimen, "you sure are a strong little woman."

"Little?" I said.

"She's fifteen," Homer shouted from the other side of the creekbed, "and she's not little. Keep your distance."

Bass glanced over at my father. "Oh, no disrespect intended," Bass said. He looked back at me and smiled. "Not at all," he said.

"Better not," Homer grumbled.

I busied myself by looking into the turtle sack. "I've got at least a dozen of them here," I said, my face red.

"Go get 'em," Flora yelled. She was standing at the edge of the water holding the white-haired boy by the collar. "Get back here, you," she said to the boy.

I picked up the heavy sack and kicked at the other one at my feet. "We got enough yet?" I called over to Homer.

"With yours and what I have here, must be plenty," Homer called back.

"I was just getting into the swing of things," Bass said.

"So I noticed," I replied. "No more hunts for a year." I yelled across the creek to my father. "All right?"

"Deal," Homer yelled back.

"Can I get out of this primeval swamp now?" Bass asked.

"Sure," I said.

Flora came up with a cloud of kids around her. I handed her one of the sacks. "Flora, can you take those kids somewhere else? Maybe back to the house. Let Brenda keep them busy. She's good at that. Then maybe you can give me a driving lesson later, hey?"

"Dolly, you want to get rid of me?"

"Not you, Flora. "

"I mean about the driving lessons. It *is* a new car. I'd like to keep it running. Did they remember the sherry?"

"Maderia this year. Aunt Ruth did, I think. We'll see. If Mae is in a stupor, Ruth is giggling, and Mom is moving real slow, they got it."

"You don't say." Flora rubbed her hands on her jeans. "I'll see what I can do."

Flora whistled the kids together and after some protests— especially from one boy who had gotten hold of one of the poles and was wading into the creek—they climbed the hill. Once Flora and the kids were over the crest, I went over to the wagon. Bass followed me while Homer gathered up the equipment. When I stopped short Bass almost ran over me.

"You lived here all your life?" he asked.

"More or less."

"What do you mean 'more or less'?" Bass edged his glasses back as I turned to pull the wagon out from under the tree. When I looked back he grinned at me nervously. I noticed three overlaps right in the middle of his smile.

"Well, to answer your question," I said, "I think I'm not really *here* when I'm dreaming, for instance. How about you?"

"Oh no?" His nose looked very large to me, maybe a little dimpled too, something like a flesh-colored golf ball between the lenses of his glasses. Decidedly unappealing, I thought.

I pulled back the tarp. The yellow eyes of the giant snapper rolled up to meet mine. "Spared again, Percy," I said.

"That really your pet?" Bass asked.

"More or less."

"What do you mean by *that*?"

"Well, he belongs to himself, doesn't he?"

"More or less," Bass said. He wobbled on his weak ankles trying to get out of my way as I rocked the wagon.

"You could help me," I said.

"Glad to." He limped forward. "Now what?"

We turned the wagon over and the snapper lumbered off toward the water, its long tail dragging over the muddy ground.

"There's something mighty beautiful about turtles," I said as I watched Percy slide into the brown water.

"Good thing all of us are different," Bass said.

"They live a long time. Somebody told me about one that lived a hundred years."

Bass was looking at the downy hair on my arms.

"Tell me," I said looking over at him, unable to get what was beginning to be a painful grin off my face. I glanced down at the back of his waders. "What do they mean by 'jelly heels'?"

"If you let me hang around a year or two," Bass said, wobbling a little as he spoke, "I'll show ya."

I decided, right there and then, that I'd let him.

"Maybe I could talk to you about—" I paused for dramatic emphasis, "—healing."

And that's how I met my man.

Skin

Wallace flipped off the lights and ran a film, which opened with the Technicolor debridement of the stumps of a young man who had both legs amputated at the thigh by a train. Amy fell back into her seat, appalled, slightly sick at her stomach. She might have had some experience, but she had been away from trauma nursing too long. The veil had lifted, she realized, and she was just like other people, sickened, offended even, at the gore on film in front of her. But she was in graduate school, she needed the job. She would get used to it.

"Well," Mrs. Wallace the fat Inservice Director said when the film had ended, "see you tomorrow at four for the evening shift. That's when you start, isn't it, Miss Vogel?"

"Ms. Vogel," Amy corrected her, emphasizing the "z" sound, but knowing it would never stick. "Yes, that's right." She rose from the chair, a hand on its back to steady herself. "See you then."

She stumbled out of the small, windowless office.

Amy avoided glancing into the patient rooms through the half open doors. Tomorrow evening would be soon enough to see what was here. Sure, she had worked plenty, even had orthopedic experience, but that had been Ortho Surgery, nice clean bone surgery, with all of the surgical sites neatly bandaged in clean white gauze. But this was an Orthopedic Trauma Unit, to which the worst cases in the Midwest were air-vacced. Here came the cases that couldn't be treated in the small farm town hospitals short of supplies, expertise, and doctors. Here came the mutilated, hardly human remains, Amy thought, of accidents with farm machinery, fast cars, and cross-country freight trains.

That night Amy couldn't sleep. She kept seeing the bloody meat of those severed thighs before her, on the body of a young, good-looking boy of about nineteen.

∾

"Good, Miss Vogel," Mrs. Wallace said, "You're here for report." The matronly Inservice Director saluted her with a mouth only smile when she saw Amy walk by her office door. Wallace stood, grabbed her black coat, locked her door, and headed down the hall without looking back.

Amy wandered into the nurses' station back room and hung her sweater on the rack.

"Hello," she said to the young blonde nurse seated at the table, the Kardex open in front of her, "be right with you."

"Okay," the seated nurse said, "name's Colby. Got to go. I have a class at four forty-five."

Amy listened to the fast report. She was glad to see two more well scrubbed young nurses come in and quietly sit down to listen. She tried to take notes, but missed much of the information. Amy did get that most of the patients would get acetic acid soaks and IV antibiotics. She could handle that, she thought. The first night on a busy unit was like jumping in on a relay race. The new team member grabs the baton and runs with it, adjusting to the terrain in a harried flight to the end of the shift.

∾

Amy walked down the hall to room 314, a couple plastic liter bottles of quarter percent acetic acid solution in her arms, wondering what a Midwestern Indian might be like.

Henry Rain Cloud greeted her with a grunt, then perhaps because of the look on her face, a surprising smile. He was a hulking big man with straight black hair and a big-nosed, pockmarked face.

"Time to do the packing, huh?" he asked.

"You know how it's done?"

He nodded. "Do what you have to."

He sat up in the hospital bed as she flipped on the overhead light and grabbed one of the green cloth covered packing trays that were stacked on the windowsill. She spread the tray open on his overbed table and poured some acetic acid solution into the stainless bowl on the sterile tray, being careful not to contaminate anything. She put the bottle aside, and pulled on sterile gloves.

"Oh," she said flustered, "I forgot. Could you unwrap your leg, Mr. Cloud?"

"Rain Cloud," he said. "Both of them, you mean."

"Yes," she said, "both legs."

He threw down the sheet, leaned over, and unwrapped the roller gauze, which went from thigh to ankle on both legs. She stood back and watched, her sterile gloved hands suspended in the air in front of her. He dropped the gauze and the soiled gauze pads that were under it, into the plastic-lined waste can shoved between his bed and the nightstand.

Amy studied his legs. She had heard in report that he had been peppered in both legs by a shotgun blast. The story was that Henry Rain Cloud had been stepping out on his wife, and her brother, a full-blooded Sioux from South Dakota, didn't like it at all.

Looking at his legs, she saw that much of the flesh had been blasted away. The shaft of bone was visible in some places and in others, once she removed the deep packing, nothing was there but white space. She realized she was seeing through the shotgunned Indian's legs to the wall.

Henry Rain Cloud stared down at his exposed wounds. "Looks like I'll have a lot of scarring."

"Well," Amy said, "it will all be covered by your jeans."

"No, I'm glad to have scars." He grinned at her. "When you die the old hag eats your scars. But if you don't have any, she eats your eyeballs. Then you're blind in the next world."

"Oh," Amy said.

"Yeah, I don't really take to blindness. Go ahead."

She threw the contaminated forceps and the old packing into the trashcan, and with new forceps, dipped a strip of sterile accordion-pleated gauze into the acid solution and stuffed the wet strip of gauze deep into one of the holes in both legs. She packed his wounds as tightly as she could, going methodically down one side, and then up the other of both legs. The entire time Henry remained perfectly quiet, his teeth clenching down on a ball of bedspread he had stuffed into his mouth sometimes when she wasn't looking.

As soon as she finished the packing, Amy placed sterile squares over the holes and wrapped as she went with roller gauze from the toes up. She gathered the equipment together, making sure she had put all the soiled gauze into the plastic trash bag, tied it shut, and then dropped the bag into the red contaminated waste receptacle beside the sink. She washed her hands.

"I'll see you later, Mr. Rain Cloud."

"Okay," he said, "thanks. You should have seen them weeks ago. I'll tell you a secret. Don't tell anybody. Rain Cloud isn't really my name. It's Harland McCoy. That's why I got shot."

"Yes?"

"One day I looked in the mirror and said to myself, "Harland, what do you look like? Why, you look like an Indian, I said to myself. And you know, right then I was one."

She looked at his dark, pock-marked face. "I like the name," she said. "Rain Cloud."

He grinned. "So do I."

∼

In the next room, a blonde three-year-old girl slept in a crib. In a chair beside her a scrubbed, neat-appearing young woman sat, staring out the window.

"Hello," Amy said. "I've come to do the dressing."

"Oh, no," the woman whispered, "she just got to sleep."

"Has she been medicated?"

"Huh?"

"Did one of the other nurses give her something for pain?"

"Yes, I think so."

"That's probably why she's sleeping now. I'll want to do the dressing change before the shot wears off." She glanced at her watch. "Four-thirty. Before dinner, okay?"

The woman nodded. "That's better," she said.

"Your daughter?" Amy asked.

"My niece."

Amy nodded, smiled, and left the young woman again staring out the window as the child slept. The little girl had wandered around her grandparent's farm and fell into some machinery, Amy had heard in report. Lost half her foot. Amy hadn't known there would be children on this unit. She had avoided pediatrics all her nursing career. Each time she took care of a sick child she saw her own son lying in the bed in its place, raising his arms to her. She was glad to avoid the little girl's screams for the moment.

In the next room Amy found Mr. Koch sitting on the windowsill, looking out into the courtyard.

"Hey!" he said when she entered his room. "Someone new. How are you?"

With a big smile he jumped up and came over to her. His right shoulder was covered with a massive dressing; his right arm was missing.

"What happened?" she asked without thinking. She hadn't heard in report. "Sorry—"

"Not at all. Not at all," he said. "I just had a little disagreement with an auger."

"An auger?"

"Oh, just a piece of farm equipment. It's used for boring holes in the ground. It's got a shank with a handle, and a tapered screw in the middle with cutting lips. Looks like a big corkscrew if you want to know. Somebody's going to have to persuade John Deere and International Harvester, and all the rest of them, to install some safety devices."

"They don't?"

"Nope. It's been all in the papers out here though. Some guy even won a Pulitzer Prize reporting on it in the *Des Moines Register*. No fooling. He even came in here, right here, and interviewed me."

"Makes you angry, I'd guess."

"Me?"

"Might do you good to vent a little."

"Nope. Not worth it."

She looked at him for a moment. His broad face was brown, serene.

"Let me do the dressing change," she said. "Okay?"

"Sure," he said. "First, let's get rid of this gum."

After Amy removed the dressing, she packed Mr. Koch's shoulder cavity with acetic acid packing and redressed the wound with a tight pressure dressing so the many large blood vessels ruptured by the injury would remained sutured and closed. During the procedure she was extremely careful, knowing there was danger of severe bleeding, and when finished, she affixed a large Kelly clamp to the sleeve of Mr. Koch's hospital gown so it would be handy in case a large blood vessel should burst.

"Done," she said, as she retied his hospital gown. "You did fine, Mr. Koch." On the back of his neck she saw a patch of psoriasis.

"It could be worse," he said, staring out the window. "I still have my left arm. And I don't write much. Why, I had an uncle lost an arm in a farm accident, my father lost his left eye chopping wood when he was eighteen and lived fine 'til eighty-two without it, and most of my neighbors have lost a finger or two along the way."

"I'm from the East," Amy said. "You don't see this kind of thing very often."

"Farming's always been maiming, darling. East or west."

∼

Amy left his room and stopped off at the nurses' station to see if there were any new orders before she saw her next three patients. One of the other nurses, a dark-haired young woman in her early twenties, sat at the desk taking off doctors' orders. Her name pin said Miss Ferguson.

"What about Mr. Koch?" Amy asked her as she sat down beside her at the desk. "He says he has nothing to worry about. Takes this lost arm too easily, don't you think?"

"Oh, you have to understand these Iowa farmers," Ferguson said looking up from a chart, "he'll act it out soon enough, don't worry. These country people are hardy," the young nurse said getting back to her chart, "but you'll see."

Amy got up, stopped at the supply closet, then went down to room 320. Inside, an eighteen-year-old paraplegic reclined on his side, propped up on his elbows.

"New here, aren't you?" the dark-haired young man said as she approached carrying her liter bottles of acetic acid solution. "Let's see if I can run you off too. My score has been 5-0 so far. One look at me and they're gone."

"Why is that?" Amy asked.

"You'll see," he said.

She approached the bed and moving to the other side, lifted the sheet and took a look at his dressing which covered his entire buttocks. Pulling a pair of utility gloves from the box at the bedside, she unwrapped it, smelling the odor of necrotic flesh she recognized from all of the worse cases of her nursing career.

"How did this happen?" she asked.

"Oh," he said. "I did it."

"You?" she asked.

"Yeah," he said in a matter-of-fact voice. "I drove my parents nuts until they finally let me get my own apartment. I'd had this car accident see, and I couldn't move from the waist down after it. But I had this great wheelchair, motorized, my own wheels, and I was doing okay. Going to school in the chair, you know. Then I guess I wasn't paying enough attention. You know, keeping clean and all, keeping off my butt as much as possible, lifting and airing, you know. I didn't know the pressure sore had started—didn't know anything about it until I kind of started to smell it, you know."

"Yes, I know."

"Well, it got away from me."

"We'll take care of the pressure sore. Don't you worry."

"You haven't seen it yet."

She uncovered the largest decubitus cavity she had ever seen.

His tail bone was visible, ringed by a circle of black, necrotic flesh. It will have to be surgically debrided again soon, she thought. She'll be sure to write a note on the chart.

"Not bad," she lied, "I've seen worse that's healed okay."

"You have?"

"Sure." She turned away to get a breath of air. "Now help me out by keeping real still."

~

Amy stood at the sink and scrubbed her hands repeatedly with the antibacterial soap. Don't think, she told herself. Don't think. One more to go and then back to the little girl.

Amy walked into room 310 and saw before her the star of the training film Wallace had shown her, a young man about nineteen with an anxious looking face who was leaning over his stumps, moaning. She could see that both legs were gone at the thigh. Train, she thought, drunk and trying with his buddies to hop a train on a dare. That's what Wallace had told her when she had asked. Amy had thought the film was an old one, but no, there he was in front of her.

"Look ma'am," he said, "you've got to do something." He leaned forward and pressed down on the sheet that fell off his aborted thighs. There were tears in his eyes that he quickly wiped away with a fist. "The damnedest thing," he said. Pain where you don't have nothing."

"Phantom limb pain," Amy said quietly. "The nerve endings don't know yet. I'll get you something for pain, Charlie. Your name is Charlie, isn't it?"

"Yes, ma'am. Thank you ma'am."

Amy hurried out of the room. Only a little older than her son, Tommy, she thought. What did she really know about Tom's drinking habits? His response to dares? What did he do when she wasn't around, she wondered? Did Tom try to jump trains? Was he just lucky so far, and this boy was not?

She went into the drug room, flipped open the medication Kardex and found Charlie Dunn's orders. Demerol 50-100 mg. every four hours for pain if needed. She got the keys to the narcotic cabinet, signed out 75 mg. of Demerol for him, and drew it up in a disposable syringe. She noted that he had had his last dose six hours ago. The boy might not know to ask for it. She'd have to tell him to use his call bell when he started to get anxious with the pain, not when he got to the point of tears.

She went to give Charlie his shot before she started the dressing change. She'd have to wait a while for the medication to take effect before she could begin. She'd do the little girl first.

Amy barreled into the nurses' station after completing her dressing rounds. Mrs. Wallace was sitting at the desk, her coat on the chair beside her. Why didn't she tell me Charlie was on the ward now, she wondered. Amy could see that Mrs. Wallace was checking the nurse's notes on Amy's patients. She tried to keep her voice under control.

"What's this 'What me worry?' attitude with Mr. Koch?" Amy asked. "That went out with Alfred E. Neuman."

"What?"

She sat down in a chair beside the older nurse. "Maybe bring in a shrink. The man's just letting his skin say it for him. He's screaming for attention. Have you seen that flare of psoriasis Mr. Koch has all over his back?"

"Just a minute," Wallace said, "I'll be right with you."

Amy crossed her arms over her chest and quietly fuming, thought about Mr. Koch's skin. She remembered the first time she had seen psoriasis. There had been an English teacher in high school, Mr. Simms, who had the worst case imaginable. The man's skin flaked over everything. Flakes would fall off onto student papers. His face was red. His eyebrows and lashes were crusted. His fingers were red and raw looking, his fingernails thick, ridged plates. He walked slowly, with a cane and always wore tweeds covered with shed flakes. Forever after every time she saw a tweed jacket she would think of him. He must have had psoriasis too on his feet, because his shoes seemed over large, as if covering logs, and he walked with a slow shuffling gait. Mr. Simms was the father of one of her high school classmates, which made his situation even the more horrible to Amy. Imagine coming home from school to such a man as your father, she thought, in long delayed sympathy for the girl, to know that everyone in the school knew what a horror he seemed, how he flaked on their quizzes.

In class students would openly shake out the papers when they were returned, as if the affliction were somehow catching. Seeming not to notice, Mr. Simms did something no one else had done. He read poetry to them, and in his rich sonorous voice Amy first heard Auden: *About suffering they were never wrong,/The old Masters: how well they understood/ It's human position: how it takes place/ While someone else is eating or opening a window or just walking dully along.* For some reason she had not forgotten that poem. She could still evoke the sound of Mr. Simms's voice.

She realized now that he had been the one who taught her what she had considered was the first lesson of nursing school, not to show on one's face the horror perceived, and she had forgotten that lesson had come from him. It took real courage to sit in class and pay attention, courage to look Mr. Simms in the eye and not shudder at the red and flaky skin on his cheeks, courage to listen to him and discount his appearance, to give him the same measure of dignity he squandered on the students. How well he treated them, how poorly they had responded. Skin.

"Now we have to treat Mr. Koch's psoriasis too," Amy said when Mrs. Wallace at last lifted her head.

"So, is that so bad?"

"What do you mean?"

"I mean," Mrs. Wallace said tapping her pen on the desk, "who are you to dictate how Mr. Koch has to react? Maybe this is more acceptable to him. He doesn't have to talk it out, to act weak—in his own terms. So fate strikes him another blow, he thinks. He withstands that too. And in the meantime there has been enough time for him to get used to the idea that he doesn't have that limb."

"You mean his good right arm, don't you?"

"Yes, his good right arm."

"But that's head in the sand stuff," Amy sputtered.

"Oh, Vogel, cool it would you? There's a long night ahead and the unit is understaffed. Let him be. Don't you like Mr. Koch? He's a dear."

Amy was silent.

"Don't you spend a lot of time in his room?"

"Of course, I have to."

"Precisely. Amy, let him be." Mrs. Wallace's face was earnest. "He's doing his best. Don't embarrass him. Don't make him cry. I know these farmers. Grew up on a farm myself. He's been up before dawn all his life making the best of things. Let him use that hardiness now when he needs it. Forget the textbook grieving for lost parts. People grieve as they can. Our Mr. Koch grieves with his skin. So let him."

"But the psoriasis can be avoided."

"Probably. But not to him, honey. He knows it will fade with time. He needs it now. You don't think this is the first time it's flared on him, do you?"

"Maybe you're right." She thought of Mr. Simms from long ago. Why had he needed that skin, she wondered.

"Of course I'm right. Amy, you'll be okay. It takes a week or two of doing these dressings for any new nurse to calm down and get a little numb to it. Familiarity breeds blindness, maybe. Or maybe you just start seeing the person who has these wounds, and you see the small progress. It makes you strong, honey."

"Tell me about it."

"In wounds up to your elbows and John Q. thinks you're playing hankie pankie in the linen closet." Wallace smiled. "God damn, we don't even have linen closets. The laundry comes up in a cart." She laughed and winked at Amy. "Ever tried fooling around in a cart?"

Amy laughed with her, thinking of fat Mrs. Wallace fooling around anywhere.

Amy stood. "I think I'll take a break, Wallace."

"Sure, I'll tell the others where you are before I leave. I'm just about to go. Your charts, by the way Amy, are fine."

She nodded.

"Fifteen minutes. Then it will be time for dressing rounds again."

"Don't remind me."

∿

She took the elevator down to the first floor and wandered into the small employee lunch room. It was nine-thirty p.m. She went to the vending machines and surveyed them one at a time. Candy bars, cheese crackers, Lifesavers. The next machine had soft drinks, coffee, hot chocolate. Another machine, more candy. Why no fruit, milk, or yogurt in an institution supposedly dedicated to health? She pulled some quarters from her pocket. The peanut butter crackers, the ones without the orange dye, might be the closest to real food. She fed several coins into the machine. They dropped noisily into the coin return. She went to the next machine and tried again. Nothing. Okay, a candy bar. Baby Ruth, maybe. Empty. She tried all the candy and the crackers, the hot chocolate, even though she had been avoiding chocolate most of her life. All empty, the only things remaining in the machines were the display items.

She paced the lunchroom several times, then sat down at a sticky table on one of the molded orange plastic chairs. She glanced at the tiled floor, the plain white walls, the dark window onto a closed-in, plantless courtyard. Like a prison, she thought. She glanced at her watch.

Amy remembered she had gotten some empathy for Mr. Simms when she picked up impetigo in a swimming pool locker room. She supposed that's how it came about. Maybe it had been the universe's way of presenting a lesson. She was still in Mr. Simms's class at the time. She had scales on her face in a circular pattern—maybe it was ringworm—and she felt like a leper. Certainly people stared at her, or at least she imagined they did until one morning, after all those painful days scrubbing her cheeks with peroxide and slathering on ointment, the crusts were gone and all that remained was a pink shadow which gradually faded.

Amy glanced up as an orderly came into the lunchroom. He surveyed the empty vending machines, shook his head, and left.

She looked out the dark window. Amy remembered her mother's younger sister Ruth had taken her under her wing for the assault on acne. Amy was sure she was the only ten-year-old in the world with pimples. Aunt Ruth plied her with Noxema, then urged Amy to visit her in the country for a week or so. Aunt Ruth leaned over Amy solicitously, brushed her long curly hair and convinced her—it did not take much—that teenage girls got their never-cut hair clipped, and thinned, and wore ponytails. So she had agreed to the haircut and grew to worship her redheaded Aunt Ruth who had given her so much attention. Aunt Ruth, of course, was a nurse, and the only woman in the family Amy thought had any spunk. Aunt Ruth was her freckled idol upon whom in gratitude, Amy modeled her life.

Later, she became concerned with marks and scars: the birthmark mole on her ankle that looked like England, the chicken pox scars on her jaw, the scars on her legs, souvenirs of a childhood of chronically skinned knees and gashes from bicycle falls, the scars at her hairline where her brother and cousins had thrown waste glass at her for spending her time at the old black typewriter in her grandfather's office instead of coming out to play softball.

She had a strange keloid-like lump on her shoulder from the BCG inoculation she got in nursing school for those likely to encounter TB. She thought of the brown shadows, like butterfly wings, over the noses of people with lupus, a disease that left them wolf-like in profile, and unsure about the progress of their lives. She thought of those with the cystic scars of *acne vulgaris* who had their skin sanded by dermatologists, and of middle-aged women who agreed to have their faces lifted right off of their skulls and sewn back on, a slender scar circling their hairlines. One step less, and theirs could be the faces left on trees, as warnings in El Salvador's war. She thought of the clear, small-pored buttocks of the dying, never tanned by the sun, in sharp contrast to the weathered skin of their hands as they unconsciously scratched themselves. She thought of the piebald skin of some American blacks whose cutaneous selves announced the mixture of their origins. And she thought of the healed eyebrow of the trusting boy, Willie, with no sign of a scar. She thought of the dimples on babies, and on knees, precursors of the dimples of cellulite in the thighs of the sedentary.

And she thought of the decubitus sore of the young man, the severed thighs of Charlie, the torn arm of Mr. Koch sweet with denial and psoriasis. She glanced out the window to the blank wall of the dark courtyard, down at the dirty table and the orange chair, over to the empty junk food machines. And she said to herself, enough.

She took a big breath. She didn't want to wait two weeks until she got used to it. She didn't want to "get used to it" any longer. She didn't know where she would go, or what she would do, but she couldn't do this any longer. She'd take her son Tommy and be a hermit in the woods. Anything.

Amy pulled out her pen and a piece of paper. She opened the folded paper in front of her and thought a minute. She could go in to a long explanation, she supposed, but she wouldn't.

ENOUGH, she wrote on the page. She signed her name: Amy Vogel. And after considering a minute, added R.N. She folded the note into her uniform pocket, left the lunchroom, climbed the back stairs to the nursing office and slipped the paper under the door.

Animal Mischief

Maggie closed the side door behind her quietly so Bert would not know she had left the house. She stepped off the porch into a drift of knee-deep snow. The hemlocks bordering the driveway were bent under the winter's accumulation, and the wet snow slithered further down into her boots as she crossed the driveway and trudged through the white pasture, leaving a herringbone pattern behind her. She knew tonight she would finally see it.

Walking to the deserted road, she remembered another evening like this one, when Edward had lain beside her at the foot of the bed in front of the open window—the shade raised, the snow falling silently outside—the room heavy with moisture.

She turned right when she reached the snow-covered road, and headed toward the river. A soundless light snow was falling.

Edward had held her so close she thought he would suffocate her as they slept. In the small of the morning he pulled her tighter to him whenever she moved to breathe deeply or break free. She suspected he hadn't loved her, yet he wanted her warmth, her body close to his, and he tangled her in sheets and desperate hugs.

"Don't do that," she said to him, "it's too much for me," knowing he would hold her close, make her stir, make her breathing fitful and warm against his chest, and then say, "Go to sleep, Maggie. Go to sleep."

Yet that night in front of the open window the falling snow had a strange affect on him, seeming to peel away his leathery indifference and make him very human.

She closed her eyes. On the lonely road Maggie was as unconcerned with navigation as if she were on a large deep river after all the boats had been called in and the storm had ended. The sound of the wind mimicked the flap of a breeze through half-lowered sails.

Edward had let go of her as he had let go of everything, absent-mindedly; his love for something else simply had superseded his love for her. In the years since that time she often dreamed of him suspended in a cloudless sky, holding something—she could not tell what or who—close to himself like a lover.

When she opened her eyes she noted the snow had changed texture; a fine-grained snow was falling. The air was crisper as the sun went down and the new moon escaped from behind the flocked trees. On the unbroken surface on the road's shoulder thin, mica-like flakes glistened like small golden disks.

~

After an early dinner of boiled beef and potatoes, Bert had eased her into his sparely-furnished living room that smelled of dust. As soon as he left the room, Maggie rummaged in the logbin by the fireplace and found a dog-eared *Readers Digest* in with the discarded newspapers and rotting wood. She carried the magazine to the old sofa, clicked on the floor lamp, adjusted her glasses, and in the chilly room read about allergies, Eskimo snowwalkers, and Mohini, the white tiger at the National Zoo. The allergy article irritated her, scornful as she was of people who choose to be allergic to life. She thought the white tiger might be interesting to see, but she was intrigued by the snowwalkers. When she finished reading, she put the magazine face down on the coffee table and listened to the sounds of running water and the clatter of dishes coming from the kitchen.

Bert wandered back into the room and dropped into the lumpy brown chair opposite his mother. He was in his early thirties, and with his dark wavy hair and blue eyes looked a lot like his father.

"Bert?"

"Yeah?"

"Oh, nothing." Maggie looked past him to the straggly wandering jew that was hanging in the window opposite her. Beyond it, Maggie saw a few scattered snowflakes were falling.

"Your baby needs watering," she said.

"What?"

"Light and water. The plant." Maggie nodded toward the window and pulled herself out of the hole between the sofa cushions. She smoothed down her blue dress, then moved around the coffee table, careful to avoid the ashtray of her shredded cigarette butts that sat precariously near the table's edge. "I'll go rattle some dishes with Sally in the kitchen," she said.

Bert glanced at the dying fire. "Come on, Mother, rest. Sally has it under control." Bert sat back in his chair, yawned, and stretched his arms out in front of him.

Maggie shook her head and paced in front of the sofa. "Got to keep moving, Bert," she said.

She walked over to her son, glanced down at his hands, and noted the black grease under his nails. "Mechanics can have clean hands too," she said. "Why don't you use that Boraxo? Your father used to wash his hands clear up to the elbow with it." She sat down again on the sofa. "Doesn't Sally object?"

"She has never objected to me or my hands."

Maggie stared at her son for a minute, then picked up the magazine she had left on the table. "Have you seen this?" She held the *Readers Digest* up to him. "There's a story in here about a white tiger." She flipped the pages, looking for the article. "It's here somewhere." She wet her fingertip and turned another page. "I wonder if your sister's seen it."

"The tiger?" Bert stood up, "or the article?" The familiar tic jumped on the side of his face.

"Well, I mean," Maggie said, momentarily stopped, "Ellie's—"

"Would you get off that? Ellie doesn't know everything."

Bert yanked back the fire screen.

"I just thought you'd be interested." Maggie glanced down at the magazine in her hands.

"Okay. I liked animals when I was a kid. That was a long time ago. Mother, you've pointed out every animal story to me since I was four years old."

"Animals have a kind of power," Maggie said. "They're still magical to me."

"You simply have a child's imagination," Bert said slowly, enunciating each word. "Come on now, Mother," he added quickly, "maybe it's time you grew up."

"Me? Never!" Maggie slammed the magazine down on her lap.

She thought of those years in Canada, the evenings reading stories to Bert and Ellie, the mornings standing rigid at the frosted window watching Edward wave goodbye with a smile. In the three years since he'd died she had lived with her children a season at a time— three months at Bert's Wisconsin farmhouse, three months at Ellie's in Virginia, and back to Bert's again—and in all that time neither of her children had understood her, even for a moment.

She turned to the window beside her and pulled back the curtain. As she watched the powdery snowfall she saw something leap across the yard. Maybe a deer, she thought. Didn't Bert remember how they used to sing together in the mornings? Didn't he remember the Sambo story he insisted she read over and over each night until he fell asleep?

"It's March, Bert, this might be the last snow." She turned back to him. "Do you want to take a walk?" She glanced out the window again, and whatever it was, had gone.

Bert ambled over to the logbin, selected a sturdy piece of hardwood, and tossed the log into the fire. "It's too cold," he said. "I've been out all day working for a living."

He reached for the iron poker, then jabbed the fire until the room filled with the odor of ash and wood smoke, and sparks exploded in the air around his head. "You women that never had enough to do," he said, "prize that marriage certificate in the gold frame above your bed, but it's just a license to sleep together with your backs turned."

A blue flame leaped up at the back of the fire. Maggie watched Bert's plaid flannel back as he poked the logs around on the grate. "Oh," she murmured. "Oh," she said again in a whisper.

Maggie considered her son's muscular back a moment longer, then quietly walked out of the room. She pulled her overcoat down from the coat rack by the side door and leaned down to retrieve her boots from a pile by the entryway. She jumped back as the yellow-eyed cat, sleeping on the nest of hats and scarves, woke wide-eyed and hissing.

~

In the cold wind Maggie smelled the sticky tar-like odor of the creaking pines on either side of the road, and with it, another odor she couldn't name. Frozen ruts of mud under a light dusting of snow made walking treacherous, and in the damp air her face was beginning to sting. She turned her back to the wind and looked behind her for the depressions in the road where some of the white had been blown away and a hint of the black macadam appeared beneath. As the snow-fall grew heavier, she struggled into the drifted shoulder, her hands dug deep into the pockets of her overcoat.

Maggie heard the sound of a motor. A dark car was barreling down the icy road toward her, its snow-chains flailing and clanging against the wheel-wells. When the car was a few yards away she stumbled back into a roadside drift. Brakes squealing, the car went into a spin in front of her. The car slid diagonally across the road, then came to a stop with a thud, its nose buried in a snow-bank. From where she had fallen, Maggie watched the motionless car. The snow fell around it. After a minute or two it pulled out of the drift with a furious spinning of wheels. The car came to a sliding stop beside her. Maggie stiffly got to her feet.

She watched the car window roll down. Through the thick veil of falling snow the hatless heads of two teenage boys appeared.

"Why don't you watch where you're going, lady?" one of them shouted. The car sped off, its snow-chains clanging.

Maggie brushed the snow off her coat as the car fishtailed away over the icy road. She stood there until the small red lights disappeared into the haze.

She turned around to be sure the road was empty behind her. Rubbing her bare hands together, she squinted through the steady snowfall. Maybe Bert was talking to Sally again about her undrinkable coffee, over the soapy water and the clatter of dishes in the grey clapboard house. She started walking again toward the river.

Maggie had found that if he made the morning coffee very strong, and sang to herself in a voice that had grown embarrassingly harsh, through sheer power of her will she was able to steel herself for another day. The decision was one she made each morning as she spooned the coffee into the pot. She never seemed to have time to establish friendships, even to know each morning with certainty where she had put her shoes. She vowed to her children that this didn't matter. But often as she rode the bus between Wisconsin and Virginia, the uphol-stery soiled and stiff behind her, she wished the bus would go careen-ing off the road into a ditch. Then she would force her head back against the padded headrest, close her eyes, and dream her recurrent daydreams of Edward, or the other thing that appeared in a form she did not understand.

Her body ached in the increasing wind and her legs were as heavy as the large desiccating logs at the bottom of Bert's woodbox. She paused to rub her ears with numb fingertips. As she walked on the deserted road she let her mind drift.

In a young woman's lust for conception—her body roaring before her mind—Maggie had named the infant she was sure she conceived the night before the open window. But in a few weeks the idea had been washed away in the red river of her blood.

Edward was not sympathetic when she told him shyly of this lust for children, and her disappointment.

"Don't expect anything from me, Maggie," he told her. "I know how things are, and I'm a glacier."

"Yes, I know," she said, looking into his pale eyes in an attempt to find a thread of understanding there, a minute indication that he might in some small way bend to her will. "But a glacier, melted, moving," she said, 'is a river."

Bert was born later out of an ordinary need. Then came the ever-crying Ellie.

Maggie passed a stand of pines that whistled and shuddered in the wind. Behind it was an empty pasture. Drifts were piled high against a faded red barn, and snow eddies rose from the sloping roof fringed with icicles which seemed ready to fall like clear daggers into the soft snow beneath. Seeing the icicles, Maggie thought of the place on Lake Erie where they lived as caretakers after the Second World War. In the black mornings Edward got up at five to plow the parking lots, and by the time everyone else was rising at seven and eight his face would be as purple as a grape in the cold wind off the lakes. In the late afternoons he knocked the six-foot icicles off the eaves with a long pole. As she passed, an icicle fell silently from the barn roof. Maggie pulled her head down into her collar and peered into the snowy haze on the road in front of her.

She knew the cold didn't bother Edward, but he had never gotten the sand out of his vital parts from that wartime beach landing. He told her the heat of that day changed to fog, then cold, but he never revealed the mystery, what it was that left him ever after in a fog of disconnection, the ice solid around him and unyielding. She was not surprised by this any longer, and she had been able at times to escape its sting. But she wanted for once to fight a battle that was her own. She had written too many polite, safe little letters, subdued too many passions to take this time of her life in comfort. She walked with her head down, her chin tucked into her damp coat. The sun had set in the grey sky and she was impatient, knowing her destination must be about half a mile ahead. She wanted to see the trees along the river, the aspens and elms she remembered from the summer before when she had spent the season with Bert, and he and Sally had taken her there for a picnic.

That day Bert had told her the story of a woman who walked out into the snow the previous winter, folded her clothes carefully on the riverbank, and then waded into the frigid water. This was an act Maggie could not understand. She wondered if the woman first sat down on the black rocks at the water's edge to decide whether she would yield to her great temptation. Maybe she had spent months thinking of it in bus stations, or maybe she had decided as she walked there. Maggie thought the woman would have had to break the ice first with the heel of her hand, her boot, or a stick or rock found in the snow. They had discovered the woman's boots, Bert said, her coat, and her blue dress in a neat pile on the shore. The searchers then followed her bare footprints in the snow to the river. Maggie thought it would be easier and somehow more comforting to be clothed at the moment one sank beneath the icy surface.

◦⁓

As she walked on the snowy shoulder Maggie briefly considered turning back, but instead encouraged herself by thinking of warmer times. She thought of a morning at her daughter's house in Indian summer, the yellow tail end of fall. A tulip tree had been gold outside the kitchen window, and the house smelled of lemon furniture polish and toast. At the table Ellie bent her wiry head over a coffee mug.

"You can stand a spoon up in this stuff, Mother," Ellie said laughing. "I can't drink it."

Maggie had glanced out the window at the buttery ring of leaves at the foot of the tulip tree. She thought she saw something dart away from the base of the tree.

"You know, Ellie," Maggie said, turning to her daughter, "I could never go to work each morning like you do. I spent my life waving at the window. Just like your father wanted me to."

"Mother," Ellie said as she scraped the crumbs off the table into her cupped hand and dumped them on her plate, "times are different now."

"Remember how we used to dance in the kitchen after he went to work?"

"Mother, don't talk like that." Ellie pushed her coffee mug away from her and looked down at the tablecloth for a minute. "I read this really interesting book on creative dreaming," she said looking up.

Maggie stared out the window. Ellie was still talking but she couldn't listen. She glanced down at her empty plate and silently upbraided Edward for leaving her stranded; her mind slipped so often into the past that she felt she must grasp it with two hands and hold it firmly in place in order to attune to even an ordinary breakfast table conversation.

"What, Ellie?"

"I was saying that instead of saying 'good morning' to their children these Malaysians ask them what they dreamed the night before." Ellie folded her napkin and placed it in the holder. "If the child says he saw a fierce animal and woke up, his parents tell him to go back and dream again."

She still has the same face, Maggie thought. Her body has changed, but Ellie still has the face of the little girl who cried all those alligator tears. Maggie took a long drink of her coffee.

"They teach their children to learn from their dreams, you know." Ellie stood, gathered the empty plates, and took them to the sink.

Maggie nodded. A familiar story. So many years telling my children bedtime stories, Maggie thought, and now my daughter tells me breakfast stories, as if I were a child. She pushed her chair back from the table.

"No, don't get up, Mother. I can do it." Ellie was running the water, the steam rising up through her wild head of hair. "If the child is smart," she said, "the next morning he'll say he saw a tiger and when he faced it, it disappeared."

"You mean if he was brave," Maggie said. "Yes, Ellie." Maggie watched the yellow leaves on the tree outside the window fan the breeze. "That's a good story."

"Mother, don't you believe it?"

"No, the only thing I believe in," she said with a smile, "is a good strong cup of coffee."

"But, Mother." Ellie came back to the table and sat down.

"I give you this," Maggie said looking at her daughter steadily, "at least you haven't put me on the bone pile."

Ellie looked down into her mug. "I won't put you into a home."

"Thank you, Ellie." Maggie poured herself another cup of coffee from the pot on the table. "But—I might have some friends there and we could talk. Maybe embroider pillowcases."

"You never embroidered a pillowcase in your life! You don't mean that." Ellie gazed at her mother for a minute, her eyes pale brown on a wide face. She pushed her mug toward Maggie.

"Is it too strong for you?" Maggie asked. "I'll make some more."

"No, it's all right—give me some warm on top."

Maggie poured the coffee and then turned again to the window. She noted the brown edges of the leaves lifting and falling. It was time for another bus ride to Bert's. Soon the leaves would be decaying in the Autumn rains.

"Ruth McGrory," Maggie said, "remember her?"

"No." Ellie changed her position on the wooden chair.

"I used to talk about her all the time. We used to play under those trees at the side of the house."

"Grandma's house?"

"It was my house."

"No, I don't remember." Ellie gazed out the window. "What's out there?"

"Well, she's not much older than I am."

"Who?"

"Ruth McGrory. She's in one of those homes."

Ellie stirred her coffee silently.

"I went to see her once. She was all tied up and sitting in piss."

"Mother."

"Okay, sitting in urine. Same thing."

Maggie looked at her daughter's dark hair as she bent over the coffee mug. She hoped when Ellie lifted her head she would suddenly see something in her daughter's face that would remind her of herself.

∾

The moon was obscured behind a greenish haze that hung over the road. Maggie pushed her hands deep into her pockets as the moaning, snow-laden wind whipped past her. It was fully dark now and the road empty in both directions. If the cat at Bert's door hadn't driven her away she would have picked up her gloves. Sally brought the cat with her when she moved in, but Bert was the one who fed it. Maggie knew Edward would not have understood any of this, especially a woman moving in with their son without marriage. Maggie felt suddenly tired. Her face and hands were tingling. She squinted through the increasingly bitter storm looking for the trees she knew should not be far away. Within the snowy haze lurked the eyes of several stars. She turned off the road and lowered her head against the wet blast from the river. She thought she saw someone ahead of her in the snow and she called out, but there was no answer.

"'I went to the Animal Fair.'" She sang the child's song into the wind. She peered through the blinding snow and listened carefully. She heard her father's baritone laughter in the wind. Suddenly he picked her up and turned her in his arms.

"We'll go to the circus, Maggie." She heard his deep voice at her ear. "We'll see the big cats and the pretty ladies."

He's not here, she thought, no.

Maggie waded through a waist-high drift, her legs numb. She smelled something as aromatic as her mother's stew simmering at the back of the stove. As she walked she heard the mantel clock ticking at the side door of her mind and then the sounding of the clock's Westminster chimes, and she thought of summer evenings after dinner long ago. She and her brother would chip away at the sycamore trees in front of the house, pulling off the light grey patches of bark until the trees were peeled down to their waxy yellow souls.

She felt nearly frozen. She had not realized that the river was so far. Her lips were cracked and tight. A blast of frigid air brought the faint odor of smoke and ash. Maggie leaned down to scoop a handful of the grainy tasting snow to her lips. She gave a short cry and lost her balance as the surface caved in beneath her.

She tottered in a moment of fear and then fell into a large ditch partially covered with a piece of snow-laden plywood. She bit her lip. Her glasses shattered against her face as she landed in a painful heap on top of something hard and cold.

Tasting blood in her mouth, she pulled herself to her feet and brushed off the snow. Beside her in the ditch were frozen sections of an exposed water main. The white surface was far above her. She tried to climb the steep sides of the hole but slipped back onto the snowy wet floor. She tried a second time and fell back against the frozen mud of the cavern's wall. After a few more attempts she sat down on a section of pipe and rubbed her ankle, which was sore, and even in the bitter cold, beginning to swell.

In the thin moonlight that filtered down to her she thought it would not be difficult to face. It would be there. It would be at the river. She took off her boots and rubbed her ankles. After a few minutes her right ankle looked silver, then purple, in the moonlight. She took a handful of snow and packed it around the foot, shuddering as she did so. She looked around her.

The black wall of the ditch was partially frozen, partially muddy and slick from the previous day's thaw, and much of the hole was filled with patches of new snow, fallen branches, and dark puddles thinly iced over. The surface loomed above her head.

"Help!" she called. "Over here."

Her voice was lost in the howl of the wind. She tired again to scale the steep sides of the ditch by digging her fingernails into the cold mud and bringing her body up to them, but her arms were weak and on her painful ankle she could not get a firm foothold. She slipped, and slid back into the snowy cavern. Her ankle throbbed.

The howl of the wind frightened her now. It was the only sound she could hear and it became not a howl, but the openmouthed screech of a tiger. She pulled her damp coat collar up around her neck as a ledge of soft snow fell down on top of her. She tried to put on her boots with shaking hands but was unable to force them over her swollen feet. She thought of Bert back at the house stoking the fire and of Ellie in her house in Virginia polishing the furniture with long rhythmic strokes.

As she sat on the frigid pipe and rested she could hear her own teeth chattering. A long time passed. Maggie was very cold. She was not sure exactly where she was, as place and time were beginning to be obscured for her in an oblivion of snow. She could see in the faint moonlight her hands, red at first, were now white.

"Help!" Maggie called out in a voice she did not recognize. "Is anybody there?" Surely not Edward. It was a horror to him to reveal any secrets, although at the end he became unexpectedly joyful. "Give me the life," he'd say, his eyes fixed on some distant vision, and Maggie dutifully would give him a drink. He didn't eat. He wanted to be spirit only, Maggie finally decided. And surely the lost child was not there, nor her mother, or father, or brother. They were there only, if at all, as ghosts, as haunting as footprints in the snow.

"Does anybody hear me?"

Her only answer was in the roar of the wind. The air was thick with damp. She was near the river. The arctic wind growing ever stronger blasted down into the ditch. She sat on the section of pipe and in exhaustion briefly fell asleep.

She woke with a start. There had been no sound or movement. Five large dots had been held in front of her without comment, long enough for her to perceive the pattern, and perhaps also, the meaning. But she didn't understand any more than her impression that there was no beatific smile on the face of this dream, no creamy white lotus held high above her head. Instead, she reacted with a kind of loathing; she could not interpret the signs and symbols in the unarticulated realm of dreams. She wondered how long she had been asleep. She gained no clues from the sky above the ditch, obscured as it was by heavy snowfall and the overhanging branches she noticed now for the first time.

As she looked up the moon reappeared as a faint illumination behind the rolling haze above her. She was not sure if time exists in dreams; it exists only when one must wake and account for the progress of the world when one had been gone from it. We come back reluctantly, she thought, and must grab onto our minds with two hands.

Maggie got up and walked in a small circle in the ditch, avoiding the pipe and the icy puddles, but her ankle was still painful, and she sat down again. She felt colder than she felt in her days as a young woman in Canada when it was a coldness of spirit that held her. She would not think of it again. She would think of the heavens stretched out like a curtain—the words came from somewhere in her past.

In the moonlight she picked the caked mud from her numb fingertips. She listened for the tiger. It would be as white as Mohini but not Mohini, a white tiger blending into the snow. She had seen its footprints, so this would be the place she would meet it. She knew it was prowling silently in the snow above her, stalking her in a gradually decreasing circle. It had always been there, outside the windows, always. It had been following her during her walk to the river. Its yellow eyes had been in the small lights in the distance, and sometimes it had padded behind her in the depressions where the black macadam showed through the snow. She had turned to see it several times but it had evaded her, moving to the left as she looked right, sometimes hiding in the tree of her thoughts high above her head.

She looked upward and saw the snow in mid-air above her, suspended like blossoms amid the bare trees that bordered the ditch. A dog barked off to the right, an alarmed piercing series of barks that carried through the thick dream of night above her. The dog could also smell the sweet, wild odor of the tiger.

Maggie heard the big cat padding above her. Small avalanches of wet snow fell down on her head. She held her breath. Then she heard nothing. After a few minutes of strained listening she rubbed her ankle, huddled down in her wet coat and rested her head on her arm.

When Maggie opened her eyes the tiger was in the ditch beside her. It was sleeping on its side, one muscular leg over her, pinning her down in a fearful embrace. The huge white head rested on a grey paw in front of them, and the great expanse of trunk and legs filled the den. Maggie sucked in her breath. From the damp chest fur of the white mass came the warm odor of ash and wet leaves. She stroked the tiger's chest with a delicate touch of her forefinger. She gasped. The fur was damp, the flesh solid behind it.

With all her strength Maggie lifted the heavy white limb off her shoulder and jumped up. She pressed herself flat against the muddy side of the cavern, her ankle screaming with the pain of her sudden movement. The sleeping animal's body expanded to fill the den.

In the moonlight the tiger's ear was a convoluted cave of pale red, its nose and paw pads glistening triangles of black. The rest of its body was a mound of grey and white shadow.

Maggie was trembling like the small leaves of the aspens she had seen by the river. Her feet were bare. She forgot her throbbing ankle and the dried blood on her lips. Her mind leaped into confusion. She thought of a dozen lions yawning and sleeping in a small den, surrounding a quiet man whose name at the moment she could not recall. If the man's friends threw hunks of meat down to the lions in the dark of night to save him, would that be less of a miracle? Are lions more docile than tigers, she wondered, less fearsome than leopards, more inclined to spare a small man who believed in something?

Maggie stroked the rough wool of her overcoat. It was soaked through to the lining. She took it off and folded it neatly in a pile at her feet.

The white tiger lifted its large head, blinked, and then stared at Maggie, its vertical pupils black, shining, unseeing. As she watched, black stripes shot from the tiger's eyebrows, and its slanted, intelligent eyes focused and gleamed with bright inquiry. The tiger gazed at

Maggie for a moment and then opened its black mouth in a yawn of white teeth that soon was transformed into a roar.

Slowly the tiger stood and stretched first forward and then back on its haunches. A second roar echoed in the small muddy den and in her fear Maggie had a sudden urge to release her bowels. Not even wild animals foul their own dens, she thought, they groom themselves and their young with barbed tongues and cover their wastes with the brown-edged leaves of fall, or the dry ash of spent fires.

Mohini stared at Maggie, the tiger's black pupils large within the yellow irises. The tiger roared again, with a piercing sound that vibrated through Maggie and obliterated her thoughts. She moved further against the cold side of the ditch. Maggie wondered how in a dream or no dream she had happened upon Mohini's secret place. The tiger raised an eyebrow and then swiped at her with a bared claw, knocking Maggie against the opposite wall of the ditch. She slid to the floor. Maggie felt as if all her bones had been flailed against the loose bag of her body. She pulled herself up on her swollen ankles, her numb feet, and lunged at the yellow-eyed mass. The tiger's head was cocked to one side, and it peered at her with one surly eye a slit over its open mouth. As she watched black stripes swirled up the tiger's chest, met at its jaws, and curled around its neck. Maggie took a deep breath.

The sound of the wind blasting into the hole became louder.

"Maggie, Maggie." Somewhere in the treetop of her mind she heard her name being called. She lunged at the tiger and knotting her fingers into its sides she climbed onto its back. Black stripes zipped around the animal's broad trunk and locked her legs against its thick fur, which was pale yellow in the changing light. She fell forward onto the tiger's head. The cloud of moisture from the creature's nostrils smelled of straw and rain.

Maggie rolled with the beast in a tangled embrace over the ice puddles and the black mud of the den's floor. She crashed again and again against the frozen water pipes as blood streamed from her eyes and face where the giant's claws had torn the flesh of her eyelids and cheek.

She pulled herself up on numb feet and then fell back against the wall as her breath came alternately in wheezes and sobs. The tiger stood facing her, its head down, a low vibrant growl coming from deep in its throat.

She knew she could not walk away from her fear as it stood all spark and moan before her. Her body gave off a sharp scent of despair.

Above her she heard the deep rumble of the ice breaking up on the river, the thunderous rumble of the thawing, moving ice floes growing louder as the boulders broke loose and crashed against the black rocks, scooping them up and hurling them ahead in a glacial roar downstream.

Maggie lunged at the tiger a third time. Her breath came in painful gasps as she fell upon its muddy, straw-colored coat. She could feel the tiger's muscles tighten beneath her.

She fought the tiger as fiercely as Jacob met his foe. She called up all her strength by calling off the gasses of defeat, drying the blood on her lips, denying the frostbite of her hands, the emptiness of her womb, the pain in her ankles, the numbness of her feet. She forgot the dreams of her childhood, the sadness of her young womanhood, the anger and fear of her mid-age, the despair of her most recent loneliness. She gathered all the courage she had forgotten she had been born with, the joy, the pleasure, the pain of small things done well and grand things believed in. And when she had let go of it all, when she had seen the pettiness of even these concerns, when she had given it all away in order to muster the strength for this one grand battle, the white tiger roared, its hot fragrant breath upon her face, and disappeared.

Maggie kept very quiet and listened. She heard the wind whistling through the trees and the lonely howl of an animal far in the distance. Then she heard the sound of a motor being cut off and muffled talk.

"For God's sakes, Jimmie—" Maggie strained to listen. "—the ditch has got to be here somewhere. The storm hit and the laborers just left."

"Damned stupid thing to do."

"Yeah. Well, you find it and I'll get the flashers up, and we're gone."

Maggie wiped the blood off her face with her sleeve. Maybe Bert told Sally she had gone off to bed. Maybe first they had searched the house for her. She took off her soiled, wet dress and folded it neatly on top of her coat and boots.

"'I went to the Animal Fair,'" she sang the song into the waning blizzard above her. It came in a harsh whisper. "'The birds and the beasts were there.'" Her voice was a rasp. She tried again. "'The old raccoon—'"

The muffled voices of the men faded and then came near as they combed the dark roadside. The snow fell steadily.

"Do you hear anything, Jimmie?"

"No, just the wind."

Maggie stopped singing. Above her were people allergic to life. She knew it now with certainty. She saw Edward with the blue behind him, heard the clink of dishes in a sink, dipped her hands into the warm suds of an understanding as someone coughed. The yellow eyes of a portable hazard sign blinked above her as a small avalanche of snow fell into the ditch.

She shook the snow from her head and steadied herself on legs that had lost their feeling. Mohini stared down at her with curiosity, tail hanging into the hole like a rope, yellow eyes glowing.

Maggie leaned down and picked up her dress from the top of the cold muddy pile of clothing at her feet. She stood, holding it in her hands.

The men's voices were fading. To catch them before they left, to let them know she was there, she would have to yell. She would have to yell above the yawn of the tiger, yell louder than she could yell above the swirling moonlit snow and the loose luffing sail of the wind. Some small fear made her want to shout, but then she remembered that snowwalkers are silent as they walk into the river of their dreams.

JOYCE RENWICK: A BIOGRAPHICAL NOTE

"I've invented three spirit guides. Muses. They help me center myself, focus my energy when I begin to write, escape the world of traffic and newspapers and television to the world where I can write."

JOYCE LOUISE TITUS (1942-1995) was born in Woodbury, New Jersey. Before she was able to read, Joyce was fascinated with words on a printed page—as a child she lay on the hallway floor copying newspaper headlines word for word. At the age of twelve she started writing poetry and short stories in a daily journal, which she kept until her death on August 14, 1995. She first published at the age of thirteen having won first place in a poetry contest.

Following the example of a favorite aunt, Joyce trained to be a nurse at the University of Pennsylvania. In 1963 she married Jack Arthur Renwick and had her first child, Lynne Robin, in 1964 and her second child, Susan Mary, in 1966. Due to her husband's career with the Naval Investigative Service and later the Secret Service, Joyce moved six times in six years. She was divorced in 1975.

Deep down Joyce knew she was a writer disguised as a nurse. Her turning point came in the late sixties when Joyce was working in a nursing home. She met a woman who told her, "I cleaned my house for fifty years, was gone one week and it was dirty. What good was my life?" When asked about this in an interview Joyce said "I realized life is very short, that entire lifetimes pass quickly, that I had to do something now if I wanted to be a writer." Joyce enrolled at the University of Virginia in 1970, transferring to George Mason University where she received a Bachelor's degree in Individualized Study, which encompassed Nursing and English.

Joyce studied for a Masters in English at Middlebury College in Vermont and attended the Bread Loaf Writing Conference for seven summers. To pay for her tuition she was on call twenty-four hours a day as the school nurse and lived in the infirmary. Joyce met her mentor, John Gardner, while studying at Bread Loaf. He taught her to "Just Tell the Story." She had this motto hanging above her computer, typeset, and framed in bright yellow. She used to say this gave her such freedom, such permission to write. John Gardner was an inspiration to Joyce and, while at Bread Loaf, she interviewed him and many of the other writers (including John Irving) for an unpublished collection of interviews she called *The Bread Loaf Dialogues*. The Gardner interview was bought by NPR and broadcast nationwide.

Joyce received her MFA from the University of Iowa's Writer's Workshop. She moved to Maryland in 1985 where she taught Creative Writing and English at the University of Maryland, the U.S. Naval Academy, the Writers' Center in Bethesda, Maryland, and American University. While teaching, she wrote and published. Her short stories, interviews and reviews appeared in such publications as *Horizon*, *The Southern Review*, *Sewanee Review*, *The Crescent Review*, *The Mid-American Review*, *Newsday*, *The Houston Chronicle* and *Best American Short Stories* and many more. Joyce was also very active in arts groups, woman's groups and writer's workshops. While in Maryland, she and her then companion, poet Paul Grant, started the New River Readings to bring artists together. She began her own Writing Consultant Business at this time.

In 1991, after the D.C. area proved too crowded and noisy for her, Joyce moved back to Iowa, which she had always loved. Looking for beauty in everything, she seemed to find it in abundance in Iowa. Joyce continued her writing consultant business. She taught classes at the University of Iowa occasionally because she enjoyed it. She was active in the artist community and was a contributing editor to *Mediphors, a Literary Journal of the Health Professions*. Joyce did, however, bury her nursing shoes in her backyard in a ritual of farewell.

Involved with personal exploration and discovery, Joyce reached the point where she could expose her true feelings, in her living and in her writing. Through meditation, she entered a magical nourishing world, which encouraged new and rewarding directions. In an interview "The Beautiful and the Disturbing" by Joan Peternel (*Writer's Digest*) Joyce explained, "I've invented three spirit guides. Muses.

They help me center myself, focus my energy when I begin to write, escape the world of traffic and newspapers and television to the world where I can write. The Peach Lady is a kind of cartoon-like fairy godmother with rosy cheeks and a frilly hat and apron. She gives me peaches, mason jars, and jars of canned peaches. She's at the entrance of the pit. She's the messenger who takes me to the bottom of the pit, to the sun lioness, a powerful medusa-like character with great primitive powers. She's fearsome, but I needed her when I wrote the horror in the nurse stories. I'll need her for the novel, too. When I write of beauty or need comfort, though, I go to Alexis. She's motherly, quiet. Her house has music and flowers, soft couches, a view on to the water." A fourth Muse, Titus, emerged but Joyce never disclosed her characteristics. This spirit guide was inspiring Joyce to write her last work, which was autobiographical with some aspects fictionalized. Joyce's Muses were facets of her personality, her higher self.

In the last two years of her life, Joyce began to paint. Instead of using canvas, she painted chairs to remind her of the people she loved. She would start with an idea then let go as a whimsical thread emerged, finding inspiration for new stories by the time she was finished. For Joyce "other things bring me joyfully back to writing."

Joyce lived her art. As a teacher and writer, she shared her love of beauty, honesty, and language with many.

—by Susan Renwick DeBardi

Robin Renwick Riehemann
9342 Bluewing Terrace
Cincinnati, Ohio 45236

513 - 794 - 9342

mriehemann @ cinci.rr.com